THE POCKET GUIDE TO BEING
AN INDIAN GIRL

B. K. Mahal was born and raised in Derby. After studying English Literature and Media at De Montfort University, Leicester, she began writing her first novel. She is a primary school teacher and is currently working on the sequel.

THE POCKET GUIDE TO BEING AN INDIAN GIRL

B. K. Mahal

BlackAmber Books

Published in 2004 by
BlackAmber Books
3 Queen Square
London WC1N 3AU
www.blackamber.com

1 3 5 7 9 10 8 6 4 2

A full CIP record for this book is available from
the British Library.

ISBN 1–901969–23–1

Typeset in 11/13pt Garamond Three
by RefineCatch Ltd, Bungay, Suffolk
Printed and bound in Finland by WS Bookwell

F121,716

£12·00

Acknowledgements

To
the father that I revere,
my mother, for daring my dream,
brothers Jazz and Jit for putting up with me,
and sister Sharan for her zany ways.
Thank you Nani and Manjit for your ever lasting support.

The deepest gratitude also to my true friends and family

Forever a doomsday

'You will die a sorry death.'

'Yeah, yeah. Well, you'll die a happy one,' I screamed back, before pulling down a handful of those long straggly ribbons she hung over your head in the doorway just to mess up your hair. OK, so she'd caught me borrowing some M&Ms, but there was no need to spread rumours about my dad in front of everyone. What's he ever done to anyone 'cept me?

Only my third week at Mrs Kaur's as general lackey and already I was in trouble. I heard everything Mrs Kaur bleedin' said when I was stood by the out-of-date crisps piled so high you'd wonder how her five-foot-nothing got it that tall without a ladder. Don't know what I was thinking when my hand knocked her carefully stacked packs of chickpeas over, but Mrs Kaur's a right witch and a half. I've seen white boys and girls steal everything from right underneath her moley eyes and the most she ever puts their way is one of those 'I'll tell the police next time' looks. Even when my mate Indy helped himself to some Brylcreem 'cos his mum had confiscated his styling mousse, on account of his head sullying the pillows, all Mrs Kaur did was tut disappointment and give him a lecture on how his parents had struggled. She also told him some other stuff

1

he didn't know, like he'd be the second child in line instead of the first if it hadn't been for his mother's miscarriage.

But me? I don't get the 'Why have you come to steal?' treatment. I get the insults straight away. Hope she goes bankrupt, the stupid, slimy maggot. Anyway, how am I supposed to know that everybody but an Indian girl can steal? Yes, your honour, I broke Rule No 1: Never, ever steal from a corner shop.

Legging it out of Mrs Kaur's, I hurried to tell Mum about this disconcerting incident. My family rely on that tab like Mr Dindsa did on us gluttons before he upped and hopped to Delhi to manage his hotel. Now I'd put the tab in jeopardy and all for a bunch of M&Ms. I might well have to eat marrow dhal from the allotment for the rest of my adolescent years, not forgetting a hastily pack-your-*banain*-and-*kachi* arranged trip to Handsworth with Worzel and her brethren. Ugh.

Thank the almighty take-away industry. Mum had been coaxed into doing an extra three hours for the grand overtime rate of £4.12 by a bunch of scammy chimps, meaning she wouldn't be home for another hour. I found Budgie sitting in the corner with his headphones blaring and dribble fermenting down the side of his gob. A comb poked out of the pocket of his baggy corduroy jeans. His hair style that looked like it had taken inspiration from a hedgehog looked as pokey as his beige face which turned paler each passing moment. India were heading for their highest test score against Australia and Budgie could barely believe what he was seeing on telly. Neither could I.

Grunting to acknowledge my presence, Budgie combed his spikes for that added assurance.

'Laxman, you beauty.'

Sitting down far as I could from him on the same settee, I cheered on the batting duo. Some days I imagined myself to be hitting a six, other days I was lucky even to be googlied. Today was one of those days.

'What ya doing?' asked Budgie, frowning.

'Same as you.'

'Watching cricket?'

'Yeah, why?' I asked.

'Girls don't watch cricket.'

'Well, don't consider me a girl, then,' I told him – a simple solution to his problem.

'I don't.'

In no mood to argue, I turned my eyes back to the screen. Tendulkar and Laxman, still on the batting crease, eased the bat this way and that for easy pickings. With the flow of runs flustering the Australians, the Indians quickly notched up to 527 on the board.

'Get me some *roti*, will ya?'

'What?' I asked, all dazed and glazed.

'*Roti*? Get me some.'

I huffed a little and chuckled a little because some things in the world are said just to kill you. 'You'd starve rather than get *roti* yourself, wouldn't ya? I mean, how lame is that? All you have to do is to put the *roti* and dhal in the microwave and eat. You're telling me that's hard?'

As Budgie began with the verbal tirade and all wasn't quiet on the Eastern Front the telephone began to bleat, and yes our telephone bleats. What does one expect from

3

Guggi's Electricals? That's where Budgie works, you see. On the second bleat I pounced into the air and sprinted from our front room to the living-room.

'Don't pick it up!' I shrieked to Kully, although there was little danger of her picking up anything, not even a disease in an epidemic, since over the past year she'd honed her lazy-cow skills to Olympic level. I yanked the telephone flex from its socket and was satisfied that Mrs Kaur wouldn't complain by phone, at least.

Kully came to life. For the whole afternoon she'd been gawking out of the window waiting for the right man to walk by – and she was about to marry the wrong one. While waiting for the big day she was reading self-help books. 'I'm enlightening myself on the social differences between men and women,' she said. At the moment it was that Mars and Venus one. *Haiyo Rabba*! Oh God! Education really has gone downhill since the days of Charlie Brown.

I have another sis, Kiz, who was born after a five-year drought. A drought's still there in her head, too, because she's hoping to become an Indian film actress or a *bhangra* star. The idea first took root when her good friend Gurminder (who lies all the time and eats garlic pickle) said that Kiz had the makings of a star. I suppose Kiz is rather glamorous. When she gets up in the morning all her eyeliner and pastel lipstick is still pasted to her face. Her bouncy curls, which hardly need combing, look wonderful. Even her pyjamas aren't creased. Kiz says sleeping carefully is the secret of real beauty: 'You mustn't put too much pressure on your face.' Anyway, her friend Gurminder said that she'd never seen anyone more ravish-

4

ingly adorable than Kiz and that one should go with one's gut instinct and do one's duty in life. I said one should really brush one's teeth but Kiz thinks I'm just jealous. Don't you hate it when people say that? 'You're just jealous. You're just jealous,' in that self-satisfied tone. It's the easy option, and a civilised argument thereafter is impossible.

'OK,' I said to Kiz. 'Learn to speak Hindi, get reborn into the *filmi* mafia and change your outfits more times than I can call you a Gorm, then we'll see where you get.'

'What about you?' she asked in that smug 'I know something you don't know' voice.

'What about me?'

What about me? Well, it's hard to talk about yourself and I don't really like to, but for rapport's sake I'll reveal all. People say I'm the first Indian girl in Dudley to leave school without a qualification to her name. They're partly right 'cos I stink at everything – except art, that is. I got a B in art. Mind you, that isn't a proper education, they say, so I've got to go college to get one. In my opinion college is the last place you get educated but I'm going anyway, just to get them off my case. I'm going 'cos there's nothing else to do around this jail of a town. I've been advised by Saira to do all I can to climb the social ladder. I call her cliché cow.

And that's it. There isn't much else to know about my family except that we're dirt-poor, sodding third-world-debt poor as schmuck, and I guess that's why Dad went loopy-lie. He went round the bend at a hundred miles an hour and is certified officially kerrazy. Everyone thought he was an alkie before that, but that award should be given to Budgie. He's my brother, but like most girls in my position I don't go exclaiming to the world about it. 'O hail, ye of the wondrous world of folk, I present to you His Royal High and Mightiness King Budgie Guji, ruler of thy kingdom.' Now's as good a time as any to point out that I'm made of a sugar called sarcasm, which, as my new millennium resolution, I'm trying to get rid of, but I'm thinking it might take me the whole millennium to do it.

Budgie has a theory, and Confucius he is not. He reckons most members of our family, bar Mum, Kully, Kiz and himself, will suffer some form of hereditary mental illness. My grandmother was a schizo and her sister was a manic depressive. That's all OK with me, since I reckon anyone related to Budgie has to have a higher than average chance of being sent to the asylum. Failing a relaxing retreat there, I'd opt for prison any time – might end up there anyway, since I bet all my *qawali* collection that Mrs Kaur would dob me in.

I wished Mr Dindsa and his lot still ran the shop. At least he'd give in to that charming smile of mine. He was ever such a decent chap, him, despite his Fair Isle knitwear collection, but that Mrs Kaur, oh, she's not even fit to be a hand-me-down rollneck.

I guess Mrs Kaur's about as endearing as the Mosquito at college, who struts around and speaks real elevated English with long, long words, not to communicate but to condescend. So she babbles her never-ending confusing words all day long and can't even put enough syllables together to intro me as Sushminder instead of Sushi. What? Has she never been to school or something? How

6

hard is it to read Sushminder off the register? They always get our names wrong, pronounce them like they want to. Like it's up for debate. So thanks to the Mosquito I'm now the signifier of a delightful delicacy of raw fish. It's one of those nicknames that have been thought up for the sole purpose of having ridicule and obscenities hurled at them from meteor-like gobs. I'd only just got everybody calling me Sushminder again. Now we're back to bloody Sushi.

Behind me in class sat Nicola and Joey, dressed fashionably according to a teen-mag fashion guru. Having decided the night before to wear the same sparkly shade of lipstick, they looked content as they complimented each other. At the risk of sounding like a concerned adult, I was led to believe by Mum that Dudley College operated and adhered to a strict code of appearance which for girls, and increasingly for boys, meant no make-up – not even Vaseline. As per usual, though, in my perceptive adherence to observing mankind, I'd stared a little too long at the artificial faces looking back at me. In return one of the blonde-hairdo girls snarled under her breath, calling me something that sounded rather like 'snitch'. Anyhow, there in the space of a second I had created two enemies without even having to insult them. Bravo, Sushminder. Rule No 2: Keep your head down and be a good, demure, can't-look-you-straight-in-the-eye Indian girl.

Having made enemies before I had made any new comrades, I turned round to nobody at my side and pretended to have a conversation with an invisible companion.

'How are you?'

'Fine. How are you?'

'Fine, but how fine are you?'

'Fine fine . . .'

'Oh, right, that's good, then.' Well, being weird's the new normal, don't you know.

My seat's a middle-of-the-road, average Joe Schmoe seat where everybody can see the back of your head. Not that there's anything wrong with the back of my head, it's just that I have paranoia unparalleled by a paranoid and don't like the thought of people looking. My 'mates' usually wear motley colours, cheap designer shirts with fashion fads and accessories to match. Special attention is always given to the creation of individual hairstyles; they invariably consist of a beehive, Elvis cuts, fringes which curtail thought, and poodle perms gone wrong because they've been created in consideration of a student's budget. Add to this my own stylish ponytail with a wispy additional top layer, and it's hairdresser heaven or hell, depending on your outlook on life.

After eventually being liberated by the Mosquito from morning tutorial, I found myself walking down the Tech block with a pile of sugar paper, chalks and pastels. I was motivated, you see. While observing the finer points of inner-city-grime architecture, a temporary lapse in vision made me trip over my boots. Blood rushed to my cheeks as I scuttled to my feet, pretending nothing remotely embarrassing had happened. Of course, I was burning up inside. Just when I thought there was no one around to add to my humiliation, what looked like a young philanderer leaning against the vending machine said in a strong Canadian accent, 'They've gone under there.'

'Hunh,' I mumbled with a frown on my face, brushing the dust off myself. I wondered why I felt so strangely bereft. Does falling down in front of people make me less of a human? So vexed was I at my moment of imbalance I hardly noticed that Dad's crazy pills had been flung on to the polished wooden veneer and landed any which way but mine. Still, panic-stricken though I was, I managed to shine a smile back at the Nit sipping a can of Coke like he was in an advert or summat. Taking little notice of him, I pulled up my bootcuts, got down on my knees like a pauper looking for her last bread roll, and patted the way before me. Starting at the edge of the corridor, I worked my way backwards. Having patted only a square metre of the tiled flooring, I realised the Nit was still smirking.

'You might want to help me. I'm what some might call a lady in distress here. Do you not watch Indian films?'

'Talking to me?' he asked.

'No. I'm a loony who likes her little repartee with the vending-machine.'

I think I must've scared him or something, because when I said that about the vending-machine he squatted down pronto to help.

'You an art student?'

'Perceptive, ain't ya?' I said, looking at my sketch-book, which had 'ART' written across it.

'I'm a maths kinda guy, myself.'

'Oh, what a shame,' I blurted out. 'I hate maths. You see, I've got this inbuilt number detractor in me. Hurl a number at me and I hurl two right back at you, unblemished, untouched and unsummed.'

9

He chuckled, letting me conclude that he was impressed with the fine figure of a female before him. I agreed, looking into his black twinkling eyes while a jelly-like state took over my knees.

The stranger, missing my little internal fit, passed me three pastel boxes. Although most of the sticks were broken and I was in for a beating from the Mosquito for not taking care of the benevolently funded resources, they were in colour order so I meekly thanked him. That is when I was captured by it. Some say a smile is a person's best feature and I've often disagreed with them 'cos I think it's the eyes, it's always in the eyes, but now I take back all I said, 'cos I kid the world not when I saw this. His smile was the most delicious, delectable smile I had ever experienced. It was a smile which didn't have to be forced to be made. 'Genuine' was the only word to describe it. I could have melted right there if it hadn't been for the silence that now divided us.

What to say? What to say? 'Maths always gives me face strain. I think it's 'cos I'm too preoccupied with wondering what x – a letter from the English alphabet, as I'm sure you know – is doing in my algebra. Can you tell me? On second thoughts, I don't want to know.'

The stranger – the alien – looked at me so I stared back at him, gazing into those big black almond-shaped eyes like it was Mills & Boon's love at first plight. He was the right height for me, not too gangly and not too gnome-like. If ever you have a partner, they should be the right height for you. It doesn't matter if they resemble cowpat but they ought to be the right height. That's not what I say, that's what all the antis say (don't know what the

10

uncles say). He was a very cool-looking chappie: the face of a young man unaware of his magnetically alluring aura and possibly Shashi Kapoor reincarnated. I felt guilt as the heebie-jeebies of love raced around in my head. All of a sudden I started stuttering and st-st-stammering, coming over all girly-wirly.

'My name's Arjun. Arjun Singh Dhaliwal. Just moved here from Toronto.'

'M-m-m I'm Susham. Sushminder, really, but, er, the registrar at Births, Deaths and Marriages in 1986 was finding it difficult to identify simple sounds. Dad was also having a sneezing riot at the time. Anyway, I ended up with Susham but I still insist on Sushminder. That was my dad's intention, so that's what I go along with.'

'Right . . .'

'I'm actually quite a pleasant person once you get to know me,' I said, trying to reassure him but having the opposite effect. Don't know why that happens – if any of my romantic nerves are shaken (and I do have some) I talk gibberish. Then I shook Arjun's hand with such force he must have thought I was going to have it for a main-course meal, so I stopped as soon as he looked about to wince.

The damage, though, was already done and I'd looked more enthusiastic than I should have. It doesn't take but a second to get carried away with this love thing, and I knew I'd pay for it later. But at that moment, if he'd asked me I'd have married him right there and then and would gladly have pretended I didn't have a brain, too. Before I could wonder where our joint account was to be

11

held, a slapper dressed in a cat-suit and moth-eaten cardi walked up behind him to ruffle and run her fingers through his fine black hair. How dare she use Rule No 3 to her advantage? The rule I'd already broken: Be distant and rude to those who yank at your heartstrings.

'Arjuuuuuu, where've you been? I've been looking for you everywhere. This college is so big, innit?' she whined. Then she giggled, showing a smattering of fuchsia lip gloss slapped on and staining her two buck teeth. I was certainly not going to be the one to tell her it was there.

She was Sammy, my cousin and the bane of my existence. Her real name's something like Samrinderjitdeep. Here she was again, flirting like Miss Piggy. Most guys are thick, though, 'cos they fall for it all the time. Yes, sure, Sammy looks like she's just walked out of a salon, with her straightened brown hair and willowy figure, but any female, be it his mother or potential love interest, who shows the slightest signs of affection grabs nothing short of a guy's full attention. My theory is that it's the fault of most of the mothers in the world.

You see, some guys have been led to believe they're the pride and holy deliverance of this world. They have the sort of mother who runs about after them with a wet hanky, cleaning their faces after the meal they've just gobbled down. They have the sort of mother who doesn't mind being told off by her son for not ironing the collars on his shirts or not cutting the crusts off his toast, mistaking it for an assertion of his independence. They have the sort of mother who will get a voodoo-doll-like pin-stabbing pain when her son grazes his knee and is in desperate need of the care he'd require if he'd been run over by a truck. They have the sort of mother who chants her son's name like a mantra and raises him to godlike status.

Those mothers all belong to a special clan called the Over-Protective, Over-Burdening, Over-Annoying Indian Mothers. You can spot them a mile off because they all have that uniform hoity-toity look and haul their bedraggled daughters along behind them on leashes. David Attenborough's description would go something like: 'The daughter, the donkey of the family, has to carry the burden, but although she is the donkey she is also the honour.' (Note to myself: I sound bitter. Another note to myself: I am.)

Because of this – us the unfortunate, and them the doted-on – there is created a cold war between the sexes, I guess. You don't know when it happened but you know that Rule No 4 has always been there: Never forget that you are a lesser human being than your brother.

Oh, God, that's not the only thing you know has always been there. Sammy stank of Anaïs Anaïs, enough to conk you out, to make sure you were barely conscious, and that's even if you were wearing a gas-mask.

While she got into one of her deep conversations, I stretched under the vending machine to retrieve the last of Dad's smarties – he depended on them. After struggling to click the cap on the container I decided to feel sorry for myself and crept out of Ken and Barbie's way. While I shuffled grudgingly down the corridor, my mind suddenly began teasing me: 'He'll call your name. No he won't. Yes he will.' Why must I be a sucker for optimism? As it turned out, he didn't call my name, but that's what happens when you get sucked into deep talk with Sammy.

By the time I got into the hall the other students had already set up their displays. Some had been ravishingly adorned with flowers to represent their natural kinship to Mother Nature, except the flowers were plastic. Others had laid personal mementoes out on a table for everyone to inspect, a picture of a loved one, a photograph of a hated one, keys to their new cars and seventeen birthday candles.

'Come on, dearie, an exhibition or representation now,' cried the Mosquito, flapping her hands at me like she was shooing an annoying fly away.

'This is my display,' I said pointing to the blank canvas on the board. 'That's me.'

The Mosquito stared hard, first at the board, then at the chalk and pastels I was holding, then at me again with one of those expressionless faces which say something.

'I see,' she said coldly, taking an expensive marbled stylo pen out of her tweed blazer pocket. 'I see.'

But she hadn't seen at all, 'cos if she had she wouldn't have graded me U for effort, U for thought and U for creativity – what a thick breed. The other fourteen students sniggered at a distance, 'cos even the E graders had beaten me. Think they're cleverer than me? We'll see. After spouting some verbiage on the frivolous nature of the Mosquito's taste and everybody's disposition towards the glaringly obvious, I stomped out, trying to slam the door behind me but, alas, the door wedge foiled me.

At dinner in the Broadway Campus refectory I saw Indy and Saira, who unlike me had made around twenty-one friends in as many minutes. You see, Saira has a likeable throwaway personality and an inviting, open face which draws you to her. She's a bit of a chameleon, so can change just like that. Still, Saira comes baggage-free, that's why people like her so, and Indy, well, he's the nicest geezer a girl could know without making you want to hit him in the face – real *Waltons* brother material. He even looks like one of them, Jim Bob, I think. Indy's the kind of guy who looks out for a girl like me without making her feel beholden to him.

While Saira went to the toilets to see whether she'd left her mobile there, Indy waltzed over to me.

'Here, you want one?' he asked, sliding a neat metallic mobile phone forward with one hand and waving to a pal with the other.

'Er, no, thanks,' I replied, hastily assuring him that it wasn't that I couldn't buy one of my own, more that I really didn't need to be contacted 24/7 when there were plenty of taxi drivers around to do that for me.

'Oh, go on. Here, it's my seconds. You'd be doing me a favour.'

'No, really, it's OK,' I protested. 'I wouldn't use it, anyway.'

'You're going all poor girl on me, now ain't ya?'

'No.'

'Yes, you are. I can tell 'cos you go all flushed in the cheeks.'

'Oh, get stuffed,' I said, losing my patience and getting up to go into the college field to sulk.

'Wait up. I'm only joking. Sorry.'

'How sorry?'

'Cheese and chips sorry.'

Happy with that reply, I sank back into my seat and waited for Indy to grab a plate of chips from Pauline, our friendly dinner assistant. When Saira returned, she slowly and painfully intro'd me to Kirpal, Purvi, Jazz, Rubina and Sheila. I didn't think anybody named their kid that any more, but then again what's in a name? – no one can ever get mine right. I said hello to each one. Hello, hullo, heylo, hallo. While they spoke about their future alma maters, I nodded with some enthusiasm and peppered the chips, chewing strands of melted Red Leicester.

'What's up with you, Sush? Why are you being such a muppet?' asked Indy abruptly.

'Shut your mouth, thick breed. I'm normal, you know.'

'Put an *a* and a *b* in front of that, then you're talking.' Quickly changing the topic of conversation altogether, he asked 'Has your mother dearest found out what you're doing here, then? Mine sent the police out when I was sixteen and some D graders were becoming a bad influence on me. Ah, I remember it well. Over-reaction big time, ain't it?'

'You're telling me,' I said. 'She reckons I'm doing business studies. According to her most artists are a bunch of lowlifes who haven't set their goals high enough. Of course I have. I've got plans to be a cartoonist, perhaps even a courtroom sketcher, depending on what gets flung my way. I can't tell her straight out about my arty-farty course 'cos she's still not talking to me properly, but I manage to get a grunt now and then. The trauma of showing my intellect has taken its toll, though. The reasons she's not talking to me are mangled but basically they boil down to a question of my human rights. All I want is to be able to choose my own hairstyle in the morning, but she still likes to comb it into two plaits.'

'Well, you do look cute in plaits,' kidded Indy.

'Get knotted! Nowadays I need to look a bit decent and more with it, so I go downstairs with my hair left loose and those beady things girls plait into strands of hair to give them a bit of an edge. Mum sees me coming and blows her top. You see, for years she's combed my hair like a ravaging pit bull terrier. "It's our quality time," she says, but I know the fun she's having as she pulls out another handful of my hair – her snorting chuckle gives her away there.'

'Why don't you put some mustard oil on?' asked Indy, looking up from counting some money.

I didn't bother to reply to such a silly question but let him know that the stuff stank, and then I rattled on about being made to sit on the floor with hair long and knotted enough to put Rapunzel to shame. I used to have to crouch on the floor to be given the beating of my life. Mum was lucky I didn't invite Social Services round for tea.

My mum lacks patience. So do I. 'That's what happens when you bring up four children,' she says. 'When the babies are born the patience dies.' Then she'd slap some mustard oil on my head to minimise the friction of comb on scalp. Keeping my head still proved a challenge greater than an SAS assault course, 'cos any involuntary movement to interrupt her delicate plaiting acted as the cue for my head to be jerked back against her knees.

Every day I bore five minutes of excruciating torture known only to me and my God, so yesterday I broke it to her as gently as my subtle-skills deficiency allowed me to.

'Mum, I don't want to look like you.'

Rule No 5: Your mother is another human being who is better than you'll ever be, and don't you forget it, 'cos she won't. She has power. You haven't.

I know my shouting didn't help, but there's always been a bit of a gulf between knowing and doing with me. Mum wept a little, but that couldn't be helped 'cos I mean she bawled her eyes out like a burst waterpipe when Zee TV stopped *Amaanat*. She even threw a wobbly when she found out that Kully didn't wear a bun any more because Doctor Sharma had advised against it – the bun was why her migraines were getting more and more severe. It had nothing to do with Kully being made to do lots of washing up.

When I finally managed to deter Mum from combing my hair to look like Pippi Longstocking, even if it was only a short reprieve, she started on my clothes.

'Why don't you wear this?' she said, holding up a blouse with frilly sleeves and a doily-hanky draping round the neck.

'In our family,' I told Indy, 'when Mum asks a question there's no reply expected 'cos the question really means "Do it or go to Hell, where even the devil won't play dominoes with you." As if that doily-hanky thing wasn't embarrassing enough, she'd made the special effort of ironing on a flower transfer. I tried hard to

18

explain to her that I really did not have to wear that blouse, which would have called for instant exclusion from the primordial gathering of my peers, but do mums understand? No, of course not. That would require them to like you.'

Indy's an amiable listener, and it's just as well because sometimes I do go off on one.

'Your mum likes you. She just doesn't want you knowing it,' he said, still counting a wad of notes like a boring banker.

His cropped hair flicked over his broad forehead, and he pushed it back in annoyance every time he'd counted £50. Sometimes he gives the impression that money is the only important thing in his life but it isn't anything like that, it's just that he's an only child. A real anomaly. Indy's parents, Mr and Mrs Kang, own the Pind Pub and they think he'll naturally want to work there when he gets out of college. Indy hasn't said he won't, but then again he hasn't said he will either. In the meantime he organises gigs. He reckons daytimer gigs have gone down the pan, and late-night gigs are, well, too late, so the next natural step is the evening gig. How clever is he?

'It's the only thing that satisfies my soul.' Indy says. And there was me thinking it had something to do with him being a party animal.

'All that gig money, then?' I enquired, hoping for the invite that would at last let me show off my *bhangra* skills.

'Yeah. Should be at least eight hundred plus. I'm expecting more but those Birmingham venue holders line their own pockets first.' After counting some more Indy asked, 'Seen your dad anywhere?'

'Might have,' I replied, kidding no one. I hadn't seen him in over ten days, not since he broke his section order. I thought it was him in the fish and chip queue but that turned out to be some Charlie with an allergy to nuts. I'd even foraged at the Gurudwara, the allotment and the market, but my dad was having none of it. The rest of them have given up looking for him ever since he went that way – they think he's lost. When Mum said 'I love you' to him, though, Dad knew they thought him dead and we've been in the pits ever since.

Indy said he reckoned my dad had been seen at the Pind Pub with the rest of the Folk Friday lot on Monday. I said if that were true Rai would've called the loony lot in a snap, what with him being the helpful guy he was.

'How did Rai get into Folk Friday?' asked Indy.

'Contacts – says he knows some Punjabi singers who'll sing for them free.'

After stuffing all the money into his college bag Indy drew up a list of the possible destinations in Dudley that Dad might visit. It didn't take long, 'cos Dad isn't the meandering man everyone assumes he is. He's too fond of the familiar. Just when Indy'd established that Dad would definitely not be hanging about suburbia (Dad isn't that sort of man) and I'd begun prising a speck of pepper out from between my top front teeth, the refectory door was flung open.

It was him, our Arjun – darling Darjeeling Arjun. How can a guy walk in as though he's floating on air? I'd like to walk up to him right now and let loose my black hair. I'd like even more for him to come over and do it for me, and in a moment of bashfulness I'd shy away and protest at his lurid and dangerous intentions. I'd like music to blare out of nowhere, the lights to darken and all eyes be hypnotised by us as we sashay along the refectory and up some golden-banistered stairs. How I'd like to bloody poke his eyes out for letting Sammy be so near and me so far. *Aaaaaagh!*

I've often found that ideas work out so differently in reality, when they wreak a havoc all of their own in my head. You have things all planned, make allowances for that odd mishap which might drag you down, but when it comes to the real reel it just scorns you.

Eating my chips as daintily as possible, I avoided staring at the happy couple as they caressed each other's hands softly enough to make me want to hurl what I'd swallowed all over them. What a bunch of regurgitators they are. Then Arjun looked up at me, which made me feel uneasy. I know it may sound like I'm lying an' all, and an honest person like me does occasionally, but to tell you the truth when I sat there staring at them I didn't feel all that jealous. You see, I have these mind-reader feelings sometimes so when I look into a person's eyes, stare at them straight, I can almost instantly tell what they're thinking. With the more sly ones it takes an extra minute or two, but I can tell even with them, given the time. It's the best gift I've got besides drawing, and I let nobody know in case they start acting different. I'd say behaving different, but it's all acting.

When I looked at Arjun that first time I knew he liked me. The thought comforted me on my walk home when I dragged my heavy feet into the Jammu Kashmir Tandoori to pay sixty pence for some tough chicken to chew

F121,716

on the way home. It got dark at half four now, so there was only minimal danger that somebody with nothing better to do would spot a Punjabi girl eating ungracefully outside.

My mum's always had a problem with my masculine way of eating. A masculine way! Once she got so angry at the way I put veg in my *roti*, rolled it up like a taco and tore it to shreds with my incisors that she stopped me eating until I'd had a lesson on table manners from Kully. (Oh, that reminds me, here's Rule No 6: Eat like you would if you were being filmed.) 'You put your elbows on the table again, Susham "Kauray" and I'll paste them with oil.'

Now, is there anyone in the world who can explain why elbows on the table are disrespectful? I say that any-one who feels insulted by elbows on the table is a smidgen lacking in self-confidence.

Today, though, Mum was positively radiant with the stuff, because when she opened that door to let me in she squeezed the eyeballs out of me, mumbling congratula-tions and jubilations.

'What's wrong?' I asked. What terrible atrocity had occurred in my absence?

Mum didn't answer. She didn't have to.

I could tell from the coats taking up the whole width of the corridor that my uncles were here. The chinking of bottles and glasses from the front room confirmed it. Dad used to display his whisky bottles in order of expense, then a little later rearrange them, this time in order of size in the front-room. I pushed my way through the coats I made my way into the living-room.

There on the mirror above the gas fire sprayed in silver snow was *Congrats to Kulvinder Kaur Dillon and Pardeep Singh Rai*. Finally I had to face up to the fact that my sis was well and truly shackled to the mafia of Brummie Land.

Last spring Kully had said yes to the guy in the brown leather blazer that must've cost a bomb. I think that's why she went for him, you know, 'cos if he could afford the jacket she'd have naturally assumed it meant he could afford her. Of course, I totally disapproved of it and stated my intellectual stance on her behaviour, with a thorough description of my disgust at her superficial, super-inflated, super-cogitated ego. She ignored me, in the way a girl does after she's seen some major sloppy lurve on the big screen, in that dreamy 'I'm not here on this planet' way.

She hasn't a clue about all the shenanigans in Pardeep's family. Mind you, neither had I until I earwigged on Dad's chit-chat with himself at the allotments.

It all happened the night Dad went over to have a *glassi* at the regular Folk Friday get together at Brummie Uncle's. It's usually held at the Pind Pub but Mr Kang had to close due to unforeseen circumstances. Brummie Uncle's a bit of a hyperbolic alcoholic. 'Fantastic' or 'Stupendous' is his answer to everything – oh, and alcohol, of course. 'How are you, Uncle?' 'Fantastic.' 'Would you like some *cha*?' 'Stupendous.'

Anyway, Dad went round to try and convince the Folk Friday bunch that Punjabi karaoke was the next big thing. He didn't know it back then but Brummie Uncle's appetite for the big time had landed him in trouble with Pardeep's clan. Now, their clan is not one to be messed with, 'cos they've developed the knack of being three steps in front of the police and one step behind their conscience. They're not a right bunch of *kanjar* for nothing, Dad says. Anyhow, Pardeep's dad is that Rai, and he's the one to blame for all the trouble.

Rai's a self-made man; that's what he's said – or, rather, bellowed – a thousand or so times to us Dudley folk. He and his sons own at least seven corner shops in the poorer part of town. I've even seen them buy out the most Calvinist shopkeepers with a bribe so easy that you'd think they'd been shotgunned into it. But when Rai bought the last corner shop, *our* cornershop (not that we owned it or anything), he made a point on his first encounter with my dad at the Folk Friday get-together of harping on about the huge tab we owed him.

Dad, being the good man he is, ignored him and carried on singing Punjabi folk louder than ever to drown Rai's voice. Rai was relentless, though. On and on he went like an Oscar-winner. What made an already tense evening worse was that he insisted on tabbing up the bill in front of all Dad's Folk Friday chums. Now, it should be known that pride never comes before a Punjabi man's fall – a fist maybe, but not pride.

'One pound twenty for black boot polish I see,' huffed Rai, looking down at Dad's worn, torn Hush Puppies. This set off the first of many smirks in the evening during rummy.

Dad was agitated enough to say that he didn't owe Rai sod all, 'cos it was Mrs Kaur who'd been gracious enough to allow us to get the things we needed. 'Besides,' he said, 'you may intimidate everyone else, but you don't intimidate me, you leech.'

That did it. Rai's power complex went into overdrive. He's bidding to run for mayor of Dudley even though he lives in Birmingham, and slanderous accusations like that would just kill his chances. After telling everyone that he was a philanthropist, Rai said he'd kick anyone's behind who made it look otherwise.

An hour and a bit later, after yet another comment besmirching Dad's reputation had been uttered, Dad flew off his chair and lunged a rock-packed punch into Rai's jaw. No one had ever dared so much as spit at Rai before, so this was big news. Dad might have felt some satisfaction in making Rai wheeze a little, but he was dismayed later to find that he hadn't been able to position the blow accurately enough, because Rai could still talk. Later Rai informed Dad that ten per cent interest would be added to our account until the sum of £333.67 was paid in full. Well, Dad never paid the sum 'cos he never had the money, which must mean that the tab's at least a million pounds now, or thereabouts.

Despite all this, Mrs Kaur's the only one in Dudley who's ignored Rai's rule that our family be barred from tabbing, even though she's their franchisee. Actually, I reckon she's a clever cow, 'cos she makes a point of letting everyone know what a kind person she is. She don't do owt for nowt. 'I help the needy' she says, pretending to be all modest.

Later that week Mrs Rai – a Sri Devi lookalike – came to see us, and told us there were no conditions attached to the Pardeep–Kully proposal. I knew then that the clan

25

were after something, though what it is I have yet to find out.

Apparently, Pardeep has quite a thing for our Kully. He's had it ever since she bumped into his Jaguar with her Fiat. While they were exchanging insurance details, he took it upon himself to make sure she was covered for personal accidents.

'It wasn't just the jacket, Susheeeee, that was just the icing. No, my Pardeep has a nice face, nice teeth, a nice voice – oh, and nice hair, too.' So let's conclude. Kully went for Pardeep 'cos he was nice! Now ain't that a real corker she's got herself there?

They've been in the thick of wedding prep a long time, and I've avoided all altercations with an irascible soon-to-be-married-off sister, but she's still been kind of *X Files*-ish and only ever talks in non sequiturs, so if I ask where she's put my Pritt Stick she replies, 'Go to the dentist and get your filling put in.' Doesn't make sense, does it? What that has to do with her wedding only she knows, but she reckons that my back tooth best be fixed because ever since the filling fell out when I was eating Bombay Mix I haven't stopped playing with the chasm it left. God forbid the family photos don't turn out right. God forbid.

It's good and all for Kully to be so concerned about my facial features but really she, along with my other two siblings, shouldn't be worrying so much about me when Dad's the one who could do with their help. It's nearly four months now since the NHS took him in, and the only thing I've learnt is that section orders have their uses.

After saying '*Sat sri akal*' to a few uncles and antis who had turned up to help with yet more wedding prep – mainly uncles drinking and antis squabbling – down Crack Alley she towed me. We ended up in Mrs Sidhu's 'no car parking space' dentist and makeshift reception in a shiddy-shoddy terraced house. Death must feel like the moment when she rammed that syringe into my gum as if she were an Eskimo harpooning a seal.

'You bitch!' I screamed, fleeing into the corner of the room. 'Go inject yourself.'

Mrs Sidhu wasn't impressed with what she termed my 'hormonal outburst', so I kept stumm for the rest of my treatment and listened to her lecture on the social sacrifices she made to serve the oral needs of the community. Shortly thereafter I was allowed to wait in her woodchip-wallpapered Reception to watch the ordeal of the trainee receptionist working out how to hold a pen.

As I sat clutching my jaw, Kully chatted to her la-di-da fiancé on the new mobile he'd given her. It's one of those picture ones so he can see her and she him.

'Here, look at Sushi. She looks like a guinea pig,' she tittered, shoving the mobile in my face.

I smiled half-heartedly at him. He was wearing another pair of designer spectacles to make him look more intelligent, even though he has 20/20 vision, and was dressed in another designer suit but I figured it was gonna take more than a wad of weft and weave to give him a whiff of class.

Kully then apologised for my rude and disrespectful behaviour, which irritated me even more. I'm perfectly capable of apologising for myself; when I want to, that is.

Ignoring her, I occupied myself with the informative and multilingual literature placed over the cracks in the wall – as if we patients wouldn't notice that subsidence was to blame. Well, it was either that or the road drill the Bitch used on my gob.

After the final radio tribute to ABBA had been made and 'Waterloo' had been etched into my memory for the rest of my living days the receptionist paid attention to me.

'Three p.m. two weeks on Friday suit you?'

I nodded, accepting that if I wasn't dead by then I just might be back.

'So that's Sushi Kaur?'

'No!' I half mumbled and half screamed 'My name is Sushminder Kaur Dillon – occasionally Susham, but it certainly isn't Michael Cain. It isn't even James Bond. It's Sushminder Kaur Dillon.'

This minor outburst caught the receptionist a little unawares, for intimidating behaviour was subject to a £20 fixed penalty charge. The Punjabi/Urdu/English poster above the mantelpiece reiterated this point for people like me. Kully apologised on my behalf again.

Annoyed that she had to stop murmuring sweet nothings to her 'feeeeonsay' and that the dentist-come-devil-woman had let me go, Kully made sure I staggered home in a straight line. 'You wouldn't want to look like a girl with a secret appointment at Alcoholics Anonymous,' she said.

Every half a mile or so she took a tissue out of her pocket and rolled it up to shove in my gob. This made it difficult to speak, though not difficult enough to prevent me from demanding she buy me a chocolate from Mrs Kaur's for my troubles.

Kully sighed. 'Chocolates are bad for you.'

'Yeah, yeah,' I replied. 'Never heard that one before.'

'Life without my Fiat is unbearable,' moaned Kully, tweaking her matching hat, gloves and scarf.

Life without your two eyes is gonna be more painful, I thought, as she yanked me back towards her again. With her being four inches taller than me, she has longer arms This made me wonder whether she'd been fed more than me.

'I'll miss Dudley,' she sighed with a little sadness in her voice

'Yall uny be in Bumingam.' I mumbled painfully. The paralysis in my mouth still had a hold.

'I know, but I like Dudley, you know.'

I nodded – I knew exactly what she meant. Dudley was our home. It was defined by what the South wasn't. I remembered when Mum took me to Heathrow Airport in Brummie Uncle's car to drop a *bibi* off. I was little then and very terrified of that *bibi*. Anyway, we lost Brummie Uncle at the airport so ended up in Hounslow. I bloody hated it. The streets were so tight, all packed in. People lived on top of each other, not raising a smile, not saying hello, not stopping a while. Their monuments had history but none of that included me 'cos if it ever did I'd have walked right on into Buckingham and then there was shop upon shop upon shop. There was the crampy skyline. I tripped over a cone, banged into Darth Vader on his phone, and some of the places were strictly out of bounds 'cos Mum only had coppers and £23. Eventually we got the mainline to Midlands for a safe return. I'd been to hell where I could have been burnt. Oh what a yokel am I.

We arrived at Mrs Kaur's soon enough but I didn't dare go inside, so Kully left me waiting observing the mottled paved bricks. They'd seen a lot of battering. If I were to trip over one accidentally in front of a respectable member of the public, I could sue the council for more money than the Rais could horde underneath their mattress. This plan, although hasty, just might work so I waited until a family car appeared up the road, and walked twenty metres in the opposite direction, towards a brick with about an inch of its corner sticking up in the air. Slowly I gained enough momentum to hurl myself on to the floor, but before I could even do half a sensible dive a bodiless head rushed past, nearly knocking me off my boots. It was my dad.

'Wait up,' I cried, though not nearly loud enough, my gob being restrained as it was. Dad couldn't have heard me, because he went on running.

Whooshing across the road I dashed round a Royal Mail van at my peril, chasing a man who looked as if he'd just realised what legs were. Half staggering, a quarter sprinting and a quarter jumping, I went up Cavendish Street, down Anderson Road and back up Cavendish Street, running like a dog chasing its own tail.

'Oy, you silly cow,' screamed Kully behind me, finding it hard to keep up with me and Dad in her maroon leather sandals. 'Don't you want your Double Decker?'

'Get lost. You're scaring Dad,' I screamed back. She

was, too. Dad would never, ever run away from me. He just wouldn't.

Dad ran ever so straight, as if he was being pulled or pushed by something other than his own will.

'Stop, Dad! *Tehr ja.*' But he didn't, 'cos he was too busy running to something or away from it – I won't lie and say I know which. Running hard, like a whippet on its last legs, I cursed as the divide between us got bigger and bigger. '*Dedi*, Dad, it's me. Just stop, will you?' Dad did not.

When the asthma kicked in and my legs could carry me no longer, I slumped into a mess right in front of Mrs Kaur's. Gasping for that bit of air which would free me, I clutched my ribs and wheezed uncontrollably. If my lungs had been so kind, I'd have sobbed right there without shame. I missed him.

Sitting in between a bush and a small van parked up on the pavement I watched Mrs Kaur's shop windows. Opposite me, customers coming out of the shop smiled nervously at me with their groceries in hand.

' 'Ere you go,' said a concerned voice in something other than a Dudley accent.

With a pound coin thrown at my feet and rolling about on the pavement, I looked up, a bit embarrassed.

'It's you, Susham,' Arjun pointed out, grinning.

Great, I thought. Pushing the rain-drenched hair from my face, I tried hard to breathe daintily and not like the idiot I was who never had an inhaler to hand.

'But your real name is Sushminder?'

'Er, yeah.'

'What you doing down here?'

31

'Me?' I asked.

'Uh-huh.'

'Oh, I'm waiting for my sister.'

'Right,' said Arjun, looking ever so becoming in his baggy jeans and unironed grey sweater.

'Don't get me wrong, though. I'm not a beggar, just had to sit down, that's all. I had an operation on my legs when I was four, you see. Someone ran over me with their wheelbarrow and very occasionally I still feel the pain.' I don't know why I lied when I could have just told him the truth. Go away, I thought. Go away. Why can't you talk to me when I don't look like a drenched dweeb?

'Do you want to go over there? Get a hot drink?'

'No.'

'You sure?'

'No.'

The café opposite Mrs Kaur's was one I'd never been into.

'Thank you,' I said. It was the first time the door had been opened for me – usually I just walk into them. So I asked Arjun, 'Why do some guys do that? Open the door for you, I mean?'

'It's just plain old good manners, I guess.'

'My mum says if you ask a man to iron your clothes or fix a leak, they come up with a whole book of excuses. Instead they do real hard stuff like open your door or get you seated in a chair. Well, that sure makes a whole difference to our lives.'

'Look, if you're going to get crotchety just because a guy thought you special enough to open the door for you, well, forgive me but—'

'That door-opening thing may be manners and all, but at the time women were having doors opened for them weren't they being denied the right to vote? And isn't that bad manners?'

'Er, yes, I suppose it is,' said Arjun, looking annoyed that I'd interrupted him. 'Now, what would you like to drink?' I seemed to be getting on his nerves.

While I scanned the chalkboard menu I sensed a cherry scone and hot chocolate might be able to thaw my mouth properly. Together they'd cost £1.50, and I had just enough.

We sat down at a table for two and a young girl came over to take our order.

'I'll have two cherry scones and two hot chocolates,' said Arjun.

Ah. He'd chosen what I'd chosen.

'Tell me about yourself,' I said, knowing this tricky question might set him off.

'I'm an only child. Moved here a month ago from Canada and am starting anew. There, will that do?'

'Very concise. I think I'd like to go to Canada.'

'And do what?'

'There's only one thing for me to do there . . .'

'Go on.'

'I'm gonna go and find Sesame Street.'

Arjun laughed so hard that he nearly jumped in the air. I thought I'd have to slap his face.

'Sesame Street? Hahahaha.'

'Yes. I'll have you know I'm gonna be a cartoonist or a courtroom sketcher some day, and that Jim Henson was the king of the best characters in the world.'

'Right,' said Arjun, apparently trying to take me more seriously. 'But hold up. Sesame Street isn't in Canada, you know.'

'Liar.'

'No, listen. It's somewhere in America.'

'You telling me the truth?'

'I've no reason to lie.'

Feeling slightly flustered and a bit out of sorts, I thanked the waitress – she'd brought the scones at just the right time.

Arjun went on to tell me about his former life in Toronto, and what he planned to do here. He wanted to be an architect and seemed to have everything finely tuned.

'You're a map kind of guy, aren't you?' I said.

'Never been accused of that before. Care to elaborate?'

'Well . . .' I sighed with the burden of enlightening him. 'What I mean is, you like things all planned in advance so you can map the route, traverse uncharted territory with the right brain gear. Am I right?'

'Maybe, but you're no better yourself. A no-map kind of girl, that's what you are. Likes to go her own way even if it does mean she'll end up in the quicksand.'

'I ain't!'

'You are, but don't know it yet that's all.'

Just then a blonde wig tapped on the café window. I'd stuffed a big piece of scone in my mouth and I began spluttering, for in paraded Sammy wearing cropped blue jeans which if she wore them much longer would surely give her arthritis.

'Arjun,' she cooed, 'I was just going to yours, innit.'

'Hi, Sammy,' said Arjun with great enthusiasm

Interrupting, I asked, 'How are you, dearest cousin?'

'Fabulous. You?'

'Much better now I've seen your lovely hair.'

Rule No 7: Don't ever go blonde. Who are you trying to kid? Sammy didn't realise that her face and hair seemed to blend into each other.

Getting another chair, she squeezed herself in at our tile-sized table.

'I'm not really a straight-brown-hair sort of girl,' she told Arjun.

'Make yourself comfortable,' said Arjun, before complimenting her further on how wonderfully dressed she was.

What bad manners, I thought. I'd been sat there nearly ten minutes and not one compliment had flown by me. Well, I certainly wasn't going to watch them and their animated expressions adoring one another. So I did what I did best.

'Oh, look, there's my sis. Must go,' I said, avoiding their eyes. Leaving £1.50 on the table, I jogged out of the café – running when I'd only just got my breath back would have been silly.

When Kully eventually located her sandals somewhere on Anderson Road, she frog-marched over to me in a strop.

'Don't you know I'm getting married? I have to follow decorum. What if my in-laws had seen me running like that? What if somebody else had seen me and gone and told them? What if I'd twisted my ankle? What if . . . ?' Kully carried on asking me questions my gob didn't care to answer.

I let her drag me back home, only to find Mum had invited the whole of our extended clan, all bloody forty-one of them! That flamin' recurring nightmare had come back again. Rule No 8: Don't be alarmed when you find that guests turn up like lemmings – soon as you've killed one, there's another twenty round the corner.

Tip-toeing along our short and narrow corridor, I was met by Worzel (Mum's stirring sister), complaining about the crockery not being up to scratch. I ignored her and entered the lion's den, where I greeted guests (some of them, I'm glad to say, were happy to see me). Taking a polystyrene plate off the stack on the coffee table I helped myself to a bit of all the food within reaching distance, minding my own business, as you do. Then I saw Dadoo, aka the Twit, standing there in his usual annoying ten-pin way; it makes me want to get a bowling ball and knock him over. He held a throw-away plate ready to pile it with samose and pakore. His gangly body reminded me of a scarecrow stood alone in a barren field, except this scarecrow had no birds to scare because even they couldn't stand the sight or smell of him.

I smiled back at him as if somebody had Sellotaped strings to the sides of my gob and was yanking them. It's near impossible for me to do a convincing smile when I don't mean it. Soon I wished I hadn't shown even that much good manners, 'cos that's when it happened. Dadoo, standing only three and a bit metres away from me, had the nerve – had the bloody nerve! – to wink. Ugh. I felt dirty.

Dadoo is next-door-but-one's twenty-something son

and Budgie's best mate. Dad's never banned anyone from our house except him. I think it was that day he rapped me on the knuckles with a pack of cards because I'd lost a game, the rules to which I still do not know. It could also have something to do with the day that Dadoo decided to take up rapping as his future career.

Apparently he's MC Didoo Dadoo or something like that. Now he talks like he's a rapper, walks like he's a rapper and, worst of all, dresses like he's a rapper. The funny thing is – wait for it – he can't rap. Hah! So really he isn't a rapper at all. He's just a baseball cap, Caterpillar boots, signet ring, designer jersey and bomber jacket. Dadoo's like that in summer, too.

The thing I don't understand is how Dadoo can have such a genial giant as a father – I mean his dad can do all sorts of things with his arms and legs in a real nimble way and can levitate you on just one hand. Not only that, but he can put his arms right the way round his back and twist his legs to look like flumpalump marshmallows. Dadoo's elder sister, Jagdev, is pretty decent, too, and I can talk to her for ages and a lifetime and not know it. She knows loads of stuff but doesn't ever brag about it. She's away at university doing Economics, probably just to get away from that rapping.

I once told Dadoo he wasn't his parent's real son 'cos he'd been left on his mum and dad's doorstep by some girl who'd got herself impregnated with alien bits and bobs. Naturally, he thought I was using warped psychology and he started telling the whole of Dudley I was a big softy. So now when he winks at me I dimiss his sign

of flirtation and take it as an insult 'cos I really mean this when I say it: Dadoo is one thick breed.

Exchanging my polystyrene plate for a china one, I began piling on the second helping of food until the mango chutney threatened to spill over the edges on to the maroon deep-pile carpet. Dadoo stood there staring like it was his hobby and was joined by a few uncles, who must've thought me greedy for not offering them more food like a dutiful buffoon, but what was there to ask? They already had their hands full with the shot glasses of Bell's from Blackpool. Some people! '*Main jat yamlaa pagla dewaana* . . . oh ho ho.' Then they all started singing like drunken Punjabis with only one mission: to get bladdered on their sorrows. The Folk Friday uncles kicked up their feet and frog-leapt into our furniture, all twelve of them doing the Cossack dance Punjabi-stylee. When Wally Uncle nearly kicked the shins of a beleaguered toddler gone astray, I saved myself from being crushed by darting straight to the cupboard under the stairs. The dancing was getting far too dangerous for me. The stairs would have to be my sanctuary – well, it was either that or go to the girls' room and listen to them talk about their fates.

Inside the cupboard, 'Dad!' I screamed, hurling myself into his arms for a bear hug.

How he'd got past the three witches in our house with their body-heat-sensing eyes amazed me. Crammed into the cupboard, Dad's five-and-a-half-foot frame reminded me of Dadoo's dad, the contortionist. I wedged myself between him and the door, and he giggled while making a shadow picture with his hands – I think it was a dog. In

the faint light that forced its way through the cracks of the MDF doors, I saw his bleak smile. His beautiful wispy grey hair hadn't been combed in days, and his normally large black eyes were only half their former size from lack of rest. His hands were cold, too, so I rubbed them in mine to force the blood to circulate, but try as I might his fingertips would not thaw.

Tucked into a pocket of Dad's blue parka, I could see a small Nivea container. In it were assorted smarties to control aberrant thoughts – funny that: coloured pills to dampen coloured thoughts. With only a few of the pills remaining, I added the ones that had been saved in my duffel coat to his collection.

The noise outside of chatter, crockery and *bhangra* was strange as it filled the silence under the stairs. The two of us, hiding in our own home.

Dad found a loose screw on the floor and, with shaky hands, used it to etch his name on the sloping ceiling: '*Amarjit Singh Dillon wasn't here.*' When he'd finished, he chortled again and whispered, 'There. I'm permanent now.'

The cupboard was a snug fit and we had to crouch in tight so that our knees touched our chins. Them lot outside couldn't get at us, making it all the more cosier. Near my feet was a small bottle of Bell's, which had probably been hoarded by Brummie Uncle or Budgie. Pouring a little into the cap of a Mr Sheen can, I offered it to Dad. He refused it, but a convenient ledge just above my head allowed me to rest the shot (talking like a real pro there) and on my lap was the feasty plate ready for me to devour. The samose were still warm, so I offered Dad

39

one straight away. If there's one thing I hate, it's eating cold food which should be piping. Dad refused again, shaking his head. He shouldn't have, because he looked frail and grey, so I shoved one into his hand anyway, and without argument he took a bite of it. Afterwards me and Dad played count the woodlice; six altogether. Although we didn't talk much I was glad he was nearby.

We must have been there forty-something minutes before we realised it would be at least another six hours before the clan dispersed to their various parts of the world. 'Stop the wedding,' mumbled Dad over and over again. One way or another I knew he'd try.

Dad isn't like either of his brothers – he's by far the noblest of the lot. If he says something you take notice. Even his face is straight to the point. His long, defined nose, jaw and forehead have aged well. His poised stature gives him an air of gracefulness; not at all like me, all gangly and cumbersome like, banging into things I can clearly see. Like I say, of the three brothers Dad is the most noble. Dudley Chacha's all right. His name isn't really Dudley, that's just where he lives – come to think of it, he actually lives in Croydon. Come to think of it, I don't know what his real name is. Anyways, there's also Wally Uncle from Wolverhampton who's divorced now with two children. I'm quite fond of his youngest daughter, Guppy.

On Mum's side of the family there's Brummie Uncle, who's married to Mum's youngest sister, Worzel (aka Gurmej), and Greavsie from Gravesend is married to Bimla, Mum's other annoying sister. We don't often see much of Greavsie on account of him thinking that he's all

40

wondering what mad Mr Dillon would do next did not budge too far. Someone might steal their view.

'He's trying to kill us, see? He's throwing knives at us now.'

Someone at the back of the crowd giggled, and an old woman standing near Mrs Kaur remarked how much fun her day had been and that the small circumstance that thundered above her had made her trip to the local library all the more worthwhile. Better than any soap, she thought. Now she was content that her day had not gone to waste. Her first-hand evidence, experience and account of this new piece of gossip-fodder would take her far.

When I was new here I carried all my dreams and nightmares in a canvas satchel which accompanied me wherever I went. Though the satchel flapped in the strong wind, looking as if there was nothing in there to hold it down, I felt its strap across my shoulder pull down on me, as if its thoughts weighed heavy, waiting to be let out into the white wide world that blinded me. Once I had walked by these very same people to be met with a 'Hello', a *Sat sri akal*, an *Adaab* or, when the weather was too cold for people to open their mouths, a nod of the head. I used to smile as widely as possible until my cheeks ached with the effort, for I was grateful to be known.

Now I only want things to be the way they used to be.

Dad's transcript made me numb. I'd been presumptuous in thinking I knew him. Somehow I had to make things right.

Dad and I had been living at the allotment for two days, and he was at ease with spiders running up and down his trousers. I was still getting used to the idea of crapping in the compost patch, and had realised very quickly that it wasn't the best-thought-out plan. Hey, desperation can make even the cleverest girl go all twerpy.

How were the occupants of Ward Sixteen supposed to know that Dad could abseil down from the second storey, using the washing-line that had been bulging from his blazer pocket? Down on the grassy verge I waited with a stretched-out white T-shirt to break his fall, just in case.

When I'd left Dad humming '*Mere Desh Ki Dharti*' in his bleak magnolia bedroom I'd informed Miss Hodges that he was asleep, so shouldn't be disturbed for at least a couple of hours. Miss Hodges thought that was good but didn't he want his Ovaltine? 'Oh no,' I replied, 'he won't want it now,' and with that I hopscotched out of her way.

It cost more than I could afford to live at the allotment, so I resorted to enlisting Indy's help. Sure enough, he turned up trumps and brought us the works: cans of beans, matches, toilet rolls, two sleeping bags, samosas, everything in his fridge, and even *barfi*. I held out for a long time, but in the end I took his mobile phone in case of an emergency,

Dad and I were getting good at hiding in the shed, coming out only at night to warm ourselves up by lighting a fire. It wasn't until the third afternoon that we gave ourselves away: I fell over in the spinach landscape. Twice.

I pretended not to notice the man, but he was having

none of that 'I didn't see you' thing, and as I shut the shed door behind Dad, he rat-tatted, pushed the door open, nodded to us, told us his name was George, and displayed the widest grin I ever saw – his teeth were as white as the thick plaster on his right leg.

'What's that on your arm?' asked Dad.

'A gecko.'

'Where from?'

'Madagascar.'

'Why don't you let it go?'

'All right, then.'

After letting the creature ramble up his arm one last time, George unclung it from his brushed cotton blue shirt, turned away and let it lose itself among the long leaves of the onion patch outside.

'What happened to your leg?' asked Dad.

'I tripped.'

'You trip as well?' I wondered.

'We all trip, but some just pretend not to and—'

'I don't smile,' interrupted Dad.

'You don't smile, huh?'

'I smile but not enough, and I laugh but not enough.'

'Why do you want to?'

'Because I used to.'

'And why did you use to?'

'Because . . .' And there Dad halted, at the dead end of a sentence waiting to be completed. It seemed that he'd arrived at an answer by himself.

All excited, George took Dad and me to his patch of land and pointed to a row of sausages hanging on wire which had been poked through them and stretched across the top of a big tin bucket. Under the bucket burnt a few stones of coal, while bigger flames came from yesterday's *Dudley News*. The wind blew in one direction, and I found it odd that the ashes blustering in the air chose to fly in directions all of their own.

George prodded the sausages to gauge whether the inside was cooked. If there was one thing he disliked as a meat-eater, it was raw meat. 'Tastes of dead flesh mash,' he had told his wife, who promptly told him to cook meat himself. George had done so for the thirty-three years that he and Corrine had been married. He'd fed his eldest son, now a doctor, his daughter, who was a social worker, and his middle son, a lecturer in sociology.

George said he'd have much preferred them to have earthy jobs but his wife had honed her educating skills on them well, and they'd bloomed from seeds into fully middle-class civilians and moved away to the south, visiting only in the holidays. Their possessions were the only things that gave a stranger the clue to their origins – these too, George felt, were creative lies told in order to obfuscate.

> Bistro dinner sets in wooden racks – market china teacups in a display cabinet
>
> Checked tablecloths – plastic dinner mats on mahogany
>
> Impressionist prints – Jamaican landscape water-colours
>
> Plain, painted chic walls with dado rails and covings – maroon flowery and busy wallpaper
>
> Fresh hyacinths and petunias in a vase – plastic roses collecting dust

A comprehensive bookshelf – *The Voice*
Lawn – mud with gnomes
Birchwood laminated floorboards – deep-pile blue carpet.

'I hate comparing' said George.

I agreed. 'It saps you.' He was right. Compare was a dirty word that didn't let you be.

George went on with the dramatic tale of his life so far. 'Don't put hot drinks there! You'll stain the beechwood.' 'Please, Father, use a napkin.'

And Father George would cry out, 'I am eating jerk chicken. A man from the heart of Jamaica does not use a napkin.'

'You're British now.'

'Mi accent tell me otherwise and anyways I'm a British West Indian, got that? Two things,' he said sticking up two fingers at his son and Evelyn, 'and you, my son, ain't even one. Now shut your mouth and pass me a yam.'

Dwight passed his father the basket promptly, with hands quivering and a face straining in fear that George might get up and belt him one. All the while eyeing the fool with contempt.

'Dad, please be careful with the Royal Doulton. It's antique.' Dwight just would not stop.

'My son, some things in life we know for certain. There will never be black people on *Antiques Roadshow*.'

Corrine, cooking in her son's brand-new kitchen, caressed the catering-industry-recommended new oven, which could have taken pride of place in the most chiquey-chic restaurant. She was in there because, although daughter-in-law Evelyn had invited them round for a house-warming meal, daughter-in-law hadn't paid attention to the most important thing the visit demanded: food and a cook. Evelyn's tasteless dishes lacked herbs, spices, meat or fat. Her dishes were like her, lean, mean and bland, and the Dutch pot . . . Well, that was a plain pot to her.

'Everything in its proper place,' moaned George. 'No wonder I hate visiting them. Children, they drain away your whole energy and then blame you when you try and preserve some in your resting age.'

He loved his children but he loved his life more, so spent much of his time at the allotment. He had visited it every single day but three, in the four years since he'd finally snatched it from Dudley Council. One day was missed because Corrine had been mugged in the street and sought comfort from her husband. The second was because daughter Joline was to be wed at the West Indian community church.

'I need mi carrots,' George told Joline, as her horse-drawn carriage was about to pull up outside their three-bedroom terraced.

'I may be a social worker but you, Father, need to be dissected under the eye of a microscope to give man a chance in damnation of understanding what goes tick-tock inside your head,' said Joline.

The third and last day was missed because Frederick at the barber's shop had had a cataract removed but neglected to tell his customers who, not knowing, put their hairstyles in danger.

George was one of the first customers when the shop

opened that day, at the more relaxed and easy time of 1 p.m. 'Jus back and sides and a glass of cider,' he said.

'Sure, sure,' said Frederick. 'Can't see your missus in her tabard round these days. She gone left you or sumtin?'

'You hopin she come looking for you, aren't you?' laughed George.

As the conversation turned into telling stories, the stories into nostalgia, Frederick shaved off more than he should have and flicked the grade button switch from four to zero. Unaware, he carried on shaving, not being able to appreciate fully the change in shade, as more hair was shed, from a thick dappled grey to the brown of the skull. All the while, George gazed out of the window and sipped cider, paying no attention to Frederick's hands. A woman would never do such a thing.

In the end George vowed never to return, in the moment's anger when he saw his reflection in the mirror. 'I look like a used-up scuffed cricket ball. You tampered with mi head, man!'

Frederick, in accordance with his type of customer service, let the £1.50 charge go, hoping thereby to induce George to come to a reluctant compromise. 'And you don't have to pay for the cider, either.'

'When have I ever, you burnt-out fool?'

George did not return to Frederick's for the next eight months – not for a haircut, anyway. Maybe it was age, he told us, but his hair seemed to have slowed down. It grew at the rate of a centimetre every twenty-eight weeks. At that rate, he had calculated, it would take him five years to have even a praiseworthy head of ordinary hair, and he wasn't sure he'd live long enough to have an afro just the right size, meaning not so big that it took him back to the seventies.

He shook his head. 'May I temp' you with a can of shandy?'

'You may,' Dad said, thirsty from listening.

George ducked into his shed and returned with not only the cans but a battered trannie, which he switched on. 'In all the time I've been here, you're mi first guests. You run away, yeah?'

'Yeah,' I replied quickly. 'Hey, hold up, how do you know?'

He didn't reply 'cos he was too busy piling food on to plastic plates for Dad and me. We were more than happy to oblige in helping him finish the sausages, and scoffed away heartily.

'Haaaa,' sighed George. 'Paradise is where my soul is. What more could any man ask for? A sausage butty, can o' shandy, beautiful company and the voice genius Mahalia Jackson. I could die here right now, but have to wait until the spinach has been picked.'

'Mahalia?' I asked

'Yeah. You know her?'

'No. You know Rafi?'

'No.' replied George.

Trying not to choke on the last bite of the butty I poked at the fire. I was still hungry, so went over to it and helped myself to another two sausages. George smiled and said he was glad to see his guest felt at home enough to help herself.

As I handed him some more toasted bread with home-made mango chutney, I observed his skin. The fading light brought out the beauty in his dark, aged hands.

'Did anybody ever tell you that you have perfect dark-brown skin?'

'Does being called a black bastard count?' shouted George, making Dad laugh so hard that he booted his can of shandy into the fire, nearly dousing it. Fuelled by laughter, we kicked our feet in the air and slapped each other on the back. Mahalia sang only for us.

'You know when a song is right for you? When it doesn't sound like another man's words.'

'So true,' said I, sipping the last drops of shandy.

'Like to dance?' I asked Dad and George with glee.

'*Hanji.*'

Dancing in the fading light, that's what Dad's life had been so far. We jived slowly then fast to the sax beat and felt the earth beneath us, solid. Our steps, so light, kicked up only a few lumps of soil.

'Do you plan on staying here a while?' asked George

'Just until things get sorted.'

He didn't ask what 'get sorted' meant, but looked as though he understood. Before leaving for home, where another feast would be awaiting him, he shook Dad's hands with both of his.

'See you around.'

'Bye, George.'

I watched George as he took his own good time to secure the allotment gate. Then, waving back at us, he limped over the railway track, shortcutting to his home. The fire had gone right out, but we were still warm.

'I can save time,' Dad whispered, grabbing at the air.

'No, it is time that will save me.' Then he stood up and swayed from side to side, only very slowly coming to a stop. As he sat down on a crate to warm his hands, he sniffed at the air, which although chilly was strangely serene. His cheeks and the tip of his nose glowed red, and his wispy hair hovered above him in the mild wind. We hadn't washed in over four days, but we felt the cleanest we had ever been.

I looked at him. How content he is here, I thought. Taking him out of that ward was the best thing for him Although he was still eating those smarties, at least his hands had stopped shaking.

'Sushminder, you all right?'

'Dad, don't worry about me. I'm fine.'

'Sometimes when I look in your eyes you seem sad.'

'No, Dad, not me.'

We sat there singing *'Mere Desh Ki Dharti'* and revelled in our glory. Never had we felt so good as we did about having beaten those *kanjar* good and proper – always trying to stamp on you the moment you had anything to say. When Dad's teeth began to chatter and his face turned pale, I gave him an extra blanket. The fire needed relighting but we had only one match left and it refused to spark.

Dad assured me he'd still be in the shed when I returned from the shop. 'Get some candles as well.'

So off I went.

It felt strange to go beyond the perimeter of the allotment, almost as if as soon as I stepped out I'd be nabbed, just like that. I'd tried phoning Indy but was welcomed by a toneless cow. It was probably just as well. I mean, I didn't want to burden him – or Saira, for that matter – with two fugitives.

As I emerged into the high street, my heart began to beat faster. My usually 'go at them' nerves had taken a holiday. 'Avoid eye contact with passers-by,' I ordered myself, but the more I did this the more each passer-by scrutinised my face. At least, that's how it seemed. The hood of my duffel hid some of me, but not enough to avoid the gaze of the odd shopper with French bread in hand. Why was I so bloody scared? It was fourish in the afternoon and still light. The cold wind buffed up against my face like it had a grudge.

Ghettoes are the muckiest places, people tell me, but they're wrong because last year I'd seen Kofi Anan walk down Doveridge Road. It was him, I knew it was. So I ran up behind, poked him on the shoulder and said, 'Aye up, Kofi. Sign my hood, won't ya?' And he did. Kofi Anan signed my duffel coat.

To help myself keep calm, I counted the steps it took to reach the nearest matchseller. I looked straight down, seeing brogues, trainers, boots and moccasins passing by. Two hundred and forty-one, two hundred and forty-two . . . Ah, Somerfield. While I was doing the foot waltz with a man in blue canvas shoes, a woman behind me pushed me in.

I was quick going in those revolving doors but let me tell you I was way quicker going out, 'cos there, slap right in the middle of the *Dudley News*, was my face as it had been three years ago! Three bloody years ago I was a skew-whiff alien without a planet. Oh, that got my blood curdling. Rule No 11: Indian girls only make the front

63

page if they've landed a role in an Indian flick, had a forced marriage or run away. I had apparently done the last.

Run away? I'd done no such thing. Dad and me had walked to the allotment with as much cool as Amitabh Bachan in flares.

After I snuck back in I loitered warily by the newspapers to read further. Although there was no reward offered for my capture, the police were concerned about my whereabouts, as was Mum. Dad was a patient with a mental illness, so would benefit from NHS care, and anyone who saw us should telephone the Dudley police straight away. Oh, great. Then my heart began to beat faster than I had ever known it to. Before long my knees joined in the party, nearly giving way so that I had to hold on to the counter ledge.

Mustering up whatever dwindling courage was left inside me, I fled through the vacant-eyed shoppers waiting in line for the snail-like scanning of Betty. 'Don't run,' I ordered myself, 'don't run, damn it. You don't want to call attention to yourself.'

After a few hundred metres I brought myself down to a brisk walk and huffed and puffed, huffed and puffed. Oh, God, I'll have an asthma attack any other time but this. Crashing to my knees in some grubby shale, I wondered whether I should phone Saira, who had my last lot of Ventolins. She had pretend asthma to save her from dire situations such as baby-sitting, visiting relatives or when proposals came round, but by the time I'd got the mobile out of my duffel pocket the numbers had all merged into one another.

'You all right?' asked a woman passer-by. As she bent down I flinched, worried that she was probably looking to do a citizen's arrest.

'Y-y-yus,' I huffed.

'Ooh, you look a bit parched to me.'

'C-c-c-c-comp-comp-complexion,' I said, nearly dying on the last syllable. Now wasn't the best time to have a conversation.

'Don't worry, love. You'll be fine.'

Before I could say 'Get stuffed' a crowd had formed round me (getting to be quite a habit). Murmurs of 'Is she going to make it?' were all I heard before I collapsed into somebody's arms – I didn't know whose. Rule No 12: All personal, physical and mental disabilities should be kept within the confines of the home. We don't want people to think you're a wet mullet.

The girl who could

When Kiz suffocated me on Thursday morning, putting her dustmite-bunged pillow over my face, I was hallucinating severely in the aftermath of the preceding days' horrors. In hospital I'd been tortured like a mouse in a research lab, questioned by the police and, even worse, by antis who were convinced I'd done something way more debauched than running away. Smiling pathetically, I looked into oblivion while being told that running away to get attention wasn't gonna find a home in their land. Rule No 13: Don't ever expect sympathy – especially when you're no Meena Kumari.

Dad hadn't come to see me once. Everyone was still searching for him by interrogating me on his whereabouts. But I wouldn't tell any of them that the allotment was his last refuge, not even if they offered me all of the world's happiness gift-wrapped.

Kiz took the pillow off my face and decreed, 'You have to come Glasgow with me.'

'What for?' I asked, still half asleep.

'You know Shah Rukh?'

'Yeah, we're long-lost siblings.'

'Don't be daft. Well, Gurminder says that *Stardust* says that him and his crew are shooting *Bhangra Kings and Gidha Queens* here in England, except in Glasgow.'

'What the bleedin' flip-flop are you on about? Be serious for a moment, will you? Have you seen Dad lately? He looks more shattered than you after your beauty sleep.'

'Look, if we go now we'll get there at one. Come on, what's up with ya? Come on, come on, come on,' cried Kiz.

I could have whacked her on the nose and shaken her like a rag doll, yelling, 'Do you even care?' but instead she yanked at me like I was an unhappy dog on a leash not wanting to go walkies.

'Quit whining, you lightweight,' I said.

As I lay face down on the pillow Kiz tapped my back for attention. Was she serious? Today, when there were only two days before Kully was not to get married, she wanted us to go economy-class all the way to Glasgow to see some man woo. Even if we were lucky and the trains ran on time, there was no way we could get back to help with the prep. We might just make it back for the suit fittings. What was I doing? Why was I even considering it?

Kiz can be such a slapper sometimes. Once she went to a B&B-cum-exhibition-centre in Birmingham to audition for a play called *Dogs* — or was that for the leading lady in a Dev Anand overseas production called *Shove Love*? Anyway, it was something equally cack. So Kiz went to that audition with the idea of doing the *Titanic* number. Poor cow was gonna need all the luck in the world. In the end she came back cursing Dev Anand.

'He discriminated against me because I was full of zest,' she consoled herself. Later she vowed revenge.

'Stop crying. I'll be right with you.' I gave in too

easily. I know I shouldn't have, but that's what you call a
tapped brain – oh, and blackmail. The silly cow had
found out about Dad's hideaway at the allotment and she
wasn't afraid to use her new CIA powers. Apparently, I
talk in my sleep.

'Pass us the remote or I'll squeal,' she said.

'Here you go, pig.'

'Iron my bootlegs, will ya? You know you want to.'

'Bleedin' have to.'

'Scratch my back. Fetch my dinner. Go get my
conditioner.'

'*Aaaaaaaaaaaaaaaaaaagh!*'

Kiz wept and explained the biggest crisis of her life so
far, while I groaned one of those 'I can't believe it, incor-
rigible' groans. When, oh when, will she acknowledge
that there's a thing called reality between her and that
silvery screen? She thinks I don't see those Indian women
but I do, and better than she does. When I was nine one
of them used to intrude into my dreams and tell me I was
morbid-looking and dance round me shaking her long
black hair. She was white but Indian, and wore a tank
top, miniskirt and fur coat. She came and changed her
outfit, never once stopping for a chat. I didn't like her,
and it was hard for me to think Kiz would even consider
being that thing.

'It's just that Gurminder can't come,' Kiz went on.
'Her mum says some people are coming round to see her
and she has to stay in and help with the work and get
dressed and all sorts.' She sobbed a little more, turning
her back but peeking out of the corner of her eye at me,
hoping for some hope.

Worming my way out of my snug cocoon of a bed, only to be met with an army order, was starting that 'I wish I hadn't woken up' feeling. I must have triggered some of Kiz's frightfully excited genes, because she was callous about dragging me out of the room before I'd even grabbed a pair of gloves to encourage my circulation, which always seems to give up before it notices my hands.

As we stumbled down the stairs past the mess of relations who'd stayed the night, I tripped over a woman doing her hair at the foot of the stairs. It turned out to be Mum, who was trying out a new French roll imported by style icon Worzel.

'Where are you going?' she demanded. 'There's food to be cooked and a frier is needed in the kitchen.'

Leaping in front of me Kiz began persuading Mum to let us go and pay a spy-like visit to the groom's family. 'We need to see how they've decorated their house. A blueprint to work from and beat, that's what we need,' she whispered, like it was a real genius thing to do.

Mum agreed at once: after all, this was a question of one's honour. Before she could interrogate us further the phone rang, and she went to answer it. I grabbed a tenner from Dudley Chacha's coat pocket hanging on the banister. I figured the tenner was one he owed me anyway, 'cos I bought lager on his behalf when he broke his leg mending a door.

Mum hadn't seen me, what with her being too preoccupied telling the caterer, who'd forgotten, where the venue was, while at the same time advising a relation who asked in a roundabout way what everybody else would be wearing to the wedding because clashing would be suicidal.

Only half nine and already the house was swarming with people, who, it seemed, hadn't been to sleep. Someone had used up all the toothpaste again, making Kully weep. My suspicions about the identity of the Colgate thief centred on a man I'd never seen before who had a moustache curled up at either side and three tooth-brushes in his pocket. I was slightly worried that, should there be a mass killing in my absence, I would have to be able to tell the police who was present at the pre-wedding palaver, so I asked him, 'Who are you, anyway?'

'What? What? What?' shouted the man, getting more and more agitated and ending on a tenor note. '*Ki?*' After I'd been threatened with having a chilli squished around in my gob, I legged it out into the big wide world that Kiz thought beckoned her. Rule No 14: Never ask a relation who they are. That's disrespectful.

Kiz trotted down our road to the bus stop near Mrs Kaur's, carrying her mini-suitcase. I rushed after her.

An hour later we boarded a sparsely filled train and sank into grease-ridden green felt seats. A businessman who'd obviously got into the wrong class of carriage rose from one of two seats facing each other, so Kiz and I wasted little time and jumped straight into them 'cos leg-room was required. As we heaved a sigh of bunged-up angst the whistle blew. While the train chugged up speed my eyes adjusted to the blurring of the grey indus-trial landscape to the gradual greening of boring field upon field upon field upon field.

I don't like green English landscapes, I guess because

they're too sullen and dull for me. I want depth, and volcanoes spurting lava, and waterfalls so overpowering that their currents threaten to swallow anyone within a mile radius. I want huge mountains which only the most foolhardy mountaineers dare to climb, and most of them fail, or else when they do reach the top they nearly perish and have to have a helicopter come to save them. I want snow a metre deep which is an unblemished white and warm at the bottom. I want most of all to not look at green hills after green hills. They deaden my thoughts to lead, although that isn't necessarily a bad thing because I've always had this problem of thinking too much.

Sometimes I've wished there was a long piece of string hanging from the nape of my neck, and only when it was pulled would I be able to think for a short while. Then slowly the cogs inside me would lose momentum, my eyes would close and that would be it, no more thinking until the string was yanked again. Kiz never has that problem — thinking, I mean. If she did think, we wouldn't be here in a train to her brain. Those *filmi* lot are in a world of their own, and she's in hers. It's just not possible. And anyway she could never be an actress, even though she acts all the time. Nope, we have a relation in every trade except cinema, so there's no nepotism to work in her favour. Which brings me to Rule No 15: You can dream your dreams, but make them realistic ones. There ain't nothing funnier than a failure failing to realise their dream.

I looked at her, hair finely curled with big cheap curlers, and lipstick shiny on her permanently pouting lips. Bright red clashed with her pale pink complexion.

71

She might have her chance as a heroine yet. Kiz is pretty in that aesthetics-type way, but that's all she is. No, I'm wrong again. She has a kindness gene, even if it is on the wrong side of naive. She thinks good is good, bad is bad, and that grey bit in between just needs a spit and shine. I mean, our Kiz has never even seen an episode of *Crimewatch* in her life.

Two hours into the journey and I was getting mighty bored. Although it was fun to count how many patterned diamonds there were on the vacant seat next to Kiz, I began to wonder whether Budgie was right about me ending up in the loony-bin.

'Paper, stone and scissors?' suggested Kiz.

'Get lost.'

'Paper, stone and scissors. Best of three. Loser does a forfeit. One, two, three, go.'

I really didn't want to play but my hands weren't listening to my head.

'Scissors cut paper. I win,' I said. 'One, two, three go. Paper wraps stone. Two nil to me . . . One, two, three go. Stone blunts scissors. I win.' Kiz is too predictable going in sequence like that, as if I wouldn't get it.

'Come on, then,' she said, 'what's the forfeit?'

I played with my chin a bit, feeling the dent of a dimple I was convinced existed, and looked like a lawyer in contemplation. As if they ever really are. They hit a wall called 'law' and rebound. There I go, thinking again. Must stop that. What could Kiz do to put a little oomph into this killer journey?

Then it came to me. 'Dance.'

'Huh?'

'Dance,' I said again.

'Ain't got no music.'

'Oh yeah? That ain't a ghetto blaster in there, then?'

I knew her plan all right. She once heard of a girl who made it as a background dancer by barging into Filmistan with her blaster and dancing like she was having an attack, so Kiz was going to do the same on the *Bhangra Kings and Gidha Queen's* set.

'Come on, I'm waiting,' I said, tapping my fingers in sequence on the table.

It would be quite some time before anything happened, because Kiz shuffled into carriage D to lock herself in the toilet. I warned her not to go in, 'cos I once saw on *Crimewatch* that somebody'd been attacked in there – trains are a haven for criminals, and poor passengers like us must beware. Ignoring my wise advice, she spun out of there clad in a blinding-bright cerise blouse and sequinned chiffon skirt, which looked thoroughly out of place in this dingy thing called a train. Her sequins sparkled in what little light pushed its way through the smeared windows and, although she wasn't radiant in the stylistic sense, she knew who she was. If only Bimla and Worzel could see her now. When the train travelled over a particularly bumpy bit of rail, Kiz, with her red-polished fingernail pressed the button on the remote and her remix did play.

> *'Chan vekh shoukan mele di,*
> *Chan vekh shoukan mele di,*
> *Jalva tera jalva, jalvaa.'*

73

In my head I played *funtakshri*. The rules were simple. Translate Punjabi, Hindi or Urdu words into English. Now you have yourself a complete riot.

> 'Love look at the buzz of the fair.
> Love look at the buzz of the fair.
> Your charisma, charisma.'

The music echoed through her head and she gave her whole self up to it, for she belonged to nothing but the lyrics. Her hips swayed one way, her heart another, and her hair was all over the bloody place, the curls bouncing back and forth like a shimmy-spring spreeing down some steps. All the while, the music throbbed ever louder as she accidentally but purposefully grasped the remote control, with the volume button pressed down. Jeez, it was only a dare. Why did she have to take it so professionally seriously? I mean, you give a person a stupid dare and they do it well.

> *'Ik punjaban. Kuri punjaban.*
> *Athra baras ki thu, hone ko ayee hain.*
> *Dillage ne dee hava, thora sa thua utha.'*

> 'One Punjabi, girl Punjabi.
> You're going to be eighteen.
> Romance gave a bit of wind. A little smoke blew up.'

Remix after remix led Kiz up and down the aisle making passengers rise from their seats to take a good look at the dancing shenanigans. One secretly nosy man peered over his broadsheet to observe my deranged sister going dipsy. Although he appeared apprehensive, he was enjoying the free entertainment. A little chubby girl behind him with a doll in her hand showed how plastic arms and legs could move just as well to the music. They were all captured. Even the older, suited woman looked as though she was getting the hang of the rhythm as the gangway became cluttered with passengers from the other carriages. They had become the audience. All of them, gobs open, stood frozen with their eyes bulging, for Rani Kiz was dancing in the aisle of a train. How novel. She danced and she pranced as if the ground beneath her was moving. Only when the music died down did her whirling halt. Applause was all she'd ever wanted in life, and this was only the second time she'd received it.

The first was when she did roughly the same thing at a poorly organised event called a cultural something or other. It seemed to her that the only way you got applause nowadays was if you announced, 'Hey, I'm a much happier human being now and the way I changed my mind was to change my body. Yes, that's right, I lost fifty stone on the die-fast plan.' O-oh, food had crept into my thoughts and I felt a pang remembering that we hadn't had any breakfast.

Kiz went and changed back into her more sober beige trousers – she kept on the sparkling blouse. Then she returned, happily huffing and puffing, and blushing every time a wolf-whistle blew past her. As soon as Kiz sat down facing me, she arose to do a West End musical bow. Right then I could tell from her eyes, the way she confidently swept back the curly tresses of streaky brown

75

hair, that she really believed her calling in her life was to be an Indian heroine. Was she my sister? Her eyes questioned my confidence in her but it wasn't me who should be worrying. I imagined Mum at home ranting about her two lost daughters, Worzel praising her own Sammy and Pinky, and Bimla chuckling with her Nina.

Before I could grind out some praise, a woman sounding as if she had a cold and a bout of constipation announced our arrival. It was 1.47 p.m., give or take a few minutes. The minute hand on my watch was in a bad mood.

'Hurry up,' I snapped at Kiz, who seemed to think I was a dutiful coolie who'd use my initiative and get her mini-suitcase for her. Well, actually, I did. Making myself busy, I loaded the contents of her vanity bag back into it – I'd accidentally stamped on them, you see. As I was chucking in her shimmering mint-green nail polish, I saw Kiz striking up a conversation with a stranger. Listening in, I could only make out it was one of those over-your-head conversations: the speakers converse in a pleasingly orderly manner, each waiting till the other has spoken before giving a nod of acknowledgement to cover the fact that they haven't listened to a word. It's an 'I'm talking to a toss-pot' conversation.

'Oh, this is my sister,' squeaked Kiz, pointing to me like a game-show host displaying a coveted fridge-freezer. This is the freezer light. See, it switches on, off, on, off.

'Pleased to meet you. How are you?' asked the stranger holding out an open hand to shake one of mine, both of which he could clearly see were carrying crap.

I smiled but did not ask him how he was, 'cos you could tell he only asked me out of fake politeness. He scared me a bit because his eyes looked shallow, stuck only to the surface of his pale skin, and they were positively popping out at Kiz in her cerise blouse. 'Pervert alert,' I muttered under my breath, but Kiz was having difficulty hearing as the radiation from the stranger's gold fillings interfered with the sound waves.

'Best go now. See ya,' I interrupted, as I got out of the carriage and walked a hundred yards before dropping all Kiz's belongings on platform 2a. She soon came plodding up behind.

'I swear, if you've given him our phone number –'

'What do you take me for?' she asked, trying to chase down a powder compact which had escaped and was rolling away.

'I take you for nothing. No, wait. A twit, that's what I take you for.'

'Don't you call me a twit.'

'A ten-pinter, then. Will that do?'

'Quite nicely, thank you,' smirked Kiz.

We stood there scowling at each other, she regretting having brought me with her and I regretting the thrombosis that had taken hold. After this brief altercation we decided that a lack of food meant a lack of temper, so headed towards the nearest newsagent, which fortunately was only a few seconds' walk away.

Three packs of chicken-flavour crisps, a Milky Way, a Drifter and a pack of Bombay Mix later, I felt a little calmer.

Kiz had opted for just a can of Pepsi Max. 'Food,' she

said, 'makes one feel sluggish.' Then she started banging her hair up and down to add volume.

'Well,' I said, 'where are we supposed to be going, and how are we supposed to get there?'

'We'll take a taxi,' said Kiz grandly. 'Look, there's a taxi rank over there.'

I scanned the drivers' faces and noticed that some of them looked like my uncles back in Dudley, so we waited a while to see whether any more options would become available. Five minutes later I was propelled into a taxi by Kiz and the glare of a driver with a cigarette in his hand. His window was rolled down just enough for him to flick the ash out without letting in too much mist. This didn't herald 'environmentally friendly', more 'I've been at this job too long'.

Glasgow weather suited me fine: dark, tenebrous clouds threatened to swallow you up, and the streets couldn't cope with the rainfall, so traipsing through the flood was the only way around anywhere. Jus perfeck.

'My hair!' screamed Kiz, alarming the driver so that he swerved sharply to the right and made me slide across the seat, thereby squashing any inkling of meaningful life out of dearest Kiz.

'What of it?' asked the driver calmly and as if he was truly interested.

'My tresses aren't . . . My tresses aren't trestling.'

Mr Taxi Man seemed none too affected by this and smiled at me in the rear-view mirror. I smiled back. He then wound up the window that partitioned us from him. Although this seemed rather rude, I reckoned I'd do exactly the same, given only the breath of a chance.

Listening to Kiz gob on is as inspiring as putting your head in a cement mixer. I hate to complain, but she's never had a problem in her life. It's all been *Just Seventeen* stuff: 'I feel lonely. I'm unpopular. Nobody likes me and my sister hates me.'

I was so busy wondering whether we truly were blood-related that I hardly noticed the buildings that towered above us giving way to dark mountains of grass. They were like those I'd seen in Indian films before. So this is where they came.

When we at last stopped, Mr Agarwal – at least that's what his dodgy torn ID card said his name was – charged us £16.25. After I'd had another argument with Kiz for making me fork out a fiver, he let the taxi doors open, and there we were: at the destination Kiz had noted from Gurminder.

'Look,' cried Kiz, pointing to her distressed face which she was surveying in one of those flip mirrors that give an enlarged view of all your pores. 'Look. This time it's just got to be the real thing.'

I paid no attention to her, and scanned the horizon. Why I hadn't worn three pairs of socks instead of just the one I don't know, but my feet were freezing and they were all I could think about.

A double coating of lip-liner and mulberry lipstick later, Kiz looked ready to conquer the world. While strolling about searching for a film crew she told me she wanted to cut a lock of Shah Rukh's hair so she could cherish it for ever. I could imagine her doing a long soliloquy to let everybody know that her life was more worth living as a result of having his hair, but before she could go gaga over his name again, there, yonder over the hills, the embodiment of Kiz's happiness appeared, trying to mime to some catchy Punjabi lyrics. Around him a whole flock of females flapped flippingly, while the technical crew pushed them out of the way. Most of them looked very cold in their identical 'I love Scotland' raincoats. One cameraman sitting on top of what looked like a robot's arm cursed a group of girls who insisted on jumping in his way.

The miming hero, on the other hand, looked like he was having the best time trying to dance. His enthusiasm was not dampened even when the pot-bellied choreographer kept showing him how to put one foot in front of the other. Behind them both were a dancing group of peacocks – girls dressed like peacocks, I mean – and behind them three sheep which had probably come to see what all the chaos was about.

From my hill Shah Rukh looked a lovely version of ordinary.

'*Aaaaaaaaaagh!*' screamed Kiz as loud as she could, which was very loud. 'That ain't no Shah Rukh.'

'Maybe not but he did star in a *bhangra* video, and look at him – I mean, you don't get much lovelier than that.' A girl who was spluttering saliva at making eye contact with the hazel-eyed hero looked back at Kiz all misty eyed. From her sequinned handbag an autograph book poked out, open at the page on which the hero had signed his name. She peered at it. 'Oh, I still don't know Mr Scribble's name.'

'But I wanted Shah Rukh. I was even getting all dressed up for him,' blubbered Kiz.

'*Stardust* tells lies. Surely you know that?'

'Yes, of course I do. What do you think I am, a novice?' Kiz said snootily.

As she edged a little closer to the main cameraman Kiz tried hard to convince herself – I can always tell what she's thinking 'cos she's got the most expressive face in the whole universe – that the hero was worth a closer look. Then, in a lightbulb moment which nearly electrocuted her, she realised that, Shah Rukh or no Shah Rukh, she could easily adore this rising star – no problem. Kiz only had time for him because she thought he was going to be a star soon. I wanted to tell her that stardom has one big flaw: it distorts reality, makes you want to talk to people you'd ignore if they were in the supermarket queue. If that hero were serving you at Asda, you might tell him to check the total again to see if he'd overcharged you, but nothing more than that.

I bent down to tie my shoelace, and before I'd even half finished Kiz was scampering up the hill and star-jumping with excitement. I clambered doggedly up behind her, slipped on the wet grass, regained my balance, then was flattened by a stampeding horde of females of all ages and varieties. 'Watch it!' I wailed as a girl fraught with desperate intentions trod on my hand, but nobody was listening. They trampled over me, shoving my face into the damp soil.

'Oh, didn't see you there. Sorry,' apologised the last girl, who at least gave me time to get out of her way.

'You didn't see me?' I asked. 'Why? Am I invisible, like?'

'More or less,' she said as she skipped over to join the horde.

More or less? I'll give her more or less!

I watched the enthralled females scream and push one another about behind the stretch of yellow sticky tape that cordoned them off. The tape wasn't exactly the best deterrent, and twice the hero had to be rushed to his dressing-room to recover from near-suffocation by female grip. Those girls wanted him badly, and no sticky tape was going to get in their way.

Every time he ran his fingers through his hair the female zoo howled, and the bulgy choreographer smirked whenever the hero messed up or disregarded yet another dance move; all this against a backdrop of the rambler's dream landscape.

I must have been hypnotised for a while, because all of a sudden, loudly enough to perforate my eardrum, a man shouted, 'Get them into the costume van now! Hurry up, yaar!' and a thin man stopped in his tracks and started manhandling me and Kiz down the hill.

'What? I'm not one of your skivvies. Get your hands off me!' I protested, but he wasn't listening.

When we stopped Kiz and I found ourselves in a dowdy trailer. At one end were rails of costumes in daring colours and daring cuts made to be worn by daring darlings. Behind me were more costumes screaming, *Wear me, wear me!* Unfortunately, before we could opt for outfits which looked remotely appealing, we were each handed a yellow mish-mash layered chiffon thing called 'a dress' by a shy dressmaker wearing something equally shameful, oh and a peacock hat.

'I'm no dancer,' I informed the dressmaker, but she only spoke Hindi.

Kiz dragged me back. 'Shut-up. Don't say a word. This is my *chance*.'

'But . . .'

'Please. You and me are sisters. Sisters help each other out, right?'

'Yeah but . . .'

'Are you going to spoil my dream?'

Well, when someone asks you a question like that, you instantly become their slave.

I won't go into what happened next. Suffice it to say that you will see me and Kiz plodding up and down at the back of a Punjabi track with twenty-one other dancers in exactly the same dress. I'm the one who looks as though she's twisted her ankle; because I had. This takes me to Rule No 16: Never, ever be a background dancer in a song picturisation, because you won't be coming to a cinema near me.

By the time we were given a tea break, I'd danced myself to a wreck. Kiz looked like she'd only just begun.

'Me and Mr Stamina, we're like *that*,' she said.

'Yeah,' I replied. 'Pity you and Mr Brains can't get it together.'

We sat there sullenly, me waiting for the sun and her waiting for the hero; as it turned out neither of them bothered to make an appearance. Eventually Kiz got fed up and went off to hunt down her prey.

It got dark and I got tired of waiting. The next train was leaving in an hour, so I wasn't too chuffed when it took a whole fifteen minutes to locate Kiz. She'd tagged up with a girl named Sanjeev and they'd made a pact to become groupies together.

As far as I could see, nearly every single girl was masked in white foundation and eye-shadow which looked like it was a disease taking hold. The poor twerps had tried so very, very hard that I felt they should have been awarded a certificate for effort alone. Then I saw Kiz pull the exquisitely curled hair of a girl about eight inches taller than herself, someone she really should not have messed with. I grabbed her and we ducked underneath a patio table covered in a satin tablecloth with drinks and snacks laid out on it.

We didn't realise it was Mr Hungry Hero's table until his shoe brushed Kiz's hair and he sat down and crossed his legs, nearly kicking me in the face.

'Don't you dare budge,' I threatened, but Kiz couldn't control herself and gave in to temptation faster than she could say the word. Launching herself at the hero, she screamed as if she was fighting off a swarm of enraged hornets.

'Girls fling themselves at me all the time,' said the hero, fending her off with one hand and sipping the drink he held in the other.

'Modesty is ever so becoming in you,' said Kiz, eagerly polishing his ego.

What made her behave like that? I wondered. Might it have something to do with the authentic Indian Nehru suit that made him appealing, or perhaps it was because he was so unassumingly thick. Anyhow, he was rather endearing. But before Kiz could ask his name another brood of marauding females appeared from nowhere and rugby-tackled him off the chair. I leapt out of their way. I still had somebody's footprint on the back of my neck and I wasn't exactly looking to complete the pair.

'Look, I got it! Look at me! I'm queen of the world! Ha ha ha.'

There in Kiz's hand was a lock of the hero's hair. Mission accomplished.

We arrived home that fateful day to be welcomed by tut-tuts and necks stretching as people strained to x-ray our heads, trying to understand the complexities of the female mind.

'Does it take that long to see decorations?' asked Mum.

Kiz tried to convince her that it did. 'Yeah, it was like the Merry Hill Centre at Christmas, all shining, like, and twinkly.'

After that gem, we were made to decorate the house, which amounted to five metres of tinsel and a silver helium heart-shaped balloon stuck outside the front door. Then it was punishment time – oh, and that's another thing. Rule No 17: Get used to parents dishing out punishment. It won't end until you're seventy or there-abouts, and that law thing that states you're an adult when you're eighteen, it doesn't apply to us lot. For our punishment Mum gave Kiz and me a whole evening's cooking for thirty-three guests. I'd never done a whole evening in my life. Ten minutes, maybe, but a whole evening was something new. Did they want food or something that just resembled it?

We began with the dhal, because after previous attempts I was beginning to think I was good at making it. No sooner had the thought entered my head than Mum grabbed my wooden mixing-spoon and threatened to mince me because I'd committed sacrilege. I stood there bemused, with only turmeric-stained fingernails to show for my endeavours, and Mum swiftly took control and began to undo the calamity. You see, there's one rule that must never be broken in the laws that govern Indian cooking. That rule is No 18: Always brown your onions.

I had fun watching Mum have a fit when I told her the onions were partially browned. 'Partially?' she screamed. 'I'll give you partially.'

Later that evening she had some more emotional outbursts, saying that the chicken wasn't washed (it was) and that Kiz and I should be shot for not slicing down the middle of the aubergines to check for maggots.

This was only after she stopped ranting about the cheap quality lentils Worzel had bought. 'We may have to be thrifty with our money, but there will never be a day when I can't afford East End. Never.'

Mum had conveniently forgotten that I was the daughter whose culinary accomplishments included trying to cook an omelette in a non-non-stick pan without butter, and boiling rice without water. I tried to flatter her into doing the rest of the cooking by informing her that true mastery of Indian cooking lay within the kitchen, which was of course ruled by the female head of the household. And that wasn't to say that women were confined to the home any more, it was just to say that women knew cooking better.

Mum did a little of what she called 'giving in', and gave a Madhur Jaffrey rendition of how to make a

86

triangular samosa. Although this was gripping stuff to watch, my mind strayed. I wondered why, in every kitchen I'd ever been in, the oven top was always covered with cooking-foil, and why plastic shelving like fruit baskets took pride of place in the corner. Not forgetting the small drinking-glasses priced at £4 for forty, available at the local suit and sari shop; the countless empty plastic containers; the metal dustbin to store a thousand-pound bag of flour, the flowery crockery, and the newspaper used to cover the cupboard shelves.

Apart from these special stylistic features of an Indian kitchen, our actual cooking accoutrements were few. All Mum ever used was a rolling-pin, to threaten us with, of course – oh, and a *thava*, the flat pan that taught us the meaning of life or helped to cook the *rotiya*. She also used lots of metal cooking-pots big enough to hold small children, and sighed with sorrow whenever she saw only a single small cooking-pot in a kitchen. That was the sign of a non-existent extended family. Shame on them.

While I wondered, Kiz was busy getting on the side of Mum's better nature and sucking up so hard it was painful to watch. I'd been demoted to chief potato-peeler, so Kiz abused this temporary change in social status by trying to suck up even more, lecturing me on the finer points of Indian cooking. She declaimed in a presenter's voice, loud enough for the antis in the living room to hear and be impressed by, 'You know, Sushi, if you ask to have a bhaji, you're asking for a sharp slap. "Bhaji", you see, in Urdu is the translation of "sister".'

'Oh, really?' I said, gouging out a potato eye. 'So it

isn't an ugly, shapeless piece of food that tastes completely the opposite?'

'Shut up and peel.'

'You shut up.'

'You shut up.'

'I'm older than you. Show me some respect.'

'I'm younger than you. Why don't you show me some? Anyway, I follow by example, you twit.'

Just then Dudley Chacha trundled in and began looking around nervously – I guessed he was after the bottle of Bell's that Mum had hidden behind the fruit basket.

'Hey,' he said. 'Now, who bought these enticingly packaged okra and chillies?'

'It was her!' shouted Kiz and I in unison, pointing at each other.

'Well, whoever it was is doing herself out of a well-deserved trip to the corner shop, with its outside fruit stall strategically placed to make you stumble and its excellent customer service. What were you thinking?'

He's a joker, our Dudley Chacha, so I told him where the whisky was. With bottle and motivation in hand, he scurried past the antis and out into the garden to share the alcohol with the rest of the men confined to the huge tent that they called a marquee in our patchy garden.

No sooner had he gone than Worzel came in. 'When are the chapattis going to be made?'

'If you want *rotiya*, call them by their proper name,' I snapped.

'Ooh, a traditionalist, I see.'

Worzel's never happy with Indian food. She says it spoils her delicate frame, but actually she's one of those

88

people who'd spread butter on already buttered toast. She makes even healthy food fatty because she's a greedy cow.

'Go away and put your make-up on,' I snarled, to which she responded by throwing a bag of *roti* number one flour on to the floor before stropping into the living-room, where people couldn't see past her green contact lenses.

A ten-kilo bag of potatoes later I was busy learning to make a *roti*. I argued relentlessly and fiercely with Mum about her insistence on rolling a *roti* into a perfect circle – after all, it didn't alter the taste and square *rotiya* were just as appealing. However, as Mum pointed out, marriages had been made and broken over the matter of an oblong or square *roti*. Now, that is what I call wisdom.

I found that a perfect *roti* would puff up in the middle but, like humans, *rotiya* had their foibles too. Making a round one was an art, and I'd need plenty more lessons in digging out the right amount of dough and rolling it out quickly enough to keep the line of *rotiya* coming. This was hard and skilled work, so I wasn't too disheartened when the first one I made resembled a cowpat. After that I tried using a plate to cut round, but found an eager anti audience jeering at me for doing so. 'Bear with it,' I told myself.

Hours later, when Kiz and I had fed the guests, thanked our helpers, and the first lot of *mehndi* – turmeric dough, really – had been applied to Kully, I crashed out on the stairs. Somebody had locked themselves in the room I shared with Kiz and Kully, and I was in no mood to find out who it was – at least, not until someone tugged a strand of my hair so that I jerked and gawked behind me, only to find there was nobody there. My eyes were finding it difficult to focus, so I let them be and lay in a foetal position at the top of the stairs. The air around me was warm with the central heating turned high. Just leave me alone, I thought. Just leave me – Then I felt the tug again, but before the perpetrator could sprint away I grabbed her by the bottom of her pyjamas. Penelope!

It is well known that when a wedding takes place everybody you've ever met in your life is invited, but I was dismayed to find that Mum had invited penfriend Penelope. She hadn't even thought to ask.

I well remember the events leading up to that particularly troublesome chapter in my school days, when I learnt the lesson that most ideas start out as harmless pursuits for interest and fun.

On a dull summer's day, Miss Petal handed out letter-writing paper and went on and on about how we were all going to have something exciting in our lives, which would enrich our view of another world and improve our grammar at the same time. I thought I was going to get an electronic Speak and Spell, and was mightily disappointed to find it was only a penfriend.

The idea of a penfriend is all right but sometimes adults don't think about the practicality of such matters. Pairing up two children who have very little in common is pernicious. I wrote those letters under the misconception that somebody normal would reply, and for all the other pupils in class that was the case. Not for me, though. I got paired with a psycho.

I don't know what I wrote in that first letter, but none

of it should have led to being punished with a penfriend. Her name was Penelope La-di-da Baxter – double-barrelled name and all that. Her letters were written in crayon, though her peers had advanced to writing with a pen. Enclosed in her letters, you might have expected the occasional small gift of some sort but I got loose pins and staples to prick the life out of me. Chewed chewing-gum was a speciality; another was talcum powder; and then there was the time she charmingly sent me a letter soaked in vinegar so I stank of it all day.

You'd think that after all this Miss Petal would have let me dump Penelope and break contact, but no, she shrugged off the threats as harmless pranks. Teachers are always reluctant to tell off pupils from other schools, even if they wouldn't hesitate to lynch a pupil from their own.

I pleaded on bended knee. 'Please, Miss, please, Miss, it's not fair. What if she sends me a nail bomb next time?' It was a convincing performance which failed to convince Miss Petal.

Three months later it was announced that we were to visit Thorpe Grammar School out there in good old country land, and a fortnight later we were on a coach preparing to meet people we'd been forced to be friends with. Being friends means different things to the middle-aged.

It was still early in the morning when we arrived out-side what looked like a government building and were greeted with faces aghast, banners and party poppers. A brown face wasn't something they were used to. The royal welcome they'd given us was heart-warming, though, and I felt optimistic that somewhere in the crowd would be a kind, gentle girl who just liked to play jokes once in a while.

While the teachers hugged one another, our school stared at their lot, their school at us lot, all the while each of us summing up the person who stood before us and hoping the delightful-looking boy or girl in the corner was our penfriend.

Before we could choose a personal favourite, we were shuffled along to a school hall the size of the Theatre Royal with a stage fit for a Broadway performance. Here we stood in a mess while the teachers tried to establish order by matching us with our penpals. I watched, saddened, as my friends left me to be paired with people who had all the dearest of qualities.

When we were down to the last lame pupils – not including me, of course – Miss Petal walked up to me holding the hand of a girl who looked like a monster. It was Penelope, dressed in a Parisian-style dress with matching purse hung over one shoulder. She wore a hat with a sunflower sticking out of one side and underneath was a fringe the colour of sodden straw. I'd expected her to be wearing a school uniform, but Penelope informed me that she'd persuaded the teacher to let them wear special dress on this auspicious occasion. Liar.

We looked each other up and down until the teacher left us to get acquainted. Then without any time-wasting I hit her and she hit me. I pushed her to the ground and sat on her back so she nearly stopped breathing until I got off her to listen to Miss Petal's itinerary of a meticulously planned day. It included a walk during which we would be able, Miss Petal claimed, to see all the charming sights of the local farms and fields.

Throughout this 'charming' experience Penelope kept pulling the hood of my raincoat over my face so that I couldn't see where I was going. By the end of the day that girl had worn out my wits. She'd snapped the handle of my satchel, stolen the lace out of my shoe, at dinnertime exchanged my tofu burger for a hamburger, and told the whole school I wore no knickers, so I had to show them to the whole room just to prove that I did.

I was finally flung over the patience cliff when she did her imitation of a Dudley accent for the fourteenth time, even though I'd explained clearly to her that Dudley was a refined place and not scabby (as she put it).

'Yow come from Dudlay, yow do,' jeered Penelope.

I was annoyed to the point that annoyance had no return so grabbed her hat, stomped on it a few times and shouted obscenities that even I didn't know I'd learnt by the age of twelve. After I'd finished yelling my monologue in her face, I pushed her shoulder. Penelope pushed me back. What is there to do, I thought, but push her other shoulder? That should work. Should it, heck!

As we pushed each other back and forth, accompanying the pushes with menacing stares, a crowd formed round us. They chanted in heavy, carnivorous voices and bayed for blood: 'Scrap, scrap, scrap!'

Only after the eleventh push did I realise what I'd got myself into. I couldn't back out now. If any credibility was to be restored to my sordid reputation, here was my chance. Ducking behind her, I hit her on the back of the knee, bringing her down. She got hold of both my legs and soon had me on my bottom. Hair was pulled out of follicles, nails dug into flesh, and punches were thrown from alarming distances before a teacher summoned up the initiative to intervene. Sometimes I think they're only in the profession to get their kicks from adolescents pretending to imitate a Lewis–Holyfield match.

Even after a week's detention and Mum's direst threats I was glad I'd made Penelope cry. Little rich girls cry louder than anybody else on this planet, and that was the only way I wanted to remember her.

But now here she was, in my own house, evicting me from my own room. I could imagine the wedding day, Mum stapling me to the rich white girl so all the other guests would think that this Indian diasporic family had at last rooted itself properly and made some proper connections.

Before Penelope could start asking questions about 'strange Indian customs', I scampered into my room and started rummaging through her leather suitcase to find contact details for somebody who'd get her away from me. It was time to call her parents.

Penelope came dashing in behind me. 'Get out, you leech.'

'This is my room.'

'They're my belongings.'

'Well, they don't belong here. Go back where you came from.'

'You wouldn't say that if you knew what I've got.'

'I bet I would,' I said, standing up straight with my back arched as if ready for a duel.

'Liar, piar, bottom's on fire,' scoffed Penelope, reaching

deep inside her pyramid shaft of hair to retrieve – the mobile Indy had given me.

'Give me that!' I shouted, charging at her like a enraged bull with no sense of direction.

'I'm the rich witch with your life in my hands,' sang Penelope, waving the phone in my face. 'Your kind are scum. My mother sent me on this cultural trip – don't for one minute assume that I came of my own volition.'

'Yes, you did. Why bother to tell lies? You know very well your family's never had any time for you, Miss Lost Cause, and I know for a fact that your mother sent you here to get you away from her.'

'Why's that, then?' she said, blubbering inside but trying hard to look as if she didn't give a toss.

''Cos she hates you.' I screwed my face up tight when I said 'hate' and increased the drama by looking her right in the eye.

Bold-faced as I was, even I didn't believe that this young woman, who had the best education and upbringing in the Midlands, would believe me. But she did. Later that night she went away, leaving the mobile on my bed. I hoped she wouldn't tell anyone anything.

I've had enough

When Arjun and Sammy got together at Brummie Uncle's the following day, the two of them near enough ignored the pants off me. Indy reckoned they thought they were above me just because they were clad in chic gear. Arjun strolled about in his rich white cotton tunic and jeans, and Sammy clung to him in her pink floaty fishtail. Still, that was no reason to go all bourgeois.

When I looked down at my own rather basic *khadar* silk *salwaar kameez*, I nearly spluttered to see all the HobNob crumbs showering it. Arjun must have thought I was a right messy twerp. Then again, maybe he wasn't thinking about me at all: he'd folded his arms in that 'I'm listening' but defensive manner of his. Maybe he wasn't enjoying the conversation with Sammy, either. Maybe he was doing lousy time like me. Paa. What was there to enjoy? Conversation? Sammy wouldn't know how to hold a conversation even if you handed her a piece of paper with *Conversation* written on it.

Saira had phoned the night before to let me know that I'd nearly died in Arjun's arms the day I was carted off to hospital. I asked her how she knew, and she said that when she came to see me in Ward Four Arjun was already there, giving my mum a detailed account in Punjabi of me dropping in the street just like that. Mum was happy with the lad-cum-legend who'd saved her daughter's life, so invited him to the party being held at Brummie Uncle and Worzel's house before the *mehndi*-night bash.

'Why there?' I asked.

'They've got a bigger, better house,' said Mum.

'It's not got anything to do with them wanting to get in with the Rais 'cos of their fortune, then?'

'No,' said Mum as if she believed it.

So we traipsed halfway across Dudley on Friday morning into Handsworth with some of my wedding clothes in a bin-liner. All the suitcases had been nabbed by Kully and Kiz. Mum had used the remaining suitcase to store Kully's new suits packed in a cellophane bags.

As soon as we arrived, Worzel started sifting through the cases' contents, evaluating them with her fashion-conscious eye. Worzel owned a fabric boutique in Dudley, which apparently gave her a licence to criticise everyone's choice of *salwaar kameez*.

'You and your rubbish bag can go in my Sammy and Pinky's room,' she said, clearly wanting me out of the way.

'Really can we?'

Mum gave me a short, sharp glance which told me to shut up, so I did. Kully pulled me upstairs to find a contact lens which she said had popped out of her eye. Once inside Sammy and Pinky's room I slung my bin liner into a corner of their just furnished, just redecorated, Laura-Ashley-style room. How old were they? Two?

Downstairs Worzel had moved on to ranting about her Italian furniture, showing off its S-shaped bends and carved detail to all the assembled antis. She was a real

97

decorator, Worzel. That four-bedroomed semi had been wallpapered five times in as many years. It was positively a ribbon-cutting ceremony at the door when her sisters and friends came round to inspect.

Once I'd found Kully's contact lens, which was in her eye all along, I nipped back downstairs. The last guests had arrived to fill Worzel's house for the second *mehndi* scrap. In among them stood Arjun, arms crossed, chatting to Budgie. With him helping me like that when I had that bad spell, I thought I ought at least to thank him, so after what seemed like for ever I went over.

'Thank you so much,' I bleated. 'Thank you, thank you, thank you.'

Arjun paused and uncrossed his arms. Then he forced his mouth into a shape which I assumed to be a smile. 'Oh it was nothing,' he mumbled, and with that he went over to Sammy and began telling her about how low-lights really suited her yellow hair. Yeah, if you like the anaemic look, thicko.

Jeez! You show a guy a few manners and what does he do? Leaves you hanging there, practically tightening the noose round your neck. And does he even mention that if you'd died he might have, too? Does he, heck. I'd like to have decked his highlights if it hadn't been for the common-sense bug stinging me. Serves me right for breaking Rule No 19: Never, ever be nice to a guy. We girls have a Mary-Poppins-meets-Submissive-Gal character stereotype to assassinate. I mean, if I hadn't said thank you in such a grateful, pauper-like way, I bet he'd have come chasing me to ask if I'd got over my ordeal and whether he could offer more assistance to ensure my full recuperation?

I guess Mum was, in her own way, making me suffer for lying about studying 'A' levels and hiding Dad at the allotment. She was mortified when Penelope told her about the voicemail from the Mosquito telling me I'd officially been kicked off a course I shouldn't have been on anyway.

I never really wanted to go to college in the first place. Mum knew that, so as an insidious way to get me into it she invited the biggest bunch of morons ever round to *mehndi* night, too – real public-school ponces. You're probably thinking that I didn't give them half a chance but I did, I did. I mean, I said hello without smirking, and gave them the correct direction to the toilets without mentioning they were a bunch of bastards, but really when they keep looking at you like a girl without a hope in hell's chance of becoming something, how is a girl supposed to be courteous? Bunch of thick breeds think they'll come out of their education and the world will be waiting on a plate at their door.

Penelope'd also dropped Dad in it. He hadn't totally relinquished his parental responsibilities, so when I failed to turn up with the matches he'd got worried and thought I'd snuffed it. He left a message on Indy's mobile telling me to come back to the allotment. Of course, Penelope got to it before I did, then Mum, then Worzel, then Bimla and the rest of the bleedin' *khandaan*. I decided to get rid of that mobile sharpish. It had got me in more bleedin' strife than the whole of the world's antis put together could.

So there I was dashing to the allotments with the witches on my tail, to find that Dad wasn't at our patch anyway. Only PCs Plid and Plod were to be seen, breaking the lock of shed 49, rummaging through our meagre borrowed necessities. I went from a police inquiry to a witch one when Mum, Worzel and Bimla picked up the *Des Pardes* and turned to the matrimonials in the back.

With them all sat down on Worzel's Italian leather suite, I did not make eye contact.

'See, see, look at these.' They pointed to the academic achievements of every candidate. 'Now tell me, where do you fit in?'

I can't even have a civil argument with them — that would be asking too much. But God, are they thick. Dad says, 'If you're up against thick people, well, that's it, you're stuffed.'

The whole of Mum's clan went ape at me, saying that I'd never amount to anything and that I'd let down the family's honour.

'That would be a fine thing, if only we had some in the first place,' I told them. Then I ran out of the room before the slippers could connect with the back of my head.

I eagerly took up an offer from Brummie Uncle to go with him and collect the bills from their second house, the one in Aston. They were renovating it to sell it on for a tidy profit. I thought it'd be only me and him going, but Worzel, Bimla and Mum plonked themselves in the back of the car and I couldn't escape: the central locking had imprisoned me.

When we reached the dilapidated Aston semi, Worzel showed Mum around.

I tried to sneak back out to the car, but Worzel stopped me. 'It's a football day. You go out and you die,' she said.

She was right: I really would have died if I'd stepped outside. You see, during the home improvements Brummie Uncle had knocked down the front wall of the garden to allow the maximum number of cars to fit in his drive; he can get six and a half Peugeots in at the moment. Anyway, he got the shock of his life when he found most of the Wolves and Aston Villa supporters on his doorstep, too. He hates them now. 'Can't they go back to where they came from?' he asked Worzel. Wonder where he'd heard that before?

Through the front room's blinds I observed group after group of men in multicoloured scarves and hats, carrying cones of chips, kebabs and beer, go by. They spoke a different language, shouted inaudible things at the top of their lungs, only to be met by someone's bodily fluids, cheering or rubbish. The purple crowd seemed jolly – I think their team had won – so I lifted the slats of the blind a little bit, not enough to invade their space, and smiled at a group of them, who waved back. This went on for quite some time, a wink here, a nod there, but a couple of hundred men later I smiled at a tall, pointy-headed bloke. His mullet-style hair was at odds with his blotchy face and he looked to be wearing a toupee.

Usually I can tell when it's coming, but not this time. 'Pakee!' he bellowed like he was the first person in the whole of England ever to say it. The cheek!

Flinging the window open, I stuck my head out and screamed back, 'Sellotape can't solve everything, you Pakee, you toupee-wearing turd.'

I shook my fist at him with the fury that only a teenage girl can spurt out when she doesn't get her way. But before my temper could make me open the front door and declare war on the whole human race, Mum took me by the neck of my *kameez* and curtly and oh-so-kindly marched me into the corner of the room.

'You're making a scene,' she whisper-shouted, her head shaking from side to side with vehemence.

'Yes, a Shakespearean one,' I said, all frustrated.

Mum took no notice but, with Worzel and Bimla spurring her on, pointed her finger at me. Next she wished that I'd never been born. In my whole thirty-seven minutes of standing there – yes, I counted: it was either the clock or Worzel – deep contemplation led me to the conclusion that if I ever came across that man again I'd . . . I'd . . . Well, I don't know what I'd do but, believe me, I'm not all sugar and spice.

Mum wasn't pleased about owing Brummie Uncle money for the window to be fixed. I think it was the brick that did it. So Rule No 20 is: Don't stare out at football crowds walking past your window. And No 21 is: Don't expect sympathy from your mum when you get called a Pakee; she'll say it's your own fault you got called one in the first place.

When we got back to the Handsworth house, Arjun and Sammy were still – still! – chatting. Even Budgie seemed captivated by the conversation about Asian music. Captivated only because he thinks Sammy's great. 'She's the best sister ever,' he says.

I'd had enough of watching Arjun and Sammy gurgle over each other, so without haste – and with thought, might I add – I took up Dadoo's offer to play three-a-side in the back yard. After much arguing, Arjun grudgingly gave me the goalie shirt and seeing as I had asthma it made good sense. Why would I want to run miles up and down, up and down? That's the sign of an idiot, which I am not.

When it came to picking teams, no one rushed to choose me. I stood there feeling like the last orange Quality Street, until eventually Dudley Chacha realised that I was a charity case. Arjun had chosen Sammy and Budgie, while Kiz and I followed Dudley Chacha's tips on how to kick a ball. Bimla threw the ball towards Sammy, then blew the whistle. Cheat. We were only two minutes into the game when I saved the second goal attempt kicked by Sammy with her kitten heels on. I sent myself off thereafter. That leather ball had left an imprint on my right cheek which people would be able to see from afar hours later. It wasn't that Sammy kicked it with any great accuracy or speed. It was more me running into it, not looking at the ball because I was staring at Dad, who kept bouncing up and down behind the rear fence of the yard.

He was making certain the other guests couldn't see him until the wedding day, but it was hard for him to control himself until then and curiosity was killing him. So when I saw him bobbing up and down like a target in that game at the funfair where you take a pretend rifle, aim, shoot and miss, I wanted to go over: tell him that I was sorry I got caught before returning to the allotment, that I wasn't like the rest of them leaving him in the lurch. But that would be difficult because Budgie was keeping his hawk eye on me in case I did anything untoward. Nobody – not even me – was going to get in the way of the S-class Mercedes that Rai had promised him.

Mum was appalled by the mark on my face and tried to wipe it away with a used Brillo pad and a damp tea-towel. It hurt, so I accidentally said something to the effect of 'Get knotted!' What made matters worse was that I said it in front of the other guests and so had broken yet another rule, No 22: Do not swear at your Mum in front of other people. Even if it's done accidentally, you'll incur the wrath of the evil anti eye for many days to come, or at least until another scandal takes precedence.

I haven't yet mastered the art of apologising – come to think of it, I haven't even mastered the basics of making mistakes. Brummie Uncle was OK about the whole thing, saying it was silly to use a Brillo pad when there was a perfectly well equipped first-aid kit in the bathroom cabinet. Thank you.

While the fifth batch of samose was being fried, the *gogley* and *ladoos* packed, Kully's bridal collection of suits, jewellery was being displayed and evaluated, and the *bhangra* and *gidha* were in full swing, I sought refuge in the front room.

Moments later Arjun strolled in. 'Good save,' he said matter-of-factly in his soft voice.

'Oh, it was nothing,' I said airily, still annoyed by his indifference earlier. 'I've always had quick reflexes.'

'Yeah, well, use your fine motor skills to dish out the *pakore*,' ordered Worzel, sorting out the pleat in her *chunni*.

'Shan't. Do it your bleedin' self,' I wanted to say but for once I didn't want to look like the girl with a whole hive in her bonnet. I wanted to be like the rest of the people around me. People who were good at making small talk, good at becoming qualified counsellors, people who were chosen to give speeches at the last minute. I wanted to be a blend-in person. A Bip. An acronym, that's all I wanted to be.

To Arjun I was already half a Bip, because when Worzel and Sammy started fussing round him not so much as the inkling of a frown was to be seen on my brow. See if I care. The only place I was needed was the kitchen, so I marched towards it.

In the hall I bumped into Kiz.

'You all right?' she asked.

'Yup. Just dandy.' I stomped past her.

In the kitchen Mum was wiping down the granite worktops. 'You took your time,' she grumbled.

'Sorry.'

Then she handed me an aluminium foil platter which she piled so high with samose that I could barely see the carpet before me. She really put my waitressing skills to the test when she thought it funny to put two cups of the best *cha* on either side of the tray.

'Serve with a smile,' she cooed, pushing me towards the door.

Lowering the tray I showed her my best grin. 'How's this?'

'Stop it. That's scary.'

No sooner had I moved from the kitchen into Worzel's huge corridor than the platter begin to bend under the strain. The samose looked stable enough but they slid around the platter and the ripples on top of the *cha milai* were giving the game away. I only had to reach Worzel's mint-green living-room: how could that be a challenge? The house was hustling with the bustle of *bibis, babays* and other folk, all of whom I greeted with a '*Sat sri akal Ji*' as they slipped past me.

I made it through into the living-room. Now there was only a few yards to cross to the pine coffee table. The platter though began telling me time was up.

'Not now,' I murmured. 'Silver platter, you're made of tougher material.' Trying to hurry even faster to my destination, I looked up and saw Sammy, Arjun, Budgie and Nina chin-wagging on the sofa. They stopped only to listen to Dadoo rap a new version of 'Humpty Dumpty'. Sheer desperation took over when Kully and Worzel placed themselves either side of the couch, smiling for Bimla's disposable camera. Only a few steps away and '*Haiyo Rabba!*'

Face down on the floor, I could feel the samosa and *cha* embellishing my long, open hair nest. Raucous laughter drowned my distress calls, so I carried on lying there, not wanting ever to get up. Of course, I had to move in the end but if I'd had my way I'd have stayed there for ever. Spitting out a bit of samosa pastry and some carpet fluff, I sat up and saw something which will always be the most embarrassingest moment in my life – well, so far.

We all have one. Some people are left retarded by moments like these. For others they are but the foibles of life. This moment would have killed even the most courageous of you all. I wouldn't have believed it had I not seen it with my very own astigmatism-afflicted eyes, heard it with my very own ears, and felt it with my hitherto carefree heart; but there it was and I couldn't ignore it.

When Arjun bared his pearly teeth at me in a broad grin, I died a thousand times over. It was as if he'd put drawing-pins in my way and I'd trodden on them barefoot.

Eventually, taking pity on me, Mum and Worzel hauled me to my feet and slapped me down to brush off the bits of food. Laughter was still rolling out at my expense. I listened not because I had to but because I wanted to.

'Leave me alone, will ya?' I whimpered to Mum like a blubbering baby.

'Yeah, leave her alone,' they said amid more roars of laughter.

As I stood there with neither humility nor grace, Sammy flashed a smile at me.

'It was you, you tart,' I spat. 'You tripped me.'

'Calm down, Sushi. It weren't me, innit. I've got big feet, that's all.'

'You . . .'

Biting my tongue, I gave each of the munch-bunch a glare which in any Indian flick would mean revenge, but they laughed even more. I suppose a samosa splatted on your head doesn't connote serious intentions.

Then like a coward I fled to the stairs in a strop. Tears escaped down my cheeks, because I'd allowed myself to become the casualty of shame. I hadn't noticed until too late that Arjun was rising from his comfortable seat. Had he been coming to pacify me? Not that I cared. It was going to take more than a belated 'Sorry' to get me back on side, yeah. I'd give him what for. Who'd he think he was? Some bloke-cum-Casanova-cum hero? I waited at the foot of the stairs, but he was a no-show.

At the other end of the hall, guarding the front door, was Brummie Uncle, who'd been employed as a temporary bouncer.

'You go upstairs and have a rest,' he advised. So I did.

At the top of the stairs sat Dadoo's dad. He'd only been in the Midlands for eight years. Come to think of it, he'd only been in England for nine. He spent near enough a year in a detention centre in Dover, 'cos he got caught by the locals for having been smuggled in. It was his own fault, really. He walked into the local chippy and said, 'I wonder if I could have some of those crisps,' and pointed to the chips. The shop owner caught on straight away and shut the door while keeping Dadoo's dad engaged in conversation about the wonders of a fisherman's trawler.

When Dadoo's dad was eventually let out, he came straight to Dudley because a Rastafarian in prison had told him a couple of months before that it was an accommodating place – oh, and because that's where his son and daughter were. Dadoo's dad hadn't left since. I met him when I was nine. I don't usually remember my first meetings with people, 'cos that type of stuff doesn't really matter, but I remember meeting him.

I'd gone to the library to pay the fine on some Punjabi cassettes I'd thought should belong to Dad. I was shuf-fling around in the Mills & Boon section, because Saira'd told me that stuff was out of bounds, when from the Indian fiction table a man's voice beckoned me without calling my name

There he was, Dadoo's dad, sitting cross-legged on the floor reading some of Aesop's fables aloud, telling it all in *Jackanory* style. You know how you see it on telly when the kids go upstairs to bed, and then their affable, good-looking, well-adjusted parents go up and read them a fairy tale? Well, that's exactly what it reminded me of. A few moments later I found myself plonked at the feet of a man with a long grey beard and roughly tied turban. His eyes, which squinted a bit because they reckoned they were still in India, had so much to tell.

He was sitting cross-legged now, too, on the top step, reading to the younger kids; he'd changed very little. I got Dadoo's dad his first job, in window-cleaning, but that got washed out on account of his vertigo. Then there was Mr Dindsa at the corner shop, whose newspapers he delivered, but I accidentally got him sacked from that when I told Mrs Dindsa to get stuffed for being such a stingy cow with the wages.

While Dadoo's dad finished his story and the children went back to sliding down the banisters, I strolled on into Sammy and Pinky's room. I felt uncomfortable, as though I was going to be done in for sitting on their neatly made beds. Only one way to solve that, I decided, bouncing on Sammy's bed. When I'd messed it up enough, off I went to sort out Pinky's. As I went I caught my reflection in their gold-framed mirror. Do I have a happy or sad face? I thought, staring at it. After making a number of faces I was still undecided. Instead, I danced alone to the *bhangra* playing downstairs. Even with some of the samosa still in my hair I looked half decent, no matter what they said.

'Knock knock,' said a voice outside the door.

'Get stuffed,' I shouted back.

'S'me, Kiz. Aren't you coming down to do the *mehndi* on Kully?'

'Can't you put it on for me? I've already done it once.'

Kiz didn't reply. She'd already legged it downstairs.

Eventually I made it downstairs, too. Although the second *mehndi* application to Kully was over, the giggles still hadn't died down. Before I could say something suitable to Dadoo, who laughed like a frog would if it could, Mum ordered me to get some *elaichi* for the *cha*: Rai and his wife were coming round and they liked spicy tea.

They turned up on time (late, I mean), and I watched Mum's little gaggle coo over Rai's every word. He sat comfortably on Brummie Uncle's leather recliner like it was his throne. His tiny grey moustache sat perkily on his small but well-defined face. His tennis ball of a head jiggled when he chuckled, and his nest-like comb-over looked as though it had been glued into place: the grooves from the styling-comb still showed. A blustery wind will catch him out one day. The backs of his podgy hands were covered with a thick mass of hair, which he picked at out of habit. His soft baby-skin cheeks shone underneath the lamp placed over him like a halo.

Rai was a small man but the whole room seemed filled with his presence. Actually, it was mainly filled with his coarse voice, which rattled me with its 'I know it all' tone. Watching him with disgust, I tried to figure out what was so stupendous about him, why all the antis behaved as if they'd hit the jackpot. It certainly couldn't be that mouth of his. I've seen a better set of gnashers on a camel.

'And your other daughter, the runaway one, er, where is she?' asked Rai abruptly. He looked as if he was enjoying making Mum squirm, as all fell silent and eyes shimmied their gaze towards me. Have you ever wanted the earth to swallow everybody else up? Well, I did. The clan stared at me as if I was a waxwork waiting to melt, but I sat there stubbornly on a footstool, pretending I hadn't heard.

'This is her,' snorted Worzel, coming over and taking me by the arm.

'Yeah, this is me. Why? What of it?' I asked.

Rai frowned. He probably wasn't used to being spoken to like that. 'My,' he said, 'my, what wonderful words you speak.'

'All the better to cuss you with,' I said, pointing at him – I must have picked up the habit from Mum.

Rai frowned again – I figured it was physically impossible for him to smile.

'Listen, girl,' he roared, getting to his feet, 'you and your father have a lot to learn about the Rais. My family are not to be messed with.'

'Yeah?' I said, my head jerking uncontrollably. 'Yeah? Well . . . well . . . Oh, go and get stuffed, will you?' I couldn't think of anything else to say, so headbutted my way out of the crowd, who looked a bit shell-shocked.

'Where you going?' shrieked Mum, pulling her hair out.

'Going to get *elaichi*,' I shrieked back, but I had no intention of doing so. *Elaichi*, my foot. The only thing any of them was going to get in their tea was a good dose of petty revenge.

I slipped out of the kitchen door, to make my way down their lawned garden, out of the back gate and along the alley that led to the road – fortunately it came out too far from the house for anyone to see me. At the end of the road was the local cemetery; what with that and all the litter, Brummie Uncle's place wasn't too cheerful. I ran a twig along the railings of the cemetery as I mused on this and other subjects, until the melody of an ice-cream van dropped me back on earth. Immediately I convinced myself that only a Pink Foot lolly would fill me up, and I ran to catch up with the van, searching my pockets for the necessary. But all I found was fifty pence: parents can be so stingy sometimes. Two pounds fifty looks like a lot for each day, but it's supposed to last me a whole week. That Budgie gets a tenner nearly every day.

Rule No 23: Don't expect pocket money to increase in line with the rate of inflation or the general cost of living, and never, ever think of competing with your brother. I only took pocket money at the age of seventeen 'cos it was a cunning plan. Saira and I had discussed the taking-pocket-money concept in great detail and had decided that in doing so we were doing our parents a favour. The theory was that if we went to them for pocket money the parents, chiefly Mum, would feel they were in control. That meant they'd be less likely to interrogate us about future misdeeds because we'd still be their little googly-mooglys. This calls for Rule No 24: Always take pocket money, even when you're ninety.

If only Dad had been here I'd have pestered him to root about in his trouser pockets for something other than fluff. He'd eventually give me a quid. With the pound safely in my grasp, I'd run out with my shoes barely on, hopping all the way to the ice-cream van in the way you do when you're wearing-in new shoes. Yeah, and I know what would have happened then. As soon as I got to the porter hole, salivating with anticipation, Mr I. Singh would have driven off. I don't know if he'd have thought it was funny but it certainly wasn't clever. I'd have had to stand there for a few moments to collect my anger and bite my tongue so hard that feeling and sensation would be lost for the whole day. 'Now, Sushminder, you will not cry, you just won't craaaaaa . . .' Through the tears I'd have seen the rest of the residents in our road licking raspberry syrup off the tops of fluffy ice-cream, chatting to each other about everything except what happened behind their own closed doors. The only sign that a girl had had her heart broken would have been a solitary shoe left stranded on the road.

I didn't care. I didn't want to live any more. I knew then that some things in life start out as great ideas but end up a waste of time when humans get involved. The idea of an ice-cream van is an Einstein one but it's rendered useless if it drives away before you can say, 'Screwball, please.' It's like the drive-through idea, where you don't actually drive through, you just get stuck behind the people who haven't yet got their cheese-burger, or like the lifts that don't take you anywhere because you've been waiting fifty minutes for them to come down. These fast things just slow you down, Dad used to say.

The October wind was cold, cold, cold, and when I eventually got back to the corner of Brummie Uncle's road, my hair was frozen stiff and I was longing to warm up. But I wasn't going to go back inside until the Rais had gone, so had to lurk there for ages until I saw their Jaguar drive away. When I reached the house the front door was still open, so I shimmied in past my beloved relations. Arjun, Sammy and Budgie were nowhere to be seen, so I thought it would be safe to hide in the kitchen.

No such luck. Worzel pounced on me, informed me that she had picked out a 'charming little pink *salwaar kameez*' for me to wear that evening instead of my samosa-splattered one and swept me upstairs to Pinky and Sammy's bedroom to try it on.

When I saw it, '*No!*' I screamed. 'God, save me.' There was no way this side of the universe I was going to wear that grisly thing. No way. I reckoned I'd have to fake my own death to prevent that marquee from making contact with my skin. The style – and I use the term loosely – fell somewhere between a Christmas tree and a sleeping-bag. The only thing in its favour was that it offered me the option of puking on it without anybody noticing the result. Weddings are a trauma prolonged to give maximum discomfort and pain, but when you have Worzel there it's far, far worse.

I remember Stinky Pinky's friend's wedding was particularly well timed: it fell right between Wimbledon, the Olympics and the football World Cup. Needless to say, what happened in those historic moments I do not know, because Worzel had dragged me all the way to Gravesend. 'There's *gulab jamun, pakore, samose, and ras milai* there,' she said, so I went. I reckon that even if I'd been alive when Neil Armstrong stepped down on to the moon, I'd probably have missed that, too, because guess where I'd have been.

'It looks better on than off,' said Mum, doing her best to sound convincing.

I tried hard to argue that it was idiotic to think that a girl my age would not have bought her own outfit in Soho Road. Indeed I had: a classic £85 ethnic trouser suit to wear for tomorrow's party.

'You can wear it on Sunday, then, wedding day,' said Bimla.

'I've got an outfit for that as well.'

'You need two for Sunday. Two,' said Worzel, bobbing her head to and fro like a pecking hen in a battery cage.

'I'm not wearing that thing. Can't make me.'

What happened then was an all-out riot: according to them I was an ungrateful daughter and a football-playing, allotment-runawaying freak.

I was very good and didn't respond by cursing, even when thoroughly provoked. But when Bimla said that my GNVQ meant 'God Knows Vot Qualifications', I stormed out and slammed into the bathroom to sulk. Who did she think she was? I was better than Worzel's Stinky Pinky and Shammy Sammy, anyway. The commotion carried on across the landing, but from what I could hear it had switched to the topic of Internet matrimonial services.

Brummie Uncle rat-tatted on the door and called to me. I expect Mum had ordered him to 'bring me round'.

After five minutes of him singing his version of Punjabi folk, I let him in on account of it being his house. I soon regretted this when he too began lecturing me. Apparently, weddings are special not because they offer the chance for the bride and groom to be married (silly old me for having thought of the obvious) but because they're where other prospective matches can be made, and Worzel had a way with fashion which I should follow if I wanted to achieve my potential and have a suitable proposal propelled my way, he said.

I told him I agreed that Worzel certainly had a way with fashion and that she was very clever at claiming she knew what real women wanted but then applauding the contents of a dustbin being paraded on the catwalk. 'Oh yes, lurvy, that hole in the knee is supposed to be there: it's designer. That sleeve is supposed to be shorter than the other: it's art. That colour is supposed to hurt your eyes and cause radioactive waves to ricochet off your brain: that's fashion.' Just because Worzel owned a boutique didn't mean she was God, I said.

Surprisingly, by the end of my verbal strop Brummie Uncle had come round to my way of thinking and agreed wholeheartedly that I had the human right to wear my chosen outfit.

'Absolutely,' I said with glee, and I allowed him to unlock the door and lead me out.

'Just coming. Fantastic,' called Brummie Uncle to the rest of the men, who'd gathered in the hall, ready for their pre-party drinking session in the back of Wally

Uncle's Mercedes. Unfortunately, before Brummie Uncle could fight my corner he tripped on his shoelace at the top of the stairs and landed at Worzel's feet. I shot back into the bathroom.

A little while later, brave Brummie Uncle returned, carrying the pink *salwaar kameez* and my trouser suit, and not long after that the bathroom became packed with men discussing the qualities of the two.

'Brilliant *kapra*.'

'No, that one clashes with her skin tone.'

'This one hangs and feels better.'

'Do you see the beautiful way the light improves the shantung weave?'

'Worzel's a right cow. Can't leave my niece to use her own fashion sense.' Of course, Dudley Chacha would never have said that in front of his sister-in-law: he was too big a scaredy-cat.

When the men had finished mulling things over, they voted unanimously in my favour: I was to wear my suit and they'd take care of the three witches for me. Mind you, even if they'd voted against me, I'd have worn my suit regardless, and been proud of it, too – I'm not scared of the witches.

They went downstairs to join the others at the drinking session, and I followed a minute or two later. I was hungry again, so went to see what I could find in the kitchen. There was a big bowl of *pistha barfi* on the table, so I helped myself generously.

Someone coughed behind me, and I spun round, expecting more hassle, but fortunately it was Indy, someone else who was on my side.

'You finished your *gidha*, then?' I asked.

'Yeah, man. It really takes it out of you clapping like that. I can't eat *ladoo* and sing *boli* at the same time, but they all try.'

Even though he was wingeing, Indy looked to be enjoying himself. A *bibi* came in, looking for more *pakore*, and cooed over him and he hugged her, pretending that if ever he was to marry it would be to a corker like her. She hooted with laughter and went back to the party.

'Get your own,' I said indignantly, as he tried to snatch some of my *pistha barfi*.

'Er, thought you'd like to know your Dad's safe. Got the best hideout.'

'Shhh, not so loud,' I whispered. There was no one else in the room, but the witches could hear through walls, and mentioning anything to do with Dad in Brummie Uncle's house was likely to incur a life sentence of hard labour in a Punjabi penitentiary. The place was full of Mum's relations getting ready for the final *mehndi*-night party at the Asian Community Centre. Kully and Kiz had reserved its parlour for their beauty regime with their friends, who never had a nice word to say about anybody.

'Come here,' I whispered, grabbing Indy's sleeve.

'Hold up,' he protested. 'My shirt cost a fortune, all right?'

I tugged him out of the kitchen and into the downstairs toilet.

'Where is he?' I asked, the second the door was safely locked behind us.

'He's waiting at the gig for you.'

'Wha . . . ?' I asked. I could hardly say the word.

'You know, my gig.'

'What d'you do that for?'

'Do what?'

'Budgie's there, ain't he?' I wailed, burying my face in my hands out of sheer fear.

'Sorry, but how was I supposed to know?'

I couldn't answer.

'We'd better get down there quickly, then, hadn't we?'

Indy unlocked the door and we dashed out of the house to his car. As we sped down to the club in real T. J. Hooker style, I wondered if a siren might help.

When we got there I shot out of the car while Indy was still parking. Time wasn't on our side. When is it ever?

A paperweight bouncer was guarding the battered double doors, clutching a doner kebab so tightly that the mint yoghurt spewed out on to his black suit.

'Please let me in, please,' I grovelled.

He shook his head.

'She's with me,' Indy butted in. 'Let her through.'

The bouncer didn't put up a fight, and I thanked him for waving me through as I dashed inside with Indy at my heels.

'Oy, you twerp,' said Indy, 'you can't go in there.' He looked at me with dismay: I'd nearly barged into the gents' toilet.

'Well, things aren't clearly signposted,' I argued.

'It's that way,' he said, pointing down a long corridor.

I should have guessed, actually, because music was thundering behind the double doors at the end. I ran.

No sooner had I bounced on to the dance floor than I wanted to bounce myself straight back out. I'd landed almost in the arms of a guy who was wearing a thick gold medallion and whose white silk shirt was wet with sweat: the BO emanating from him was enough to concuss a person already in a coma. Indy was well prepared, as he held a hanky to his nose while fighting off a frail girl who's leather skirt was riding up her tummy. She, defying all the laws of gravity, was whirling round the room like an erratic pinball.

Pencil-thin-eyebrowed girls shuffled with undeniable hate as they tried their hardest to outdo the competition. Their hands flapping about, no higher than waist level, made me think that Japetto was pulling their strings. All of them danced like they were doing you a favour, trying hard not to smile so they could appear to have just the right amount of sophistication. Their cheeks were bruised with rouge and their eyes, which looked rough from the liberal use of eyeliner, made the whole get-up very freaky indeed.

Guys hung about them doing *bhangra* moves mixed in with some *ragga* ones and some others that could not under any circumstance be called dancing. A few mimicked *Thunderbird* puppets with their feet rooted to the hard wooden floor and their necks twitching this way and that to the two *dhols* beating away. They all sweated freely, apparently not in the least concerned about personal hygiene. An older, uncle-type man clung to the bar, probably annoyed at having been told he was attending an over-thirties gig, only to find they were all under.

I stood there a little out of sorts as faces scoured me and my *salwar kameez*.

'She's obviously just been let out,' screeched Sammy so loudly that I could see her tonsils wagging. Standing there in her garish butterfly top and what she called 'sureece' lipstick with blue eye-shadow, she sneered like she knew something I didn't.

Pinky stood quietly behind her, pretending it wasn't her elder sister stealing the limelight again. I almost felt sorry for her.

'Seen my dad anywhere?' I asked.

'What if we have?' said Sammy, bobbing up and down as she did her variation on dancing.

'Oh, go and put some clothes on,' I bit back. 'Your shopping's dropping.'

Before she could answer, I was fighting off Medallion Man, who'd crept up behind me and was skimming his hand all the way down my back.

'Get off me, you thick breed,' I spat.

'Come on girl. You and me. Me and you.'

'What are you talking about? Do you actually know how to say a whole sentence?' I sneered.

Medallion Man obviously wasn't listening as he touched my hair and sniffed it.

'Ugh.'

Just as I was about to do my kung fu kick, Budgie came skimming across the dance floor, looking like the Creature from the Black Lagoon in his all-black gigging gear. 'Back up,' he blared at Medallion Man. 'Leave my sister alone.'

'Calm down,' said Medallion Man, obediently backing away. He clearly hadn't banked on the arrival of a brother who took seriously his duty to protect a sister.

Budgie jabbed a finger into Medallion Man's forehead and shoved him away.

Here we go, I thought, but before I could leg it Budgie caught me by my wrist, nearly pulling my arm out of its socket. It hurt with a hot, blazing stroke which cut straight down the middle and I started to wonder whether it had been irrevocably damaged. I'm not ambidextrous, I thought. What'll I do?

Budgie grabbed the front of my *kameez* and dragged me across the dance floor, right up to the bar, where the Guggi electrical crew loitered about sucking on fruit flavoured lollipops to appear carefree.

'You wait till I tell Mum,' screamed Budgie over five hundred decibels of Bindrakia.

'What?' I screamed. There was no way he was trying that one on me. 'Why don't you wait till *I* tell Mum!'

Dadoo the Twit, with two of his mates in tow, materialised beside me. 'You're coming home with us.' He poked his face so close to mine that I caught the stench of several concoctions I couldn't put a name to. Ignoring his smirk I watched him mouth something like 'I'll sort her. Don't worry' to Budgie, who grinned and headed back to the dance floor.

I stood there staring out forlorn at Birmingham going Soho-boho. When Dadoo's mates took up station either side of me. They wedged me in so tightly that I could hardly breathe. Red strawberry flavoured lollipops flashed danger at me as they waved them in the air at Dadoo. He had taken to the stage to do some of his rapping.

'Humpty Dumpty's in the house, oh yeah.
Humpty Dumpty's in the house, oh yeah.
Humpty Dumpty sat on the wall.
Humpty Dumpty, why ya fall?
Did ya missus give ya troubal
or ya can't get a double?
Oh yeah, oh yeah, oh yeah.
Queen Elizabeth's horse and her furry-looking men
couldn't put my man back together again.'

Oh my God!

I tried my best to smile at Budgie's friends to relieve
the tension between us: but nope, they weren't going to
fall for that. Looking around for Indy, I hoped a chance of
escape would come. For once, luck was on my side. One
of the nitwits beside me became occupied by something
in his eye, I made my move. Ducking down, I scuttled
out across the dance floor on my hands and knees past a
mass of jivers. I could see Budgie dancing with the podgy
girl – she really could do with some counselling. Damn!
Nitwit number one had caught on (I haven't started
rapping have I?).

All of a sudden an old woman who looked remarkably
like next-door-neighbour-but-one anti, mainly because, I
realised, she actually was next-door-neighbour-but-one
anti, sprang into action.

'This is your studying, then, huh? Wait till I tell your
mothers. Oy, tell that man to stop playing *keswaa*.'

Dadoo stood there smiling nervously and trying hard,
with his own invented sign language, to signal his mum to
go away. But she jostled everyone out of her way, unheeding.

'Come on, *bebe*, let's dance,' said Medallion Man, resurfacing beside me.

How thick, I thought. Why didn't he just come right out and ask for some physical abuse?

'You like dancing, huh? Catching *na*, the *chapal* dance.' Without fear Dadoo's mum, who was heading for the stage, gave him and anyone else who got in her way a resounding slap with her wooden-heeled *chapal*. She'd been trained in giving a good Punjabi beating and that's what everyone was getting.

'Come with me, *huni*,' she cackled. 'I'll show you a good dance.'

'Ma, not here,' cried Dadoo.

'Do you want a *chapal* in your face?' Now ain't that a question?

Dadoo looked terrified as his mum dragged him across the dance floor. With her doing his *besti* like that, I knew he wouldn't be hassling me for some time to come. Even Budgie's mates had fled to the toilets. I was free.

'See,' shouted Indy, straightening his dishevelled black shirt. 'The power of a mobile.'

'Thanks,' I shouted back. At least he'd had mercy on me.

After one last Where's Wally? search we still hadn't found Dad, so made ready to leave, but someone on the stage labelling the wires popped up and down behind the decks. Dad. His head jived to the beat of a Gurdas Mann track which even that DJ sample-stealer hadn't managed to wreck.

'Nobody should mess with the music of Punjab like that,' Dad had told me more than once, 'nobody.' He and the Friday Folk lot had made a solemn pact to stop the decaying of their music, their rhythms.

I put my head down and barrelled my way to the edge of the stage. Halfway there I paused and flung a look over at him. I saw him, frowning heavily, slap a white self-adhesive label marked '*Dangerous*' on to the record deck. Then he pushed DJ sample-stealer and his baseball cap off the stage and on to the dance floor, and *bhangra*'d with joy all by himself up there on the stage. I couldn't help smiling: he'd kept his pact with the Folk Friday lot.

At that moment Budgie's face flared at me. All at once my head and heart seemed to explode: beside him stood Arjun and a gloating Sammy. Together. *Aaaaaaagh!* I could have given up right there, but before I could tell Sammy I'd burnt her fishtail *lehanga* at home (I hadn't), and Arjun to go and get himself a bottle of the best loyalty, I found myself in a race with all three of them — the three bleedin' musketeers.

'Run, run as fast as you can. You can't catch me, I'm a Punjaban,' I jeered.

Shoving three white-brown-pinky, mismatching compact-foundation girls out of their choreographed dance, I got to Dad with only seconds to spare and dragged him off the stage.

He resisted. 'What is it now?' he asked, as he stuck one of his '*Dangerous*' labels on my forehead.

'Charming,' I muttered, trying to peel the very sticky thing off. Then without wasting another second I pushed Dad towards the exit.

Now, imagine there's a rhino coming at you with

horns which can tear through bricks and mortar with ease. Well, that's how we ran. Dashing through the corridors and leap-frogging over a DJ who was bringing his records in from his van, we made it outside. Then we jumped over Birmingham's answer to the Great Wall of China. Our legs seemed to know that Dad was in danger and that the girl who had asthma and always got out of cross-country in the Black Country was going to save him. Determined not to be chased down, we sprinted through alleys and back streets, clearing every obstacle with such ease that it was almost enjoyable, like being the fastest horses on a racecourse. The wind was bitterly cold in the murky evening, but at least it was pushing us in the right direction. But then, slapping us silly, came the biggest challenge of all: Soho Road.

I've never seen anything like the Kumb Mela but I'm guessing the Soho Road that Friday evening wasn't far from it. Hordes of people occupied every inch of space as they pursued their own mini-missions. Shop signs flashed disco-style. Women gathered in clumps on the pavements, so that we had to run round them and heard only a syllable or two of their conversation on the quirks of life. Smells from the Desi Sweet Centre on the other side of the road lingered in the air until they were swamped by those from the meat centres straggling along the way. Poor window-shopper girls loitered about, Lehanga House, Priya's, Khoobsoorat, Roop, Dimpy's, all agog at the new Diwali collections that would suit them perfectly. Their mothers, too, had let themselves be hypnotised. D. Ram and Son's, Sona Mahal and Ambe Jewellers beckoned those who were already finding it painful to wean themselves off the gold that by rights should be theirs. Around us, cars beeped furiously at a man in a red BMW trying to park as near as possible to Badial's Department Store.

'Surely we'll lose them here?' Dad grabbed my arm and hauled me into Badial's.

We shot upstairs, slicing through the neatly laid out shopfloor without regard for the mannequins. One of them at the head of the stairs got decapitated when I accidentally knocked her over and she tumbled all the way down, nearly knocking out Budgie, who was heading up. But even that didn't stop him or the other two musketeers giving chase, hurling apologies at every shopper they banged into.

Before we could be thrown out, Dad and I dashed out of a side entrance and skated along the pavement towards Soho Road. On the corner of Soho Road we were met by the sight of a group of retired Punjabi men sitting without a care in the world on benches that had befriended them. A man with a beige wool coat, white turban and mahogany walking-stick was singing along to some *dumbi* and *dhol* blasting out of Music World. The sound filled the air with irreverence, its heavy, pulsating throb making our legs move even faster as we shot past.

'*Babaji*,' I shouted to him, '*oh saade dushman hai.*'

Yup, no one was going to stop me now. I was going to let the whole world know me and Dad had enemies. Why? I don't know.

Dad whipped in and out of the traffic with incredible ease, but as if he had a sixth sense he took my hand and guided me across. Together we hurtled through pedestrians, their carrier bags and their thoughts. What agility, what flair, I thought as we wove in and out of Soho Road's BMWs. But as we made it to the other side and ran past Sindoor, Sangam Sarees, another jeweller's and the Quality Sweet Centre, I found my legs beginning to drag.

The pavement outside the Bollywood Music Shop was clogged by a dense queue of people, so I stopped and turned to see if we'd lost the hunters. Budgie and Sammy came dashing out of Badial's, tripped and went sprawling on the pavement. Arjun high-jumped them, then bent to help Sammy to her feet, all the time looking deeply concerned. Budgie was screaming Punjabi obscenities in the air at no one in particular. The men on the bench laughed uncontrollably at the clumsiness of these foolish youths, and the man in the beige coat, who had apparently accidentally stuck out his walking-stick, seemed to be apologising. I burst out laughing, too.

'*Sheti kar*,' whispered Dad, pulling the sleeve of my *kameez*.

'Can't we walk now?' I panted, finding it panful to breathe. Surely nothing could touch us now?

No sooner had I spoken than the three musketeers took up the chase again, waving their arms in anger and looking much more menacing. Resisting the urge to scream, Dad and I looked round. Maybe he was asking himself the very question I was asking myself. What were we running away from? Them or ourselves?

'Oy, what'ch doin' here?' asked a familiar voice behind me.

I spun round to find Kiz and Gurminder had popped up out of the queue.

'Let us through, will ya?' I urged.

'You can't push in,' said Gurminder.

'Dad,' squawked Kiz, giving him a hug which squeezed away most of his energy as well as her glitter eyeshadow.

'We don't want to push in. We want to push out,' I told them. Budgie was getting closer: I could see his lips move and knew he was swearing at me.

'Ain't you gonna ask what we're doing here?' asked Kiz, ignoring my puffing and panting.

'No. Just let us through, will ya?' I said again, trying to find a gap in the queue which would allow this not-so-huge demand to be met.

Unaware that if he got caught by Budgie, he'd be back having a cosy chat with those blank walls in that ward of his, Dad stood behind me, counting the pills in his Nivea container. I tried to push Kiz out of the way, but was so puffed out that even my light-as-a-*roti* sis was more than I could manage.

'Well,' said Kiz 'Me and Gurminder, we're gonna hit the big time. See in there? That's Anon. They need some dancers, and me and her are dancers.'

'Yes, yes, that's front-page news, but will you let us *through*?' I shouted, jogging on the spot like a toddler who needed the loo.

Close behind us, Arjun called, 'Listen to me!' but I took no notice. After all, judge a person by their actions and not their words; that should be the order of the day.

'What's Budgie doing?' asked Kiz, sounding all petri-
fied that her big, bossy brother was going to sort her out.

'He's after you, that's what. Run before he tells Mum
about you and your dancing ways.'

Panic thumped Kiz in the face. *'Haiyo Rabba. Haiyo
Rabba.'* Whenever she's scared, Kiz automatically mum-
bles Mum's words of worry. 'Let's get out of here.' She
swept back her hair and hugged Gurminder like they'd
never see each other again.

'I'll save you a place,' said Gurminder, who was nearly
through the shop door and already hyperventilating.
She'd do anything for Anon – those Punjabi singers who
didn't know any Punjabi. She was already frizzing her
straightened hair for them.

'Thanks,' said Kiz tearfully.

Then before she could shout 'I love you all' she was
running with us, shoving aside anyone who got in her way
as though she was the strongest girl in the world. Her head
shook from side to side as she sprang about, making her
cheeks wobble. The wind was back on our side, behind us
again, and the harder it blew the faster we went.

Back along the racecourse we galloped. Dad took long
strides, I took jumping ones and Kiz hobbled as if her
legs were tied together in those drainpipes of hers. We
hardly noticed that Soho Road was changing, the smells
of *barfi* and kebab mingling with those from Davis' West
Indian Bakery. Only a few more metres and we'd be safe:
surely they'd lose us at the bend?

Wallop! Tripping over a stray banana box I crashed
down flat on the pavement, banging my nose so hard that
I roared with pain, laughing and crying all at once.

'Oh, Susham, your nose is fine. Bloody but fine,' said Kiz reassuringly.

She was right about the blood, if nothing else. It was trickling down my chin and dripping on to my *salwaar kameez*. The last thing I wanted was a polka dot *salwaar kameez* with samose stains so I pinched the tip of my nose hard, trying to stem the flow.

Dad had run on ahead, but soon realised he wasn't dragging me any more and came back to see what had happened.

'Go on without me,' I sobbed, partly out of misery but mostly because I had no energy left to do anything but look up at the dark clouds overhead. They looked as fed up as I was.

'Go, Dad, please go,' I pleaded, 'or Budgie'll get you.'

But he didn't. Instead he very gently wiped my nose with his shirtsleeve.

'Thank you.'

Even as I urged him to hurry, 'Stop! Stop!' demanded the three musketeers. Stop? Stop what? Living?

Just when all seemed lost we were abruptly swallowed up by a drove of people coming to evening prayers. They shimmied us into the newly rebuilt entrance of the Guru Nanak Nishkam Sewak Jatha, where we were hidden from the bustle of the road. The three of us crouched down behind the wall and peered cautiously out. Arjun's beige hiking-boots sprinted past, then Budgie's brown leather mules, and last, lagging some way behind, Sammy's pointy kitten heels. Safe for a while at least, I thought.

Dad was greeted warmly by a Folk Friday chum who'd

got separated from his granddaughter and was looking for her. He didn't seem to be trying too hard, 'cos he had time to talk nostalgia with Dad.

While Kiz pulled off her toe-pinching boots to see how swollen her feet were, I looked out across the road, feeling like an abandoned puppy. On the corner of an alley leading off Soho Road stood a building – well, more of a dilapidated hut, really – with a sign saying *'GUGGI'S ELECTRICALS'* dangling from a dirt-smeared window. Flyers for future gigs were pasted all over the red brick exterior and seemed to be the only things holding the building up. Inside, the odd manky television and a cash till could be seen.

Kiz took one look at the place and said, 'Our Budgie ain't working there.' She was right: too. Our Budgie (as she put it) had been lying all the time, God bless him.

When the devotees went in to evening prayers we scurried behind them into the marble-walled prayer hall. Making sure the hole in my sock toe was discreetly hidden I tugged one end of my *chunni* to keep it firmly over my dishevelled hair. After putting fifty pence in the money box, I knelt down on a velvety mat and bowed my head in obeisance, making sure my forehead touched the floor. Apart from a chink of coins from Kiz, who was trying to dig out some change, the only sound to be heard was of the mellow, soothing voice of the *granthi* reading the holy scriptures of the *Guru Granth Sahib*.

In the clear light of overhead chandeliers we scuttled over to the *bibi* who was handing out warm golden *par-shad*. Then we sat down to rest and let our minds be taken over by words which, although I didn't understand their meaning, sounded right.

Sitting cross-legged near a radiator at the back of the prayer hall, I watched Dad whisper the *Paath*. The words were lodged safely in his memory and could be called upon whenever he needed assurance that some things in the world would never change. He, too, had chosen to plonk himself right at the back of the hall, from where he could glance at those who sought peace. While the *Paath* was read I made a prayer myself. You don't need to know what it was.

The bloody blobs on my *kameez* had dried and made me look as though I'd been caught in a brawl. Bowing down one more time before I left the prayer room I went in search of the ladies' toilets. They were near the 'taking off your shoes' room, and there was no queue – I marvelled at this minor miracle. On turning the tap, out gushed boiling-hot water. It was no use, though. The more I tried to clean my *kameez*, the more the blood spread. For a moment I felt like screaming, but I repressed the urge and instead wiped the blood-streaks off my face with a damp tissue. Then I went tiredly back to the prayer hall, to my place near the radiator.

Dad was still muttering, and Kiz was chatting to a *bibi* who wanted to know what Pind she came from. Kiz was used to being asked this because her Punjabi was so pure; it had yet to be Dudleyfied. The *bibi* chuckled and raised her hands high in the air at the realisation that Kiz was a suitable marriage prospect for her grandson.

Kiz wanted to spend some time with Dad; she missed

him, too. 'You go home,' she said. 'He'll be all right with me.'

Dad wanted to stay there all night and listen to the words of the *Guru Granth Sahib*, which, all things considered, was probably just as well.

When I got back to Brummie Uncle's it was late and everyone had gone to bed; Pinky was kind enough to let me in. Not wanting to wake the others. I lay down on the blanket in the living-room for spare visitors like myself, and fell asleep without fuss. This didn't last too long: I was jolted awake by Kiz nearly stepping on my face.

'Watch it,' I complained.

'Soz.'

I asked about Dad.

'He's sorted,' she said.

'Good night.'

'Good night.'

Kiz and I woke up the next morning. Saturday, at half past bleedin' five, and tiptoed around the house so as not to disturb anybody. Who knew what Budgie had told Mum? In any case, I certainly wasn't going to hang about to find out. Kiz, on the other hand, mistook Sammy's hair for her scarf. Well, that did it. Next thing you know Sammy and Pinky had poor Kiz up before their court. I legged it, knowing that Kiz would have done the same in my place.

A sudden fog had swallowed the bleak road, and the air was clammy and cold. I walked buttoning the toggles on my duffel to keep me warm. Handsworth was awake even at this time. Most of Dudley was shut until nine o'clock.

When I got to the Gurudwara, a *gyaniji* told me Dad was at the Pind Pub, so off I went.

Catching the bus back to Dudley was no easy task, taking me nearly an hour just to find the right stop. After another hour and a bit I was knocking at the Pind Pub's door.

Mr Kang eventually let me in when I told him who I was looking for. 'Your dad's in here,' he said. 'Be gentle with him.'

Huddled in the corner with a packet of peanuts and a cordial was Dad. The jukebox playing one of his favourites, '*Chan kitha guzari ayee*' and he looked happy; the words of the song, 'My light, where have you been?', Played mellowly in the background. An assortment of napkins was strewn across the table before him, and he was folding them carefully into swans and putting them underneath his chair. This was a skill he'd learnt as the omelette man.

'Someone else here to see you,' said Mr Kang, looking put out.

In walked Indy.

'Here,' Dad said, 'what d'you bring him for?'

'It's all right, Dad. Indy won't say anything.'

'He will. They all do.'

Indy looked a little hurt at that, but all he said was 'I'll get myself a pint – get out your way.'

I thanked him and looked inquiringly towards Dad.

'You want to know, don't you?' he said.

'Know what?' I asked, helping myself to some of the salted peanuts.

'Why I don't want Kully *beti* to go to the Rais.'

135

'No, I don't, Dad. Honest. If you think the Rais stink, you're right. No questions asked.'

'Aah, my *changi kuri*.' Dad put his hand on mine. 'That Rai wants your mum.'

My jaw must have dropped to my knees when he said that like it was the easiest thing in the world to say. Indy, who shouldn't have been listening, spluttered his pint all over the counter, making Mr Kang look well vexed because he was the one who'd have to clean up.

'No!' I gasped. 'Mum's not like that.'

'Women are what that Rai wants them to be. I was only nineteen when my father told me about your mum, and she was a seventeen-year-old fighting with her pink *chunni*. So simple but strong that first day I saw her. She told me right away about that Rai and his ways. She had a choice, me or him.'

'And she chose you.'

'Yes, but sometimes I wish she hadn't. Years later, when Rai had become a somebody and I was still just the omelette man, the gap between your mum and me got bigger. I watch her sometimes when she walks the mile to the factory. She looks miserable, and the one thing I'm certain of is that I made her like that.'

'No one can make anyone like anything.' I said, though I wasn't certain it was true.

'You sure?' Dad asked. 'Fifty hours in that factory for the past thirteen years, and you're telling me she hasn't changed?' He popped a couple of his smarties in his mouth and with a quick swig of cordial swallowed them – a lot more easily than I'd swallowed his alarming news. His eyes were dull and his heart was heavy.

I felt a slow, cold anger growing inside me. The cause of all his unhappiness, the cause of his illness, was that Rai. I couldn't think of anything to say.

Dad smiled sadly and stood up. He said he was going back to the Gurudwara.

Indy offered to give me a lift back to Brummie Uncle's but I declined. I wanted to walk back to the bus station to sort things in my head and to get back to Brummie's as late as possible. Dad and Rai were still battling one another in my head and Rai was pinning him down. It made me angry to know that Dad was comparing himself with the incomparable. We all do it, though. Compare, I mean. You try hard not to, but before you know it you're sucked in.

The bus back to Handsworth was despairingly slow but I didn't mind.

'Let me off here.'

I walked along the cemetery-lined road as though I were walking a tightrope. Did Dad feel like that all the time?

When I got to Brummie Uncle's, it had just gone four.

The front door was ajar, so I poked my head round it to see how well the commotion had gone. A noisy quiet held the house, as if everyone was on tenterhooks, and I knew that by walking in I was going to break it up. I was right. The whole mob – Kiz, the three musketeers, uncles, antis, friends, Rais, all of them – had gathered in the living-room, As soon as I looked in, Worzel, Bimla and Mum fell on me like lions on raw meat.

'Were you doing *bhangra* at a club yesterday?' demanded Mum.

'No.'

'Tell me the truth. *Bhangra* at a club, yes or no?'

'No,' I repeated. 'I went to a club, yes, but I wasn't doing any *bhangra* there.'

Bimla and Worzel gasped, and Mum sat down and buried her face in her hands.

'Now you've done it,' gloated Sammy.

'Done what?' I asked.

'Go on, Painji, you tell her.'

Mum stood up. Tears welled up in her eyes – well, where else would they well? They were held back by some shreds of pride she held on to dearly and she wasn't going to give in.

'Sammy and Pinky are better daughters than you two will ever be,' she said, pointing at me and Kiz.

It was my turn to gasp now. Mum comparing me and Kiz with those two thick breeds was about as much as I could take. Kiz looked ready to faint into her silk *lehanga* on hearing Mum turn on her like that. What was Mum on about? I wondered. The only thing that was unblemished about her darling nieces was their cheeks, and I'd soon sort them out.

'Well, your precious Sammy and Pinky were there, too, so stop acting all high and mighty.'

'Don't you dare start telling lies to me. Not now,' said Mum in her most threatening voice.

'You're just making it up,' put in Worzel, wagging her head.

'If you don't believe me, ask Arjun. Go on, Arjun, tell them. Shut them up.'

138

'She's a born liar, that one,' sneered Sammy 'As if Arjun's gonna take your side.'

'Oh, put a mirch in it Sammy,' I said. 'Gobbing on like Arjun's your slave or something.'

I stood there staring him straight in the eyes, pleading without getting down on my hands and knees, but that Arjun said not a word. Instead he just sat there on the sofa, a shot of Johnny Walker's in one hand, looking as unfazed as ever.

'Tell them,' I ordered again half-heartedly.

But Arjun went on sitting there, staring right through me. He was lying to himself and to me and didn't look in the least affected by it.

'I think the silence speaks for itself,' said Mrs Rai.

Time for one last-ditch attempt, I thought. 'You remember, don't you, Arjun? You and Budgie chasing me and my dad down Soho, and Sammy right behind you?'

'Your dad was there?' asked Mum, with a look of astonishment on her face. *Haiyo Rabba*, I really was giving it to them today.

'Yes, he was, but that's not the point.'

Mum barely let me finish my sentence before she had to be restrained from throwing the *pakore* at me.

Budgie looked at me as if I'd created the awkwardness on purpose. Smoothing his eyebrows with spit on his thumbs, he shook his head disapprovingly. If Mum knew he was unemployed, she could pick on him for a change. I should have told her about Guggi's, but something stopped me.

Why must these dressing-downs happen in front of other people? The strangers in Brummie Uncle's living room made me feel ashamed. I wanted to cover my face with a cushion to avoid their accusing eyes.

Beside Arjun sat his shadow, Sammy, her long hair hiding half of her sly smile. It was obvious she'd put him up to it. She had that look about her. But no sooner had I convinced myself that Sammy was the problem than I unconvinced myself. Maybe it all came down to the simple fact that Arjun didn't think of me in that way. My imagination has always accompanied me to the party that I want to go to but haven't been sent an invitation for. It had done it to me again.

Mum took me by the arm. 'You are *besharm*.'

'No I'm not shameless,' I told her. 'In fact, I'm full of shame.'

'Ooh, she's got a razor tongue on her, that one,' said Bimla. 'Send her upstairs, that's what I say.'

I wasn't in the mood to retaliate, so for once did as I was told and went upstairs to Sammy and Pinky's bedroom; I'd stay out of the way until the party all right. Lying there looking up at the light of the flickering bulb, I wiped away my tears angrily.

Downstairs the *gidha* began again. Women wailed crescendos, clapped, jumped and laughed as the floorboards were tested to their full strength. I tried to block the noise out by plugging my earholes with some scrunched-up tissues and singing 'Hand me down my silver trumpet, Gabriel'. Clouds flitted behind the three-quarter moon low in the sky. The double glazing made it look as though there were two moons instead of one. The real moon shone the brightest, while the pale imitation reflection hung in the background. I felt like that pale one.

140

At around six-thirty a knock on the door disturbed my peace.

I didn't answer.

'It's me, Arjun. Let me in.'

I didn't answer.

'I know what you're thinking, but I can explain it all. Just hear me out.'

I didn't answer.

'I'm sorry.'

His footsteps went away down the landing. When they could no longer be heard, my mind began to drift into the land of explanations. You know the one: high on a cloud up there are the answers to all your problems, so choose one and be content with it. That's what I'd done for a long, long time, rather than refusing to accept things the way they were and blaming others. Not this time, though. There was no excuse for Arjun's lie. I didn't mind that all those lot down there thought me a liar. No, that's not quite true, I did mind. But not as I much as I hated the way Arjun had lied so flatly. He'd done me harm and he knew it. Now I knew how Dad felt.

Late that evening we eventually made it to the Asian Community Centre, to find the parking in a shambles and policemen apparently in charge of the whole world.

'No, you can't park next to the BT booth, sir,' one of them said, 'or the man won't be able to get out.'

Mum told everyone she had ordered the police to impose tight control so that there'd be no trouble, but I knew they were there to get Dad, and I decided to do all I could to harass them without getting myself arrested.

'I take cannabis, you know,' I told one of them in my

most convincing voice. 'I can even draw it for you if you don't believe me. I know what it looks like and everything. You might as well arrest me now before I go on to the harder stuff.'

I think I was getting on their nerves. They were distracted from my performance when Wally Uncle's Mercedes hit the back of Kully's Fiat. She was devastated, but still it was very funny. Rule No 25: Don't drive yourself to your own pre-wedding party. It looks tacky and is a bad omen for an already doomed marriage.

I went back to harassing PCs Plid and Plod until they got ruffled and escorted me firmly into the Centre. Resigning myself to yet another evening with the cashews, I found myself a seat in a corner and watched the hall fill up with family, friends and strangers.

Young women straightened their hair with their fingers the moment a strand dared to go astray. A video cameraman was leaping around treading on people's feet as he tried to get a perfect shot of Kully and her friends. They were posing as if they were going to have their passport photographs taken, nibbling a samosa each as if it was full of poison. A lifeless girl had a fit when a crumb of the samosa pastry flecked her boat-necked *kameez*. Her friend soon joined her in looking mortified when her long white bell-sleeve found its way into the *channe*. She'd never get the *haldi* out; nothing in the whole world can get *haldi* out.

Around them guys bear-hugged their security blankets in the form of a pint.

Eventually everyone stopped posing and leapt on to the dance floor to do their *jago*. I wanted to do my good deed of the day and warn Gurminder that she was a health and safety risk with that hairsprayed hump on her head – it would surely be set on fire by the *jago* candles. She ought to know that the Asian Community Centre had only one fire extinguisher and it was locked in the office. But before I could begin to help, I wondered who'd begun the tradition of dancing with a lit stove on your head. Someone having a laugh, that's who.

After some time, old Saira walked in, looking graceful. The beads on her *salwaar kameez* glimmered under the stage lights, and her glossy black hair looked superb. Almost before she could sit down, I vented my worries about Arjun and Sammy to her. She concluded that I was suffering from jealousy. I said I wasn't and anyway, even if that was an accurate analysis of my inner turmoil, admission of such ill feeling towards a fellow human being would be repressed at all times. She humoured me.

'Oh look, Jinders Catering Service,' I said before she could get on to the subject of Dad and Rai. 'Classic.'

The measure of a good Indian restaurant is whether it displays that fashionable shop sign saying, '*Caters especially for all occasions.*' '*All occasions*' generally means weddings, for it is here that the Indian food critics descend and it is here that they, with their wine-taster's criteria and palette, judge the host family's honour according to the standard of the food. Simply put, if an Indian woman doesn't like her samosa or *panir dhal*, the marriage has had it. That's why Mum was more than a little overwrought at the idea that the samose were a bit too chillified.

'When does the music start?' asked Saira, straightening her *bindi*.

'He's trying, isn't he?' I replied, pointing at Baldev, the beer-bellied DJ (as a kid he'd been baby-sat by Mum so he gave her a five per cent discount). He spent so long checking his equipment and mike – 'Testing, testing, one, two, three, testing, testing, one, two, three' – that no music at all was heard for the first part of what some might call a party. At last, after four unsuccessful attempts to get everything working, a screech and a thud followed by some notes wafted past my ears.

The music soon took hold of the two hundred-plus guests, including the Folk Friday uncles, and their movements became more and more involuntary as party time wore on. From where I sat it looked like an aerobics session on amphetamines. Things were interrupted briefly by an argument between two feuding brothers who hadn't seen each other for three years. Everybody watched, utterly engrossed, but Saira and I couldn't see much, so we went and joined the other people still considered children by British law. Here we removed the special-offer labels from Schweppes bottles to get our freebie bottle-openers.

After the feud had died down and the dancing was back to its jiggerish normality, I (all unsuspecting, just being good and sitting down like most of the other guests) was yanked up by Bimla, who was living all her life in the space of a few minutes. This was not good. She and her peers had been trained with painstaking accuracy in the art of snatch and grab and hustling poor little girls like me into the middle of the dance floor to do, of all things in the world, some dancing.

I tried hard to state assertively that I would never, ever

put my best pelvic forward – not for them, anyway – but was ignored. At an estimate, nine antis gathered round me pushing and grabbing and by the end of it, as if by magic, I'd become the handbag in their circle. So forgive me if I don't jump up at the thought of dancing. It invariably means doing the twist, shaking your bust, or doing the hokey-cokey, in which you put your left arm in and your right arm out . . . in, out, in, out – you get the picture. Rule No 26: Break your leg before the wedding, but only if you're a guest.

When I'd regained my composure I grabbed a *kulfi* for some relief; ice-cream should help me cool down. Before I could so much as taste it, a thin, gaunt lady who'd clearly found a new lease of life thrust me aside as she was ram-raided by uncles and cousins hurtling like comets towards the dance floor. Tonight was a night to be proud of, for Wally Uncle proved to all present that he was by far the most masculine man there. Not only did he hold a pint of beer in one hand while doing the *bhangra* with the other, but he sprayed everyone in his vicinity with beer, which he told Mum was Lucozade. Next a whole bunch of men hopped around doing the snake dance – where the snake bit came from I'm not sure, but I wished one would bite them.

Then came the last of the three *mehndi* sessions. First, the women had to get together and cover Kully in the orange dough, but my turn was cut short when she accused me of trying to feed her *mehndi* instead of the more edible *ladoo*. It was an honest mistake. I and some other poor, defenceless girls also had our butts branded, like western cowboys branding their cattle. Well, not exactly, but there was a bodged-up *mehndi* job on my hands, which is kind of the same thing. It was done by Stinky Pinky, who has the artistic ingenuity of a poodle.

I know what the lecturers will say when I get round to going back to college. They'll comment on how traditional the *mehndi* looked, to which I'll reply, 'There's nothing traditional in being pinned down by five marauding maniacs so they can play noughts and crosses on my hands.' *Mehndi* always looks so pretty on the bride.

I was still 'admiring' my *mehndi* design when someone tapped me on the shoulder and then immediately disappeared. I wondered why people can't just talk to you face to face without being silly about it.

'Remember me?' said a stranger, holding his hand out to shake mine.

'Er, no.'

He looked a little disheartened. 'Give you a clue, then. Does the word "guitar" mean anything?'

Yes. To me it meant 'dangerous instrument' because Budgie whacked me on the head with his once when I scattered chilli powder in his trifle instead of Hundreds and Thousands, but somehow I don't think that's what the stranger intended it to mean. I looked at him, confused. I rarely forget a name or a face, but you know when you have and you start to wonder whether they got the right person in the first place. Well, that's how I felt.

The soft round face before me, with its small, twinkling eyes and big joker-like smile, looked equally puzzled.

Slowly the light of memory seeped through. 'Ker – Sorry, I mean Gurmit?'

At school, everybody has one in their class, a person to be looked down upon because they aren't strong or nasty enough to answer you back or just don't care about fitting in. Ours was called Kermit Fleabag: touch him and you got fleas.

He used to sit alone, this Fleabag did, until each time a new kid was enrolled in the class. New kid saw the empty space next to Fleabag and decided to sit there, but as soon as new kid became integrated into the classroom culture they'd leave that seat for one that carried higher social status.

I realise now that Fleabag had a function, a function performed by someone in every group. It's an important one, because it makes us feel good about ourselves. Standing next to Fleabag always meant you looked far cleverer, prettier and more normal than you really were. Your clothes were positively haute couture compared to his. His unbranded grey trainers against your plastic sandals, his too-tight velour V-neck jumper against your fairly new pastel-blue T-shirt, and his faded, mottled grey corduroy trousers against your fake Levi jeans. We could be sure of who we were against him.

Fleabag's one interest was singing and playing the guitar. He didn't tell anybody about it, probably because we were all too busy listening to real music on *Top of the Pops*. I only knew of his hidden talent because once I heard guitar music coming from upstairs when our lot went over to his lot to eat *pakore* made by his mum, who was our mum's best friend at the time (I accidentally squirted some ketchup on Anti's new chintz-covered sofa). Somebody was playing that guitar like it was telling a story, and I remembered having heard similar music in *Peter and the Wolf* but had fallen asleep because of its kicking rhythm. Thinking somebody'd left the cassette on I went upstairs and put my head round the bedroom door.

Fleabag was sitting on the floor with a battered old guitar on his knees. Hugging it closely like a dear friend, he plucked the strings lightly and let the notes flow. He didn't even use that false nail some guitarists use, but it didn't matter because he played so well. When I went in he looked up at me and I was afraid he'd stop, but he carried on, undisturbed. Sitting there lost in the thoughts and rhythm of the music, Fleabag didn't look contagious any more. In fact, he looked like a musician. I hadn't seen him since, because shortly afterwards he'd been sent to Slough, but I'd always wanted to apologise for the way people had treated him at school.

'You want to dance?' he asked.

'Er, my mum would have something to say about that.'

'Oh, come on. We're nearly brother and sister, you and me.'

Oh, why not? I was looking damn fine and my company was pretty dapper, too, so before a second thought came into my head there I was dancing a whole *bhangra* track with Gurmit. We swayed this way and that, jamming to the *dhol* beat as the canes hit the taut leather hard. Apart from anything else, the more it looked like I was having a good time, the more likely it was that Mum and Budgie would stop curtailing my every move.

When Saira came and joined us, the three of us raved together.

'*Nava lai liya trac mere yaar ne, babiyan de chal chaliye,*' the loudspeakers blasted out.

'Ain't it funny?' I yelled in Saira's ear.

'What?'

'The lyrics of this song: "My friend's got a new truck. Let's go to worship." '

We all laughed.

Yup, we were having a good time and I wanted everyone to know it, even that Arjun, whom I hadn't seen for quite some time but who was no doubt somewhere near that Sammy; I was certain we'd never talk again. I glanced round the room looking for him in that I-don't-really-care way just one more time, but all I could see was lots of eyes flashing on and off at me. It made me feel small – or was it that I let them make me feel small?

After a while we stopped bopping, partly to get our breath back and partly because DJ Baldev announced that a new *bhangra* group had been invited to perform a track. Kully had invited them on account of they were doing it for free and knew her fiancé. As soon as he said that the group was called Anon, lipsticks which knew no colour barriers or discrimination came out. Girls lacquered their hair with enough hairspray to be a hazard to the ozone layer. They wanted to look 'bootypul'.

While the female guests strained to catch a glimpse of Anon, the younger men huddled at the back of the hall, jealousy getting the better of their usual 'I don't care' attitude. Then five pretty boys – well, one of them looked as if he'd just got out of a bad B & B – started to set up on stage. Each wore immaculately pressed clothes, creased only slightly from sitting in their limousine – how stylish. They flaunted the designer-wear logos and pearly-white smiles that Kiz found so enchanting. Give me strength.

At once bedlam resumed: all the girls dashed to the front of the hall and pushed and shoved to try to get within touching distance. I was yet again shoved aside by a jaunty-looking girl who was waving her handbag around as she danced to a tune in her head. All this before we'd even heard them sing a note.

Eventually, after we'd been told to quieten down ten times by Mum, the lights dimmed and on came the boys again. The first guy got down on his knees and said something into his microphone. Most of it was inaudible, but I made out the words 'This one's for you, babe.'

I thought I was going to die of embarrassment for him. Did he really think we were succumbing to their PR-constructed charm, or the foundation cream that gave them a flawless natural look? Yep, he sure did, and sure enough Kiz and Gurminder succumbed.

'This is the best party ever,' she shrieked, catapulting herself on to the stage and challenging DJ Baldev for the microphone.

I wish I'd realised sooner that I was standing next to the speakers. When Anon blasted out their first notes, I leapt clear off the floor with my hands over my ears for protection. But that reaction wasn't too popular, so I removed my hands from my ears and listened to the *bhangra* stroke pop song that had all the lyrical qualities of a Christmas-cracker joke. The melody . . . Well, it was non-existent, but judging by the reaction of the girls around me I was obviously the only one who thought so.

They all swayed, left to right, backwards and forwards, looking like lovesick morons. I supposed Anon could only get people to listen by hypnotising them into thinking the group could actually sing. That one song lasted ten minutes, at the end of which they looked as though it had lasted for fifty. I decided to slit Kully's wrists as soon as I could get my hands on her.

As I thanked my Guru for putting an end to the torture, though, I forgot about Kully. Gurmit stood there, watching from afar while the girls praised the talentless bunch. He, who could play the guitar so beautifully, just stood there. It was a crime. Here was a talent which everybody ignored, and there on the stage were a bunch of performing penguins – except without the breeding. I wished I could jump on to the stage, snatch the microphone and introduce the next big thing, but I couldn't.

The evening ended with Kully saying goodbye to one of her best friends who was going to a funeral on Sunday and couldn't see the bride off. Kully shed bucket-loads of tears – you'd have thought this was the last time she'd ever see any of us. I wished it was. I wondered why the heck she was getting married in the first place if all she was going to do was cry. Poor sod.

When at last we returned to our Dudley semi that night, I couldn't get to sleep. The only option was to watch QVC, which usually put me out in three minutes flat, but even that didn't work because my sinuses were becoming alarmed by a smell coming from the kitchen. No bags were going to adorn my eyes tomorrow. Determined to get to sleep I watched a bit more. A lady was performing exercises that we could all join in with, and I might even have tried the one that involved putting your knee behind your ear if the bouncy brunette and her patterned purple leotard with matching leggings hadn't put me off. I lasted another ten minutes, then I got up and slowly, so as not to get a head rush, zombie-walked towards the source of the smell.

Beyond the sliding door I expected to find Dad merrily cooking one of the best chilli cheese omelettes in the world. He wasn't like one of those chefs you see on telly using fancy words like 'sauté' this and 'bunsen-burn' that to make themselves seem cleverer. He was a true chef, never measured anything, never did anything by the book, and certainly never followed fashions in food. He made what he got and we got what he made.

His omelettes had been good to him, for they'd got him his first job twenty years ago. When he gave the owner of a local tandoori place a quick demonstration, the owner was so impressed that not only did he hire Dad as assistant cook but the chilli cheese omelette was added to the menu straight away. It's had its place in the starters ever since then, and people have come to know Dad as the 'omelette man', though I doubt if he's flattered by the name.

'That one's going to get stuck. I can tell,' whispered Rai to himself, jiggling the pan to loosen the *anda* from the base of it.

'Oh.'

Confessions over a garden fence

'I'd have long since become a Buddhist and retreated to the Himalayas if it weren't for my Sammy and Pinky,' said Worzel.

'Yes, I know what you mean,' said Bimla. 'My husband runs around me all day and night, keep me awake, give me a fright – Oh, I'm a poet!'

'That Zee TV presenter was kicked out of the Filmfare awards.'

'No!'

'Yes, even when she showed them the microphone.'

'Was it that one with the short, cropped hair?'

'No, the one with curly hair – you know who I mean.'

'Ah, yes, of course I do. That Sheena what's-her-face, though, bit of a you know, in't she?'

'She wasn't even at the party.'

'She was, wasn't she?'

'Don't know, don't care – not really one for small talk. Anyway, how did it go making that *noki* pasta thing for the Dillons?'

'The *noki* fettucini was OK. Copied it from Delia.'

'*Haiyo Rabba*, now there's a woman for small talk. Talks about cheese like it's art. She keeps hers in the garage, but you'd think with the money she's got she'd have a larder the size of this house. She can't cook a curry, you know.'

'Who says?'

'My friend Maninder.'

'Oh, right. She cooks a lot of curry, does she?'

'Practically invented it.'

'Ow! What d'you do that for?'

'It was a fly. You couldn't splat it so I did.'

'Thanks.'

'Have you seen Kully *beti*? Can you believe it? Such a cheap *lehanga*. Looks like it's been dragged in dirt.'

'Her *mehndi* is so simple – blobs of dung, that's what it looks like. Matchstick jobs, I suspect.'

'Her fingernails are chipped, too.'

'And her lips are chapped.'

'She doesn't even keep her head down. No modesty or shyness from her.'

'I must confess they've only made two sets for her. *Thoba thoba*. Where is the tradition in all of this? I wore more gold at Kamal Anti's funeral.'

'And Paji. Supposed to be head of the household.'

'Head of the household? Na, na. A walking lunatic with an appointment at the psy . . .'

'Psychiatreest. God forbid anything like that should happen to my husband. God forbid.'

'He was always destined for Loopy Lane ever since the day he started voting for the Liberal Democrats.'

'No, it was the day he came to this country he began to go mental. Some of us just aren't well bred enough to make it.'

'Sushi tells me he's getting better all the time.'

'She's one lying *kapati*. Have you seen the way she's been behaving lately? Taking right after her dad. My

Sammy's far too refined for that sort of laddish behaviour.'

'I'm not lending that family any more of my hard-earned money.'

'I know what you mean. I've already lent two hundred pounds and am getting instalments of ten pounds a week. Now is that any type of repayment?'

'They were richer when they arrived here than they are now.'

And that's where all three sniggered together.

I know I shouldn't have been listening, but when you're not supposed to it just makes someone like me eavesdrop all the more. My anger grew and festered as Worzel and Bimla damned us over the fence with the next-door neighbour anti who did not speak to us – she thought I was stealing her bottled milk. I wasn't. It made me want to do something drastic.

Bimla's hips wobbled through her too-tight *kameez*. No wonder she has such high blood pressure: most of the flow's blocked around her waist and hips. She's also very proud. All she needs are peacock feathers sprouting out of her rear so she can strut casually. Two slugs usually called eyebrows cover the whole width of her narrow forehead, and her mouth, the smallest thing on her face, is tight and pokey. It seldom has anything but hurtful words coming out of it. Her poor henpecked husband is the only one who listens to her, as he follows her here and there without a word.

Worzel's the youngest of the three sisters, and oh so modern – she prattles on like an interior designer, so you never know what she actually means. I've never had any time for her. In fact, she and I haven't had a conversation without cursing each other since I was a toddler. And another thing: she alarms me with that foundation of hers. Sometimes I think I could etch my name on her cheek and she wouldn't even feel it. I've often wondered what colour her face really is. It certainly isn't the pale pink she wants it to be. I think the main reason why Worzel sets me clawing at the walls may have something to do with her big earrings. Dad said that when I was two she nearly took both my eyes out with her golden *jhoomke* and that I've hated her ever since. I asked how else did he expect me to behave to someone who nearly blinded me?

As I leant against the back wall of our house, I could see Mum behind me through our double glazing taking another paracetamol from the living-room cabinet. Exhausted though she was, Mum plodded on with the dusting. She'd been awake all night worrying about this momentous morning but now, dressed in a pale blue *salwar kameez*, she looked calmer, as if she'd convinced herself that she looked happy. I wondered who she had in mind to comfort her. Those two out there, that was who. She, being the eldest, always had to be the pious, forgiving one, even though her sisters rarely wished her well. Mum's naive, and a daughter like me has to protect the family rep: it says so in the unwritten rules governing Indian daughters' behaviour.

So, selflessly, I went on into our garden and told the two twits-and-a-half that I'd heard everything they'd said. Next-door neighbour anti suddenly remembered that there was something to do back in her house, so she crawled away. She must have known I was seething. I'd thought at first that a bit of swearing might do the trick, but I wanted maximum effect so I twitched my left eye as if I was having difficulty controlling myself. It had the desired effect, for Bimla and Worzel instantly stopped putting lipstick on, pursed their lips, and smirked nervously. All the while I made straight eye contact.

'They were only opinions, you know,' said Worzel. 'Don't be so serious.'

With that brush-off she began to apply vermilion lipstick again, while Bimla became preoccupied with pressing her eyelids so that her false eyelashes stayed in place.

They couldn't just ignore me like that, so I let them have it. 'We all have opinions, but your lot's don't count for nothing. Your daughters aren't too prissy perfect themselves, you know. I mean, Sammy looks like she's had the door slammed in her face, and as for Pinky, well, what type of nickname is that, eh? And where's your daughter Nina, Bimla Massiji? Come on, you can tell me – you know you can always trust me. Has she run away again? Let's face it, she has to take every chance she can get with *haramde* parents like you. Just so you know, I think you're both Dobermanns who should be put down.' Now I've not got anything severe against dogs, and I quite like those cutsie guide ones, but somebody of my stature ought to share their fiver's worth of thoughts.

Bimla leapt at me – serial killer that she is – but I darted back into the house and shut the back door right into her knee, before rocketing through the living-room. Crashing head first into the queue that began somewhere in between the samosa and chutney table and the alcoholic junction, I moaned.

'Watch yourself. You'll fall if you run like that,' said Mum, apparently not noticing that I already had. After apologising to her I got up to straighten my *kameez*. The house was crammed with guests who thankfully allowed me to grab a samosa before my hair got tangled in next-door neighbour-but-one anti's sequinned *chunni*. It should have had a health and safety notice attached. I mean, she didn't even notice me flinch when a handful of my fine strands was pulled out.

'Poto time!' announced Dudley Chacha through a mouthful of *gulab jamun*, adjusting the drape of his linen blazer. He seemed to think we should wave little flags in honour of photoman's arrival and his ability to capture us in all our ugliness. I gave it a maximum of three minutes before the photographer began to wind me up. Rule No 27: Never, ever trip up the cameraman.

'Smile like this. Do your hair like that. Move like her,' said Potoman Mr Fateecha in an annoying piercing voice, as if he knew how a stylised Indian girl like me should behave.

Mr Fateecha had a bad rep for wedding photos and was only doing them for us because of the discount. The last belly-up he made was at Kully's friend's sister's wedding when he made her look fatter than she really was by snapping her against cream velvet curtains with her skirt spread in a circle round her while she sat cross-legged on the floor. The rest of the 358 shots were just as side-splitting, but Mum still insisted they came out ever so well.

As soon as the session began all the guests started

running around like frenzied chickens being attacked by a fox. The atmosphere, let me tell you, was tense. I'd already told Poor Child Prodigy that no amount of saliva would straighten her frizzy hair and that she definitely could not hold my hand for support when it was time for the flash bulb.

Unfortunately, this information fell on Poor Child Prodigy's bibi's ears, and uproar followed. After an in-depth investigation it was found that the wrong shampoo was to blame, and there was a right hoopla as all the antis wiped liberal amounts of oil over Prodigy's hair to flatten it: this failed to make any difference. You'd have thought they'd give up after the first few attempts, but a little while later in strolled Bimla with her very own concoction of superglue and watered-down gram flour. She was intercepted by Mum, who was armed with a paper bag full of hair accessories from the chemist. Thereafter ornamental slides were surreptitiously slid into Poor Child Prodigy's hair.

You had to hand it to her for keeping up that steely glaze throughout the whole ordeal. She didn't so much as blaspheme when she was mistaken for a flower patch. As soon as she'd been strained this way and that and her limbs put in the correct position – snap.

Worzel went off to change for the third time – into her Mughal-inspired sari – and I Poor Child Prodigy huffed like two old hags having a bad day watching the display of flab on show.

Then she gave me her two-bit advice. 'It is well known that photographers will always come to your school when your tooth has just been knocked out.'

'Ah,' I said, trying to look enlightened. 'You aren't a child prodigy for nothing.'

With that she disappeared into the crowd of guests.

It isn't much fun being shoved this way and that by well-meaning guests, and I was beginning to think there'd be no harm in faking an asthma attack. It would have been convincing enough, because I'd trekked up and down the stairs fifty times already that morning. Sometimes it had been because of a comb gone missing, occasionally to bring some more gold jewellery, and on my last trek it was to fetch Worzel's father-in-law's walking-stick – how he got downstairs in the first place I don't know.

All through this ordeal Kully was suffering from low spirits. I naturally assumed it was the thought of getting married to Pardeep that was depressing her, but she took away an hour of my lifetime by telling me that the real problem was that she didn't want to get married because she'd always dreamt of the most perfect wedding taking place on Valentine's Day.

'Oh, boohoo,' I said under my breath. Then I listened to her expound her huge problem, while picking the dirt out of my nails. My, my, she really did hold them close to her heart. I told her that I hated Valentine's Day and any other well-adjusted person would do, too. On that special day I tried with all my imagination not to go beyond my room because experience had shown and predicted that by the end of Valentine's Day self-confidence wasn't something I'd be brimming with. Why couldn't the authorities just declare it a holiday or something? Let the few puppies escape and wear their heart-shaped glasses, sip and gargle their beverages or drink through the double straws? But there's as much chance of that as of the next prime minister being black.

Kully instantly guessed that I had a hang-up and suggested that I control my eyes – I was twitching them in order to repel contact by anyone who might interrogate me about the Bimla and Worzel incident in the garden. Kully also said that we all had inside us those things called feelings, which directed the tender heartfelt desire that someone, somewhere in the world, admired your walk, loved the wave in your hair and the cheekiness in your smile, but in reality it was all a big fat whopper of a nothing.

We agreed that Valentine's Day was like Christmas Eve. We'd make it clear to Mum and Dad that, although we didn't celebrate Christmas, we still had the decent common courtesy to write Santa our extensive but not exhaustive lists. The next morning we'd wake up as excited as if we'd just been given the Nobel Peace Prize and race down the stairs to find . . . nothing. Rule No 28: Santa's sleigh doesn't fly over our chimneys, even if you do leave him *roti* and *saag*.

Where was I? Oh, yeah. Valentine's Day, like Christmas, is a let-down. Be aware that grown-ups do that sometimes: make you believe in things they don't believe in themselves – it's their way of asserting power. Before I could explain these facts to the rest of the guests I was caught up in yet another fight which had absolutely nothing to do with me. It had originated on the upstairs landing and ended up downstairs.

'You witch, get off my sister,' I snarled.

'What?' said Worzel, loosening her grip on Kiz's shoulders.

'Get off her, you fungus!'

I'd been wound so tight that when I did my jack-in-the-box jump everybody was caught unawares.

'You dare talk to me like that and I'll pour bleach right down that gob of yours. I'm a little teapot short and stout, tip me up and pour me out,' Worzel snarled back, edging away from the bride. She pushed me into the wall, which although hollow (it had been refurbished by builder mates of Dad's using the cheapest plasterboard available) could still concuss.

'Aagh!' I snorted, pretending to be injured. 'Nobody pushes me like that.'

'Mum *she* burnt your shawl. She did,' Sammy pointed at Kiz.

'No I didn't. Not me. Not touched. Not done nothing with it.' Kiz protested her innocence to Worzel, Sammy and Pinky, like they cared.

Worzel peered through the hole in the Kashmiri shawl she had specially commissioned for herself. With her anger now all-consuming she could never entertain the thought that Sammy just might be the one who was lying. In any case it couldn't be Kiz. That lass is the best ironer around. You should see the way she tackles creased denim.

Before I could grab Sammy and Pinky by their £350 (at least, that's what they told everyone) gold necklaces, they ran like scaredy-cats, tripping over their *lehange* as they went. I dashed into the front room, drew back the white embroidered voile, and saw Pinky and Sammy turn the corner, their bottoms swinging furiously enough to endanger any passer-by who strayed into their space.

As they vanished from sight, I let myself go: *'Die, you cows!'* There, that ought to make me feel better, and it did. I looked out at the road, which had always remained indifferent to me, even in my most vexed moments. As roads go it was a good one.

Just then two skinny old women passed by. One was carting loaves of bread and tins of Happy Shopper beans in her shopping trolley, and the other looked ready to pull the head right off a poor Labrador which couldn't distinguish between her leg and a lamppost.

As I said, Dad's builder mates were shoddy workers. The workmanship in the double-glazing fittings wasn't up to scratch either, so voices easily penetrated through the gaps. Every time there's a row I tell people to go argue in the back of the kitchen. I mean, what if people heard us arguing? We'd look like a right cheapo bunch.

But I hadn't heeded my own advice and the old women turned round in surprise when I told the cows to die. Before I could stammer out a 'Sorry, not you,' the one with the trolley stuck up two fingers at me and they toddled off, their chip on the shoulder restored.

Pressing my forehead hard against the window, I shouted, 'Wait till I undo the wheels of that shopping trolley. Just you wait.' Then I hitched myself up and sat on the back of the sofa, sighing with disgust at my fury over little things and my ability to get angry so quickly. I don't know why it happens, but I guess it's because I'm pretty near perfect so my tolerance level of other people's foibles is lower than average. Maybe I need to go on one of those self-help courses imported from America like they do on *Oprah*.

Moving to the high pine chair near the sofa I let my feet dangle. At first they moved fast, as if running, but then they began to keep time with the tick-tock of the clock. After a few quiet moments had passed with only a man blowing his nose outside to be seen, I moved to the sofa.

Closely followed by Kiz, Kully came scurrying in, looking as though her nerves were almost out of control. She looked ravishing in her maroon and gold bridal *lehanga*.

She sat down carefully on the sofa a little nervous and a little more composed, and said, 'Put the telly on.'

'Why don't you do it, you lazy cow?'

Looking hurt, Kully squinted at me and screwed up her face, so I did as she asked.

'There's nothing on.'

'There's cricket.'

'S'boring,' moaned Kully.

Sitting very straight and looking like she'd just had an enema she checked her make-up in her compact mirror for the fifth time. A smile dawned on her face when she saw how beautiful she looked. She really did look beautiful

'Your *bindi*'s moved,' said Kully, pointing to my forehead as if I didn't know where a *bindi* should go.

After five minutes Kully handed me the mirror. My *bindi* had nudged possibly a millimetre to the right, but it was nothing to correct and it disturbed me that Kully had noticed.

While we waited for Dudley Chacha, Kiz told me she'd concluded that I had a heart-shaped face. All these years I'd been thinking it was a Grace Kelly face and then it turns out to be Madhubala. I'll have to change my whole beauty regime now. Only kidding. That's the thing; I haven't got a beauty regime because I have a dusky complexion which is prone to minor oil and zit attacks, so foundation does me no favours. I have a proportionately sized nose, my eyes are black, my hair's black and my favourite colour is black – oh, and I'm five foot five.

'Change the channel,' ordered Kully, 'or we'll miss *The Wonder Years*.'

'Why don't you tell Kiz?'

'She's thick, that's why.'

'Don't pick on me, you fat cow.'

Ooops! Kiz could have said anything else in the world to Kully and got away with it, but she'd uttered the fatal word 'fat' and she couldn't take it back.

Suddenly Kully jumped up, grabbed the yucca plant, and threatened to slice Kiz with the leaves if she ever had the nerve to say 'fat' again. Kiz told her to get stuffed. Then Kully went for one of Kiz's most prized possessions, a studio portrait of Kiz in her most glamorous pose. I was curtly ordered to find a pen and, just to show how obliging I could be, I got three. When Kiz saw that the portrait might get a moustache, she responded by apologising with profuse expressions of guilt and told herself off for having such an unruly tongue. She added that Kully had a perky, prize-worthy nose, well-toned cheekbones and a fair complexion marked with not one single

165

sign of ageing. This buttering-up worked and Kully sat down again, holding herself straight and stiff as if this would make her appear to be in control.

'When's the Merc coming?' she complained. 'At this rate we'll have to get a taxi.'

As if on cue we heard a car door slam outside, and sure enough there was Dudley Chacha locking Wally Uncle's Merc. A minute later he poked his head round the door to tell us how good we all looked. There was always some doubt. He was particularly chuffed to see me looking so dandy, which was saying something given that the mirrored beads at the top of my mandarin collar were causing a small outbreak of rash.

On escorting us all outside to where Budgie was waiting in his black trouser suit, Dudley Chacha was horrified to find bird droppings on the bonnet of the car – I mean Mercedes. Angrily he told the cameraman to stop filming his car in such a state. While he wiped the droppings away with a rag from the boot. he offered me and Kiz some informal advice.

'Now, this is the most important day in all of our lives, OK? Sushminder, Susham, Sushi, whatever your name is. I want you to stop fighting with people, because it doesn't look good. And Kiran, you must stop dressing like a hooker – that doesn't look good, either.' He was trying to tell us what Dad would have told us if he'd been there. We said we'd try our best, but not before I pointed out that it was everybody else who was fighting me. I was as passive as the next person. In any case the promise was short-lived, because the second we siblings got into the Merc the shenanigans began again.

'Get off my *lehanga*, you dork,' hissed Kiz.

'You get off mine,' Kully hissed straight back.

'Shut the beep up, both of you,' said Budgie crossly, and he thanked Dudley Chacha for hooting over the expletive so it wouldn't turn up on the wedding video.

Shaking his head out of pity for us Budgie carried on searching for a good Asian radio station. A minute later he found the crackly sounds of a 'Nusrat' Oswali track. Only then did Dudley Chacha set off, so we could sing along karaokee-stylee for the mile distance to the Gurudwara. Kully sighed with happiness, for although it had taken her twenty-six years and a bit she was getting away from us. Then she began to practise crying, while Kiz moaned at Dudley Chacha for refusing to stop at the corner shop so the maximum number of people could see her get in and out of the Mercedes.

When Kully stopped crying she started telling everyone about the milestone moments of every object we passed. 'That was the first bus stop I ever caught a bus from.'

'Well, you weren't gonna catch an aeroplane from there,' said Kiz.

'That was the first post box I ever posted a letter in. Look, the sycamore's bidding me farewell – that tree sheltered me in my most vulnerable moments. Goodbye, tree.' On and bleedin' on she went making me want to grab the steering-wheel and crash the car – anything to stop her gobbing on.

Eventually, after Eternity and Timepass got it together, we arrived at the Gurudwara and struggled out of the Merc. As soon as Kully got out, a group of antis ambled over to her and said the groom's side had yet to arrive, but imagination shouldn't get the better of her because they were sure the Rais' coaches hadn't been involved in a pile-up. Kiz and I dragged Kully inside before she could hurt anyone with her *kleere*. The chandeliers dangled from her hands and were proving to be quite menacing.

Once we were in the safe surroundings of a makeshift office/dressing/waiting room, part one of the sabotage was going to be administered, by me. The rest of the family, including Budgie, had dispersed to meet our guests and were nowhere to be seen, so I could administer Kully's special drink prepared avec Dad's sleeping smarties – 'Give it to her,' he'd said, 'exactly thirty minutes before she's to be married,'

Shoving the drink into Kully's hand I confidently advised her, 'Here you go. It's full of vitamins. Got to keep your strength up.'

Kully obligingly took the drink in her jewellery-adorned hand, although she looked a bit perturbed at my sudden kindness.

'What?' I asked a little awkwardly, as she looked at me suspiciously.

'Nothing.'

After saying hello to some people who had flown in all the way from America, Kully put the glass to her mouth. Her hand quivered with the nerves of this important day.

I only wished I could make it important for the right reason, but no way was I going to let Rai the home-wrecker into our house. No way. I'd seen the power he had over Mum: Dad and I didn't even get a look in with Mum behaving so subserviently. We were never good enough for her when *he* was around.

'No, you can't drink that. It'll ruin your lipstick,' said Kiz dashing forward only to knock the cup out of Kully's hand. I don't know how she managed it, but seconds later maroon lipstick was spread over Kully's right cheek.

'Not to worry we've got more of it, ain't we?' said Kully.

Kiz played with a strand of hair which had escaped from her cane roll. She looked mighty worried.

'Ain't we?' repeated Kully, looking as if she were on the verge of a canyon-sized panic attack. 'Ain't weeee?'

The trembling urgency of the situation made Kiz blubber and jiggle her arms in the air as she wafted on about how it took such a long time to look as good as she did. 'Forgive me,' she implored on her knees. 'I'm prone to the odd light-headed moment.' She knew she was in for a beating from Kully. If you leave the bride's bleedin' make-up kit at home, you have to pay the price.

'I refuse to wear chemist make-up. I refuse to look cheap. I refuse,' went Kully. You'd have thought 'I refuse' was the only way she knew of starting a sentence.

'Don't you want a drink?' I said in the most calming tone I could dredge up. 'Wouldn't want dehydration, now. You sure you don't need it?'

'No, I bloody don't,' snapped Kully.

Before I could say any more, she was swept up and escorted out of the door by an invading party of seven women, including Mum, Worzel and Bimla, leaving me

169

and Kiz standing there like lemons. We could hear wails from the cameraman, begging them to walk slower because his cable was about a hundred metres too long and was getting coiled round his legs.

Worzel's smug voice floated back to me: 'My Sammy will save the day. Maroon lipstick is her favourite, don't you know.'

Yes, we bloody well do know, I wanted to shout. Looking rough was Sammy's speciality.

As I stood there looking at the spilt drink, it dawned on me that Kully was going to get married. *Haiyo Rabba.* I'd let Dad down. One simple thing to do and I couldn't even manage that. What was the point of it all? The Rais would gobble me and my dad up in a doddle for sure.

'You coming?' asked Kiz, wiping some of her smudged mascara away while she smoothed the tail of her *chunni*. I found it difficult to answer, so simply nodded.

I looked out of the Gurudwara window. The late autumn sun shone through, brilliantly letting its rays burst all over the room. In the car park guys and girls were loitering, pretending not to make eye contact. Near a bent tree stood Arjun, his hands in his trouser pockets, kicking idly at the gravel. Seeing him in his navy linen blazer and trousers made me feel inadequate for some reason. An immaculate pale-blue poplin shirt set off his unblemished complexion.

Kully was twittering and twirling, beside herself at being the centrepiece of such a grand occasion. Her fish-tail *lehanga* gave her what she called an 'aura', allowing her to walk her Rekha walk with her Audrey Hepburn hair. I hoped she didn't resent me for running out of the house like that yesterday. Then, I don't know why, but a thought raced into my head. Kully seemed happy in her own way. Maybe I should let her be?

Before I could console myself, 'Cheer up, love. Might never happen. It's a fantastic, stupendous day' said Brummie Uncle, tweaking the carnation in his blazer buttonhole.

'Already has,' I said under my breath. Why do people always say that? I mean, if you say it you say it to someone who's moping, don't you? And why are they moping? Precisely because 'it' has happened.

Brummie Uncle ignored my mutter and kicked me out of the room – private phone call, he said, sounding very important. I went sappily outside into the Gurudwara car park, hoping to cheer myself up.

Pardeep's guests soon arrived, packed into two coaches which shook severely, knackering the suspension. As their drivers parked in the six spaces reserved for disabled people I went over to greet the disembarking guests – anything to keep busy and stop me looking at that Arjun. I was in the mood to dismember him.

Men, women and children sprawled out of the coaches looking like they'd been involved in some calamity. One of them, a strange woman with bo-balls for earrings, walked past me complaining about the mix-up between Dudley and Derby. 'I knew our driver should have taken my offer of driving more seriously,' she said. The men were on coach A, which I found, when I inspected it, had a far superior toilet; the women on Coach B must have had a hole in the floor.

As I stood looking curiously at our new relations I realised that, if the attendance list comprised five hundred people, our family would in just one day have acquired that many friends and relations. The Rais' much superior guest list included the Mayor of Dudley and a man who held the world record for making the biggest statue of Jawaharlal Nehru from bottle tops – another artist in the family, way hey.

Bimla and Worzel plodded by on their stilts, saying loudly that we ought to be grateful for hitting the big time. The only thing I wanted to hit big time was their bouffants, which were airy enough to propel them across the English Channel.

When the bride's family had welcomed the groom's family in the *milni*, we all headed into the prayer hall to take our places. Pinky and Sammy were told to sit at the front: that was where I should have been.

Don't mind me, I said silently. I'll just sit at the back like a sad case.

After bowing my head, I picked my way through the tightly crammed guests sitting cross-legged on the floor. It wasn't easy not to step on ladies' toes while at the same time stopping my *chunni* slipping off my head so nobody would find reason to moan. I kept an eye out for Dad, but the ceremony had begun and finished before anyone noticed he wasn't there.

It was all a bit of a blur anyway. I'd nodded off on account of the central heating having been set at just the right temperature by Gyaniji. This time, though, I took my nap with my eyes wide open so that no one could accuse me of being apathetic.

'Photo time,' cried Kiz and Gurminder. In their matching pastel-shaded *lehange* they had jumped to the front of the queue – Worzel was having a hard time moving them away from the photographers.

Poor Kully was lost underneath the garlands that had been placed around her neck. She smiled miserably for the thousandth photo while Pardeep peeked at her. He looked regal in his black Sherwani suit, and the red turban made him appear much more mature both physically and mentally.

Parents, brothers, sisters, everyone was shoved forward to have their picture taken with the bride and groom. Even I was summoned eventually to rest my hands on the couple's heads by way of a blessing. Did they really want mine?

My photo was going to come out little fuzzy, because amid the shoot Kiz called across that she'd seen somebody wearing my black wedge sandals and if I didn't come right that minute I'd have to wear mismatching shoes. I never did find the thief, so ended up wearing trainers too tight for my size six and a half feet. They were lent to me by a *gyani* who said he'd got tons of shoes in the office.

'What do people walk home in, then?' I asked.

'Their feet.'

Nobody had bothered to ask me if Dad had turned up. Arjun had bothered to turn up, but I wished he hadn't. I don't know what he thought I was going to do. Fight over him? He should have known I wasn't that type of girl.

Once all the formalities were complete, we transferred

en masse to the Blue Cross Hotel – although its name should really be changed to the Red Cross. I tell you, a good lesson was being taught to a number of women in their high heels climbing up those spiral stairs. That's not including the two alkees who couldn't get up them in the first place: apparently vertigo took hold. Dad still hadn't shown.

I was only too glad of the small reprieve in social duties, so barged into the packed toilets, where women were changed into their party outfits. Among them stood Worzel, staring at her reflection like she'd never seen herself before. Satisfied that the right amount of aubergine shading had highlighted what she assumed to be her cheekbones, she began to powder her nose shining with sweat – or, as she daintily preferred to call it, 'perspiration'.

I tried to tiptoe past behind her, but my trainers let me down: their rubber soles squeaked like fury on the lino floor-tiles. When she heard me, Worzel's nose turned upwards as if I were a piece of cod gone off. I at once stuck my tongue out, because I consider this very immature, and immature behaviour more than anything else drives Worzel to question the common decency of girls my generation.

'Something stinks around here,' said Worzel to a woman who was having difficulty tying a *nala* on her *salwar* and who obviously wasn't in the mood to listen because she was complaining she'd had a bad experience with a falling *salwar* at a function like this only a week ago.

I didn't respond.

'Yes,' said Worzel more loudly, 'I believe she has BO.'

174

Worzel's Rule No 29: Change your clothes at least three times at a wedding, otherwise you'll be accused of stinking. So what if I hadn't changed my suit three thousand times like she had? She was the one who was discontented with the way she looked; at least I knew what suited me. Worzel stalked out with her *kameez* tucked into the top of her *salwar*, which cheered me up no end.

As Worzel exited, three girls entered.

'Oh, you're the bride's sister's, aren't you?' said Girl One. 'Isn't she lucky to be marrying Pardeep?'

'You know him?' asked Girl Two, busily adding more mascara to mascara-encrusted eyelashes.

'Every girl with any credibility knows of his aura,' chimed in Girl Three, clapping her hands. 'He was once the most eligible bachelor, you know. You can't tell me you didn't know?'

That's right. Talk and ask me questions like I'm not here, why don't you?

'Look here,' said Girl One to Girl Two, 'try these contact lenses. I've got blue and green and grey, but if you ask me' – she held the lenses up in front of her friend's reddened eyes – 'you'd suit blue.'

After waiting ages behind Girl Two because Girl Three had pushed her way into the free cubicle, which by rights should have been mine, I managed to free myself from the clutch of the women's toilets and fled. But things weren't much better outside: I bumped into a mad-looking waitress who had obviously never served at an Indian wedding before, Inebriated Man in search of more pints, and a woman with a bawling brat who'd choked on some tandoori chicken.

175

When I at last got out of this black hole Mum came towards me.

Fear sprinted through me.

'Mum, no. I'm not going to. You can't make me. There are lots of people here and I'll create a scene – just you wait and see.' The words scurried out of my mouth hoping to save me, hoping that Mum wouldn't make me clap like a dunce behind the couple as they were serenaded by the beating of the *dhol* when they entered the hall. Mum walked away. Reverse psychology. I'll give her reverse psychology.

A *dhol*-beat later I found myself joining a whole procession of women clapping furiously. Their arms snapped up and down like the jaws of cavorting crocodiles on a safari.

Ignoring all this, Pardeep and Kully waited patiently till the wedding-cake had been cut and their dance number began. Then he led her on to the dance floor with his right arm round her waist. His cleanly-shaven face glowed with pride and embarrassment as they swayed slowly to the music blaring out from speakers strategically placed to topple on to guests. Pardeep looked down even more proudly upon his wife of just over two hours, and beamed at those of his friends who'd voiced their envy of him for having pulled such a bird. He was a decent enough dancer, for his long legs and arms let him look as if he moved with grace. He'd removed his wedding turban and his hair, unlike Kully's, didn't look as if it had been stapled to his cranium but flopped all over the place as he hopped to the beat. He'd also changed into a grey suit and now looked exactly like the model groom on their tiered wedding cake.

The embarrassment that the guests felt at seeing a couple display their affection like that dissipated, too, when they began to crowd round the happy couple showering them with sterling notes.

That's when I saw a quick money-making chance and grabbed two tenners for myself. It was also when Bimla saw me and, in collusion with Mrs Kaur branded me a thief in front of the other guests. I instantly learnt Rule No 30: Do not take money at any function. You'll always be accused of stealing, even if you have a clean slate. When their jive was over, I was surprised by my disappointment at seeing them stop.

After this brief misunderstanding with Bimla and Mrs Kaur, I was told to stay under the strict eye of Budgie, who'd make sure I didn't reveal any more of my malevolent tendencies. Dadoo offered to cool me down with a glass of Coke, which brings me to Rule No 31: Never let your brother's friend offer to get you his version of Coke. He'll later deny all involvement in your drunkenness.

'Wait till I tell Mum,' threatened Budgie – the usual old spiel.

'Dares ya.'

'Trust me to get lumbered with a sappy-wappy sibling.' he grumbled.

'Who are you calling a sibling?' I demanded. 'I ain't no sibling of yours, because I've disowned you. Didn't you know? Just like you lot disowned Dad, I disown you.' Before he could tell me to be quiet, I screamed, 'I don't like you,' and stamped my feet in pent-up frustration.

'Oh, I'll have a sleepless night now,' said Budgie, sig-nalling Mum to come over from her *gidha*. He obviously expected her to shut me up, but I didn't care one bit. I was going to have my say.

'You lying little thick breed. You told me Sesame Street was in Canada and—'

'He told you that just to shut you up,' interrupted Dadoo. 'You're giving him hassle, girl. Just stup, stup, stup.'

'If you give people wrong locations, how is a person supposed to end up there?'

'You're no Henson, so why bother?' said Budgie.

'Well, you're no great electrician.'

Immediately Budgie tripped backwards. I could hear him asking himself, 'Is she going to tell everyone that I'm not perfect, that I'm unemployed and Guggi's is made up?' I wasn't.

'And I'm telling you all now,' I carried on, 'if there's one thing I'll do in my life, it'll be to get to Sesame Street. Just you see if I don't.' Dadoo's Coke was doing wonders for my self-esteem. Waving my hands for emphasis, while my head jerked with the force of my words, I was spinning on the spot without moving. How could that be?

Mum's antennae must have been on high alert, because at that moment she stormed over and dragged me right to the back of the hall. Despite my telling her the truth – that a twit called Dadoo had given me the stuff, which I'd naturally assumed was kosher – I was told to quit my lying, keep well out of sight and mind my gob for the rest of the afternoon. Charming.

I searched for Dadoo all around the Blue Cross so that I could enter a plea against the guilty verdict, but no chance. He was much too busy, and having much too good a time, standing on Brummie Uncle's shoulders, banging his head on the disco ball. Rule No 32: Always expect your mother to think the worst of you and expect your relations to agree with her.

There was an empty table at the back of the hall, so I sat down and passed the time by ruffling the edges of the cream paper tablecloth. Saira was busy dancing with Mum. Indy was busy dancing with Kully. They were all so damn busy. My neurosis was advancing rapidly, so when a waitress brought over some *ras milais* I grabbed three, hoping the vanilla-smelling milk would neutralise the whiff of rum that still hung about me.

'Decent turn-out,' shouted an unrecognisable voice.

'What?'

'Decent turn-out,' the voice shouted once again, this time loudly enough for me to recognise it as Gurmit's.

'Yeah,' I shouted back, looking around for Arjun and Sammy. Gurmit sat down next to me without being asked but I hardly noticed because I was watching the crazy dancers: one of the Folk Friday uncles was jigging on a table. I laughed out loud. I hadn't done that for quite some time, so thought my cheeks had cracked.

Bimla screwed up her face at me, warning me to not have such a good time. I should have guessed another rule would come into play. This time it was bloody Rule No 33: Don't be happy at your sister's wedding, even if you're glad to see her go. Guests presume that the bride comes from a family with many domestic problems.

Then, as if by a miracle, Arjun came and plonked himself next to me to eat his *kulfi*. He was all beamy-smiley and his feet tapped cheerfully to the beat of the *dhol*. Peeping at him secretly from the corner of my eye, I wondered what he thought of me and my family, whether he'd consider having my parents as in-laws. Why was I thinking like this? Only an hour ago I'd wanted to harm him, and now here I was getting all charmed again.

When Gurmit went to get some food, Arjun huffed a bit.

'Stay away,' I told him.

'Can we talk?'

'We can shout, mate, but talking over that ain't gonna happen.' I pointed to the speakers, but the hindrance wasn't really them, it was my pride.

After pondering a while he tore off a bit of the tablecloth, took out what looked like a very expensive pen and started writing. I wondered what type of guy kept a pen in his blazer pocket. A guy like Arjun, perhaps? When he'd finished, the paper was shoved into my hand. Ignoring him, I stood up, trying to be just as aloof as he'd always appeared to be to me.

Before I could sneak a glance at what he'd written, Gurmit reappeared.

'Hi!' I screamed with a big smile which was intended to make Arjun jealous.

I pushed Gurmit six tables up to where the Folk Friday lot were, and we sat down, leaving Arjun's ego hurt, I hope. Nobody would dare say anything to me on that table for I was with the respected elders of the community.

'You all right, Kuriye?' asked a Folk Friday uncle.

'No. No, I'm not.' I replied, shaking my head.

Uncle sipped his beer, 'Oh that's good, then.'

Then I began laughing at all his jokes so loud you'd have thought I was going to win a prize for it. I only stopped when Gurmit looked confused.

A go-between sat comfortably with the 'happy' new-lyweds, hugging a bulky purple sequinned purse filled to bursting with money which had been thrown and collected throughout the day. Gurmit said he knew that she had a gift for making sure that couples followed etiquette, and that wherever her nose sniffed a fiver her hands found it out.

I screamed with laughter again. 'Oh, you're so funny. Just too funny.'

Gurmit looked back at me oddly, straightened his tie and got up. 'You're a weirdo,' he said, and with that he walked away.

Before I could feel like a complete mushroom Kiz came over, leant down so that her silver earring dangled right in my face, and said in my ear, 'Did you tell the DJ not to put "Congratulations" on?'

'Yeah, why?'

'Pardeep's mum's gonna kill you, just you wait and see.' Kiz exaggerated most of the time but on this occasion I sussed that she was telling the truth, 'cos our own Mum popped out from behind her and leant down on my other side.

'No bloody Cliff? Are you mad? Do you want me to take my shoe off?' she shouted in Punjabi, a language in which 'Do you want me to take my shoe off' sounds much more menacing.

I whimpered, 'Sorry,' very humbly, knowing that would temporarily put what looked like a smile on Mum's face. She took full advantage of my guilt and ordered me to start dancing or her wrath would descend on me. Then she was dragged away by Worzel to help feed the new Mr and Mrs Rai.

One of Dad's mates from the Folk Friday group had observed all this with amazement.

'She isn't always like that,' I told him, but I don't think he believed me for one moment.

Seeing him fiddle with his empty plastic cup, I offered to get him a drink.

'Yes, *beta*, please do.'

I was breaking Rule No 34: Do not loiter around the bar, even if you need to find the earring you've lost and the man in the green and yellow Florida shirt is stepping on it on purpose. Nitwit. I was told by Brummie Uncle to stay as far from the bar as possible or the wedding film would be used as blackmail. I suppose I should have done what he said, but there was no point, because I'd already been caught on camera. Rule No 35: Avoid all cameras.

I thought now was a good a time as ever to start dancing and try to impress Mrs Kaur with my *gidha* so that she'd look more kindly on me, but as soon as I hit the dance floor she and the other guests walked away, leaving me standing there by myself.

I don't like to say it, but feeling like a twerp was becoming a habit. I know it's the most OK thing to be by yourself, but when everyone's staring at you it isn't, for some reason. I felt very alone. I wished Dad was with me.

I grimaced at Sammy and Pinky, who were skinny and

wretchedly tall in their big-clobber high heels. Their perfectly oval faces and long, freshly trimmed and decorated hair made them look adorable. Make-up was splashed on Warhol-like, and their floaty *lehange* danced better than they did. That Rai was circling a fifty-pound note round their heads. I didn't hate them or anything – that takes way too much effort – but I'd been wary of them ever since my tenth birthday.

That day Worzel and Bimla came round together to give me a birthday card and one of Sammy's leftover cardis. I was very grateful to receive it so thanked Sammy – I even thanked Pinky, too – and told them they were the prettiest girls I'd ever known.

That's when I broke Rule No 36: Never tell someone they're pretty. Soon as you do, they start thinking they're doing you a favour letting you look at them, let alone talking to you. That's why I now go around telling all beautiful people that they're the sort of cowpats flies wouldn't swarm around. I suppose I get my kicks like that. Nasty, isn't it? No, nastiness ain't got anything to do with it; just call me the equaliser. I'm a hypocrite, though, I really am, 'cos sometimes I want to copy Mrs Shee-Shee Raa-Raa Pooey with her candlewaxed legs and well-pressed clothes. But one thing I'll never do is go around billboard-style like the Rais do. Ain't it funny that you're doing all the advertising and you aren't even being paid?

In one of the two conversations I'd ever had with Pardeep, he said it was all a matter of taste, wearing designer. I told him it was nothing of the kind: taste has nothing to do with having crap written across your back.

Just because you wore Ralph Lauren didn't mean he'd want to be within spitting distance of you.

Deciding that I didn't want to be within spitting distance of a Rai, I sighed with shame and slunk off the dance floor. The Rais' and Stinky Pinky's and Sammy's and Bimla's and Worzel's shortcomings didn't change a thing. I'd let myself down, and moreover I'd let Dad down. I was the only one he trusted, me – that was a real privilege – and I couldn't even manage to drug my sister. Mum was happy, though; you could tell by the way she walked. I know I shouldn't have thought this but I did: Go on, someone, trip her up.

When the dance floor was taken over again by the drunken uncles for a good heave-ho, I headed for the exit, my head hung so low I could have dribbled it with my squeaking trainers that announced my departure to one and all. At the exit I turned for one last look. The hall seemed both dead and alive, and the heat of its flickering lights was turning the rash on my neck into an evil itch. I saw Rai accidentally wave goodbye to me with Worzel and Bimla hovering about him.

Near them was Budgie, who thought it appropriate to smile at me. He didn't do that very often, and it sent a sharp shiver all through me. He might be feeling the same way I did. I mean, this family wedding without much of a family wasn't kidding me, so why should it kid him? As I waited patiently behind a woman chatting to Kully's mother-in-law and blocking the way out of the door, my rash nearly caught on fire, for there stood Dad.

He looked the smartest I'd ever seen him. His worn shoes were as shiny as could be, his feathery grey hair was neatly combed, and his smile announced: Dad's here; make way for the crazy man. And make way they did as he tip-tapped over to the beat of the *bhangra*. You should have seen it. Guests rose slowly from their chairs, not quite like the parting of the waves but as near as you're going to get in the Blue Cross. We all stood there staring at him, not knowing what to do. My feet had turned to lead or something, because usually I was good at running away from tricky situations but there I was, stuck. A frown had frozen on to my face. What was Dad gonna do?

Suddenly, behind him appeared the two coppers I'd seen yesterday, looking like fishermen who'd landed their trout. Before they could get away from the Folk Friday lot *bhangra*-ing in their way, I made the quickest dash at Dad, my beaded trousers letting off sparks as they brushed against the guests' synthetic fibres. I had to get to him before PCs Plid and Plod did.

'This way,' I yelled, grabbing Dad and towing him down towards the stage.

Bedlam ensued, as guests dodged in and out trying to get Dad in their grip. On reaching the stage we were momentarily hidden by a group of potted palms behind the wedding-cake table. Dad ducked his head just in time as we dived under the table. Through the small gap between floor and tablecloth we could see assorted foot-wear running this way and that. The bright pink ones belonged to Worzel, the beige high heels that distressed her varicose veins were Bimla's, and those sad rubber beach sandals were Mum's. The table was only a flimsy plastic one, but between it and the tablecloth the music was deadened a little, and we heard frantic cries of

185

'Where've they gone? . . . What they doing? . . . Get the *paagals* now . . . I thought you had 'em.' Even now, at Kully's wedding, they couldn't leave us be.

Snug under the table while everybody ran around crashing into everybody else, Dad and I laughed so hard it made my stomach ache. It was good laughing together like that – we'd almost forgotten how to.

Observing him closely, I saw that his cheeks had sunken in. His former dimples had become holes. His face wasn't as robust as it used to be. Something about his smile had changed, too, or maybe that was me.

Dad stroked my forehead. 'I'm proud of you, love,' he said in my ear, in a voice so soft I wondered whether it belonged to him.

I'm not much of a crier. I know girls are supposed to be but I'm an emotional retard when it comes to that, so I found it strange that I was suddenly trying to fight back tears. I found it even stranger that they were winning. I'd never told him I loved him; you don't really have to. 'It's all in the actions,' Dad says, and he's right. I mean, what was the 'I love you' that Mum said to him that night he went away?

I thanked Dad for not holding my failure at sabotage against me. I'd promised him that we'd be victorious, and now there was Kully married into the lowlife clan, but still Dad smiled in that reassuring way.

He sighed and laid his head down on the hard wooden floor. 'Too tired I am,' he said. 'When I was insane the world made sense. I stopped putting up my bitter pretence. Now I've been jacketed, all straitened and packeted – "There, there, you're normal now, see" – and all

186

so quickly. I'll have one of those days where everything's blurred and life fades into a haze and then I'll go . . .'

'Here, Dad,' I said, 'have this.' I rolled my silk *chunni* into a small ball and slipped it under his head, hoping that this would calm his murmuring, which I suppose made sense to him. 'There,' I said, looking thankfully at the tablecloth hiding us, 'we're safe here.' Then he drifted into sleep leaving me scared of something but I wasn't sure what.

All of a sudden, as if to say 'You're not safe at all', the tablecloth was lifted and Arjun appeared.

'What are you doing here?' I screamed. 'You'll get us shot.'

'Look, I like you.'

'What?' I asked. I mean, he could have at least given me an introduction.

He squeezed in under the table and put his face close to mine. 'Listen,' he said in my ear 'I—'

'My dad's here. He'll sort you out, just you see,' I said like a two-year-old. But Dad just looked at Arjun, smiled and went back to sleep.

'Just go, will you?' I said. What was there to talk about? Oh, let me see. The way he makes me feel I ought to be something other than I am? Or should it be the way he doesn't exactly bring out the best in my enigmatic character?

'If Sammy sees you, you're dead,' I warned him.

'I'd rather be dead than have to talk to her.'

'What?' I asked again with a puzzled frown.

'Sammy's doing my head in, that's what. Keeps announcing we're engaged.'

'Well, you might as well be,' I said resentfully.

'Jealous, are we?'

'Nope. I just wouldn't want to get in the way of a beautiful thing.'

Arjun fidgeted for a moment, then peeked out under the tablecloth. 'God almighty, no, Mum, not that move.' He looked mortified.

'What? Your mum's here?'

He nodded reluctantly, as if he wished she wasn't.

'Where?' I asked, eager to get a look at the woman who could give birth to such a fine-looking but dense-thinking guy.

Arjun paused, for dramatic effect, I guess, and pointed at a crowd of around seventy on the dance floor. 'There, the one in the pink suit, see?'

My eyeballs nearly popped out of their sockets as I strained to see who he meant. 'No. How's she dancing?'

'With difficulty.'

We chuckled nervously.

'Look, look right next to your brother. She's doing "put your hands up in the air".'

I peered through the mash of people but the only ones I could see clearly were Mrs Kaur and a frightened-looking Kully, who was being dragged from one circle of dancing ladies to the other.

'There's only that wally Mrs Kaur the Kamini in the pink there.'

Arjun turned on me, his face paling before my very eyes. 'That's my mother you're talking about.'

'Oh.' Rule No 37: Don't ever take the mick out of a Punjabi son's mother.

'Look,' he said, 'I had a good reason for not saying anything about the gig and all. Just hear me out.'

But I wasn't listening. Dad's leg had sprawled right out and might well betray our hiding-place by tripping someone.

Tucking it back in, Arjun smiled. 'There, they won't get at us now.'

I wondered when Arjun had made himself part of an 'us'. From where I sat the only 'us' was me and my dad, and we hadn't invited anybody to our party.

Arjun bent over Dad for a minute, frowning. When he straightened up, he said, 'He's coming down with a fever.'

'Yes, Doctor Arjun.'

'No, really, feel his forehead.' Arjun took my hand and put it on Dad's head. He was right: Dad was burning up.

'*Rehende!*' mumbled Dad, looking well zonked out – he must have been if he could sleep in all that noise.

'We've got to get him to an ER,' said Arjun.

'No, an A and E.'

'Oh, whatever.'

I smiled uneasily, not sure what to do. If we left our hiding-place Dad would be taken prisoner, but if we stayed here, well, Dad might just . . . As if he'd heard my thoughts and wanted to shove an answer in my face, without warning Dad sat bolt upright. His head banged the flimsy table high in the air, making nearby guests dive to safety. Wails of distress from every direction greeted the eruption. Arjun and I crouched on the floor, letting the wedding cake shower down on to the floor and on to people's heads, including Rai's – he looked like the abominable snowman.

'You!' howled Rai. 'You!'

Before he could call me a name I certainly didn't deserve, I yelled 'Bog off!' at him, and skipped away to join Dad who had skated to the dance floor, laughing ho ho ho all the way

Dadoo's dad materialised beside me. 'Your father's the man he always he was,' he said. 'You have a lot to learn but we'll begin with the ending. That's as good a place as any.'

I was both confused and intrigued by his words, so said nothing, just listened.

'The way into the necropolis of the mind,' he went on, 'is a treacherous path, but those who take it wander through, not out of spite nor because of mistakes, for they hold themselves accountable to none but their nightmares. These grow stronger with each passing night, and once in a while through the sombre light they emit a smile which hovers in your heart till weeping and laughing become the same.

'Many people mask a man's character behind the label of "refugee" or "immigrant", but no one upon whom one of those labels was pinned ever bore any love for it – how could they? Your father certainly didn't. Then there were the people who enforced their own choices, their own will, upon him, never dreaming that the man in the flat tweed cap had a clicking knee and would never dance to their song. Like many others, they would succumb to his kind of wrath.

'Amarjit Singh Dillon, that gentle, humane man,

never harmed so much as a fly but he got caught in a web spun by somebody else, in silk wound so tight it dammed the flow of blood in his left arm. When he was only a small boy, the other children mocked him in a way that only callous cretins could, and it was then he learnt that neither child nor so-called grown-up could ever soothe away the pain of a boy aged perhaps six or seven: no one else could know or understand.

'He was never what one could call huggable, for when his mother held him out for people to admire he could outstare an eagle. His mass of thick black curly hair was an unfitting thing to see on a newly born baby – foreign, some would say – and it was over these minor things that women lipsticked to death worried. "Ooh," they used to coo, spinning a strand of his hair round their fingers but secretly blessing fortune for having carried in their womb babies who were greeting-card material. Amarjit Singh Dillon saw it then, from the moment his eyes could focus. He saw these people and wondered why, even when breathing the same air as he and eating the same food, they were yet so different.

'When Amarjit Singh Dillon was nine and a bit years he went up for seconds at lunchtime at school. He'd just caught Stammering Sam's eye to signal two helpings instead of the usual meagre one when, through the window, he saw two policeman slam shut their car door and plod up towards the school, his sullen uncle trailing behind them. Although perturbed, he ignored them and went back to his seat with his non-beef Cornish pasty – he couldn't eat beef. Staring down at his plate he watched the way in which the flakes of pastry first swam about in the gravy and then sank, but before he could break into the pastry mould a shrill voice calling for Ammo smacked him. He rose promptly and scuttled to the front of the dining-room where the headmistress, who was so tall and stodgy he could see only a banana nose, met him. Miss Faceless hurried him through the woodlouse-ridden corridor, making him jog to keep up. His feet ached in his holey gym shoes and he'd gladly have run barefoot if it hadn't been against the country's laws. That's when he learnt to tap-dance his way out of trouble.'

'How do you know all this, Uncleji?'

'What do you think we do in our Folk Friday group, just sing?'

'Well . . .'

'We talk.'

Seeing that I was completely dazed, Dadoo's Dad assured me that things were all right. But they weren't. Things hadn't been right since that limbo-land feeling had first begun to fester.

'Look at your father now, *beta*. Go on, look.'

So I did.

'Doesn't he look like he's coming to a head with himself?'

Actually, Dad looked to be enjoying limbo-land as he danced. He was in a world I'd never seen; and I wasn't going to be the one to take him away from it. The guests edged ever closer, trying to get a clear look at the man who danced to the *dhol* in that startling combination of tap and *bhangra*. There he was, dancing all by himself; nobody could touch him now. As I pivoted, glaring at all the people who were giggling, PC Plid and Plod backed away. That evil stare of mine had to work its magic sooner or later. Leave him this moment, at least.

Soon the beat of the *dhol* got through to Kiz, and she slid towards Dad in the centre of the dance floor. A grin spread over my face. If ever there was a time to dance, now was it. I kicked up my feet and skimmed across the floor. The lights dimmed and, with the spotlight on us and cheers filling the air, we followed Dad's lead. There was no way my asthma was going to get a look-in, not now when my arms and feet had a life all of their own and for the first time ever were doing as my brain told them. Dad had the moves all pinned down, with his tap-dancing feet the unlikely but rightful partner to his *bhangra* arms.

Mum, Budgie and Kully started clapping – out of anger and love, I suppose – then came on to the floor to join us. The music pulsated through us in a way we'd never known, and took us by the scruff of the neck. The insistent beat pounded around us and we became its slaves, doing all the Punjabi verbs in one go. Mum and Dad were getting it together like they used to, he smiling at her as if he'd never stop, and she holding his hands so tightly that I thought she'd never let go, ever again. Their feet glided in unison, and to me it seemed that it made no difference whether there were five hundred people at this wedding or none at all: as long as they and their children were together, they didn't care. Well, that's what I wanted them to think.

Dad let go only when the Folk Friday lot gathered round and heaved him and Budgie up on to their shoulders to do freestyle air *bhangra*. Mum showed her happiness with a reserved but comforting smile, reminding me of Kully when she was a little girl. It dawned on me then that maybe all Mum had ever wanted was some order among the chaos. Dad wasn't able to give her that.

As we circled round the two happy couples (King Pardeep and Queen Kully had to come off their throne some time), the room felt safe. I was no longer ashamed, and neither was Mum. It seemed to me that, for this moment only, time had reversed and we were back in our childhood.

Mum never used Dad's first name, always calling him 'Kully's Dad': 'Would you like some tea Kully's Dad?' and 'Do you want *alloo parathe* or *mulee* ones, Kully's dad?' They rarely hugged each other or talked love; they didn't have to. When Dad made Mum a swing in the garden from those stackable fruit baskets, he pushed her for ages: back and forth, higher and higher, she went. She giggled hysterically but not too loudly – after all, there were the neighbours to think of.

Then Dad had to call the ambulance when Mum couldn't prise herself out of the basket. She wasn't cross, though. No. 'These things happen,' she said, not in the least embarrassed that a fruit basket was hanging from her rear and she had to waddle like an unfortunate mallard.

Then there were all the times the two of them ate *roti* from the same tray. Dad used to finish off the *matar paneer*, and Mum the *saag*. Occasionally they'd dip into each other's favourites but they always proclaimed that their own choice was the best.

When Dad got Mum a subscription to TV Asia, well, that broke the boundaries of love. Mum was beside herself. For once she had something first. Now it was her turn to boast to her family and friends. She could have shouted to her sisters, 'I've got TV Asia and there ain't nothing you can do about it.' Instead, she became quite the benevolent entertainment fund. When antis flocked in in the evening to watch the latest offering of prime-time Indian soap, her face lit up and the glow of her was infectious. For once, she was on the inside of the circle.

'Keep dancing,' shouted DJ Baldev, who'd run on to his special *bhangra* number for professional dancers like us. Suddenly the beating-stick of the *dhol* suddenly snapped and so did Dad. Like a puppet whose strings could no longer hold the weight, he drooped to the floor. It happened slowly, right there before us, but so stunned were we that none of us caught him in time. The whole Dillon family descended on him; even Kully managed to get down on her knees and utter an 'Are you all right?'

'He can't hear you, you stupid cow,' I said. 'When he could you didn't talk, and now—'

'Oh shut up,' said Mum, losing her last shreds of patience. 'Look what you did to Mr Rai.'

'Look what I did to that Rai?' I said furiously. 'I'll tell you what I did to that Rai. I'll tell you . . .' But I couldn't because I was too angry with Mum for giving the toss of a coin about him. So what if Rai was still wiping the last of the cake off his shiny face? Here was Dad waiting for the ambulance that Arjun had efficiently called, and there was Mum worrying that we were making a show of ourselves. Rule No 38: Beware: some people were born just to drag you into the depths of despair.

'We'll handle this,' said PCs Plid and Plod, all brave like, barging in as if life would halt without them.

'No, you bleedin' won't,' I retorted. 'He's my dad, not yours.'

'Oh, shut up,' said Budgie, who was trying to wake Dad by splashing water on his face.

Water may work in Indian films, mate, I thought, but this is the Midlands and if one more person tells me to shut up I'm going to get very cross and they won't like that because I've learnt a lot from Dad and forgotten none of it. There was a plate of chillies on a table near Bimla, and I was quite prepared to force someone to chew them.

When the paramedics ran in, pushing a wheeled stretcher, some of the antis couldn't be bothered to move out of their way and had to be pushed.

I bear-hugged Dad. 'You'll be fine,' I whispered in his ear. That was all I had time for before Bimla and Worzel bulldozed me out of the way, pretending to be distraught. Then Dad was carted off again, only this time on a stretcher and without hope.

'Don't worry, ladies and gentlemen. Mr Dillon will be just fine. Don't let it spoil your afternoon,' Rai announced through the microphone, like some big orator or something. Hah! The only thing spoiling my life was him.

After wiping away a few tears, Mum did as she was told by Worzel and handed out the *mithai* packs to guests as they left. She had only one more hurdle to clear: the crying session.

Cramming ourselves back into the cars parked illegally outside the Blue Cross, we set off home. Mum refused to look at me, even though we were sitting in the same car driven by Brummie Uncle.

We got home all right, but then had to wait ages for Pardeep and his lot to come and take Kully away. When they eventually turned up, all the girls harassed them at the door for money. The grand sum of £211 was earned by Kiz and Gurminder.

After a few more formalities inside the house, Budgie led Kully outside to seat her in Pardeep's Jaguar. Worzel was the first to give way, and broke into an operatic rendition of an infirm woman who had never, ever felt, seen or tasted happiness during her whole life. Then Bimla and next-door-neighbour anti started as well, because they didn't want to be outdone. This went pretty well and all the participants gave a convincing performance of sadness. First prize should have gone to Gurminder, who cried a whole cupful.

Even I managed a dry tear to express some regret at the departure of a very bossy sister. How I'd miss the days when she made me slave after her while she sat on the settee and I had to lift her legs up to make sure the Hoover did its job. How I'd miss the other days when she got me into trouble by squealing on me whenever I sneaked out to the library but was later accused of going to a *bhangra* daytimer. Oh, how I'd miss those days.

A respected elder scattered a handful of money across the Jaguar's path as it waited to depart, making Pardeep scowl at the ching and chang of the coins – they might scratch his precious paintwork. While he got in and settled himself next to Kully, the children dashed to nab a few of the coins rolling here and there, to boost their miserly pocket money. I joined in without hesitation. Wow! There was a two-pound coin next to the gutter. Budgie revved the engine to warn the coin-pickers to move out of the way.

Kully didn't mind them at all. In fact, seeing the way she peeped from underneath her flowing, diaphanous *chunni*, I could tell that the thing she wanted most in the whole wide world was to join us. I don't think it was that she wanted to be a child again. It was just that there were some things that she wanted to do but couldn't, now that she was the wife of a big man.

I was so intent on my battle with Poor Child Prodigy and Guppy over that two-pound coin that I didn't notice an Escort coming straight towards me – or should I say at me? – skidding as the driver braked fiercely. *BANG!*

Rule No 39: Don't be too keen to pick up money off the road if cars are coming. This also brings into play Rule No 40: Underdressing is worse than overdressing, so aim to look like a Christmas tree. If I'd stuck to that last rule, the Escort would have seen me coming before it decided to send me to the infirmary. Typically, everyone said that this was a bad omen for the newlyweds. Bad omen for me, more like.

Kully watched over me in the Jaguar, which was going to drop me off at Dudley hospital on the way back to Birmingham. Then she said something which hugely surprised me: 'I'm glad I saw Dad.'

To comfort her, I told her that, seeing as I was on my way to his place – the hospital, I mean – I'd give him her regards.

As the car made its way along, the once recognisable

scenery began to blur. I caught Pardeep sneaking a peek once in a while at his bride through the silk *chunni* that veiled her. The gold embroidery framed her face as if she'd become a picture, and he thought her divine. It wasn't Kully who was lucky, it was him. To love and to marry were not terms that always held mutual regard for one another – or respect, come to think of it – but he had it all now.

How unfair I thought. All I had was two broken arms.

The aftermath

The house felt very empty, once Kully and her paraphernalia had disappeared, so Kiz thought it would be clever to go out and get a pet as a replacement. Goofy the rabbit was a quaint, ugly mite which just sat, ate and crapped where he was put down. Exciting as this was, it bored me and Kiz to the point of neglect, and so neglect him we did – accidentally, of course.

It arose from my natural assumption that Goofy was Kiz's rabbit because she'd bought him, but she later changed her story and said she'd seen me moping about the place so much that she'd got him to keep me company and therefore Goofy belonged to me. I told her three things. First, I mope about all the time anyway, so it was nothing new; second, she was abusing my personality trait; third, Goofy was no good for keeping anybody any company 'cos all he ever did was make a person feel even more lonely.

Mum hadn't got time to find out whose fault it was, like it was real detective work, so instead we were both bombarded with Punjabi profanities for a while, before she went to buy a whole heap of *karele* from Mrs Kaur, who was her new best friend.

A few days later Kiz did the stupidest thing she's ever done, and bought another rabbit for a tenner. Neither of us had the imagination to name him or her, so we called it Rabbit Two. For a whole week Kiz didn't disturb Goofy and Rabbit Two, thinking they'd need a longer honeymoon than most, because she'd chosen the pair at random, meaning they conformed to the laws of an arranged marriage.

Six weeks later, there were eleven bunnies bouncing around. They drove Mum crazy when they travelled up next-door-neighbour anti's polka-dot *salwaar* when she came round for a dose of *gupshap*. Me and Kiz were scolded by Anti: her feet would never step on our deep-pile carpet ever again. Well, at least we achieved something.

In the end we gave the bunnies away to the RSPCA. Mum thought it would have been a good idea if they'd taken me as well. So did I the next morning. Mum came hopping into the bedroom at half eight, all excited – very unlike her – 'cos the newlyweds, who weren't so new any more as they'd been married nearly two months, were gracing us with their presence. She demanded that I put on my best clothes and eliminate the bunny smell from the house. I informed her the smell was coming from Budgie's room 'cos he'd got in late last night after going to another *bhangra* gig where guys didn't know the magic word 'deodorant'. I also said Mum would have to wait until I went clothes shopping because I had no such things as best clothes. She sat on me into submission.

There's nothing more sickly than a newly married couple cooing over each other like nobody else in the world existed. So when Kully and Pardeep came round to get their blessings, and to invite the whole family round to their place to view their photographs of a first-class honeymoon in Bermuda, we all had to hide our distaste as they bombarded each other with affection. Even Budgie had to avert his gaze and put his headphones on louder. Unfortunately, there was no escape for me. Mum was still angry about the rabbits and said I should learn a lesson or five in how to treat guests in your home. I pointed out that Kully and Pardeep were no guests of mine: I hadn't invited them round.

Kully shocked me by wearing so much make-up you'd think she was soliciting. I've seen it happen so many times now it's become plain unfunny. A girl gets married, then it's time for the make-up kit to go manic. Saira says it's like in the mortuaries where the make-up artists have to decorate dead-pale faces with pink and red rouge, and that the same thing happens to a female when she marries – she gets all anaemic and colour-blindness sets in.

When I could no longer bear the newlyweds' canoodling and sharing bites out of the jammie dodgers, I sprinted upstairs and told Dad that Kully and Pardeep were openly disrespecting Indian rules about public affection in the front room. Never show affection of the romantic type to anybody except the one you're being romantic to.

It was strange tattle-tailing to Dad. For so long we'd gotten used to not hearing him about, but here he was. Who'd have thought a good nervous breakdown could do a person such an enormous amount of good? But that's what had happened to Dad, and after three weeks recuperation from his crack-up at the wedding party he was back home again. Now he had no one to hide from.

Dad left his Spot the Ball coupons, came downstairs and took the lead by telling the two to stop, with a big tut at the end of his sentence. Then he went back upstairs, leaving Pardeep mortified. I was glad to see that the hoity-toity expression he had the monopoly on was fading away. You couldn't charm my dad so easily.

Kully was acting all proper and formal, as if she didn't know us any more. 'Where are the coasters?' she asked.

'What?' I asked, bewildered. Our house hadn't seen a coaster adorn the coffee table in its life.

Kully began to twitch her nose nervously as if she'd come to a really weird place.

'Why don't you go up and see Dad?' I said. 'He's been unsectioned.'

As soon as I said that word – 'unsectioned', I mean – Kully near about died. A little while later mascara ran down her cheeks when she couldn't bring herself to go up. Only her handy pocket tissues could help as she patted her face down.

I stared at her. 'Did I say something wrong?'

'You always do,' said an unwelcome voice.

'Oh, shut up, Sammy.' I don't know when she'd arrived but she looked like she was on a mission – probably to check out the Rais' capital assets.

'You shut up,' replied Sammy in that petty way.

Not wanting to get involved in a shut-up relay race, I simply stated that just because she wore a leather jacket and catsuit round the Midlands it didn't mean a doddle. Then . . . I'm not quite sure how it happened but I ended up with her in a headlock. She tried to cop me one with her long pink-varnished nails. She might have even scratched me when she poked one into my arm, had I not bitten it off and accidentally spat it into Pardeep's tea.

'I didn't do it on purpose, you know,' I shouted as he walked out the living-room in a strop, with Mum apologising on my behalf. Hate it when people do that.

Then Kully handed Budgie the receipts for the wedding. The cameraman cost nearly eight hundred quid and the cellophane bags cost thirty.

'Were they made of saffron?' I asked. 'More expensive than gold,' I explained when they all looked blankly at me.

Budgie took off his headphones, snatched the receipts and stuffed them into the back pocket of his blue jeans. 'I'll sort them,' he lied. How could he sort them? He was still borrowing money from Mum.

'So when's Guggi's open?' I asked. 'Indy wants to get his car stereo fixed. You lot could do that, couldn't you?'

'Yes,' snapped Budgie, throwing me a look which warned me in no uncertain terms to keep shtoom.

Fortunately he was diverted when a disheartened-looking Kully and a furious-looking Mum persuaded a pacified Pardeep to drive our lot to their lot in his Jaguar. I didn't want to go, but Dad, who was taking time out from Spot the Ball, said I needed to see Kully in her natural surroundings.

'She's not in a jungle, you know,' I said.

'Yes she is, and that Rai's king of it,' said Dad, looking out of the window at Mum trapping her *chunni* in the car door.

'Why don't you come, then? See how she's faring?'

'Can't. Don't want to. Won't.' Then he clammed right up, making it clear that the Rais were like Kryptonite to him. Since the wedding party, he seemed to be only some of the same as he was before but it was self-development of some sort. I mustn't be too fussy.

When Dad and I were both in hospital, him on a drip and me in my plasters and with a bit of concussion, I sometimes snuck out of my ward to his. One day, during a long conversation about the useless cow in the kitchen who couldn't even make *saag* without killing it, Dad asked for his passport.

'Sorry, Dad, I ain't got it.'

'Your mum has.'

'What d'you want me to do?'

'It's mine.'

'That it is.'

'Get it back.'

'All right.'

Dad said he'd seen something in the hospital cafeteria that made him want his passport. There was this woman inside toying with the idea of eating the dark chocolate layer sandwiched between three fruit-layered sponges. She was scared that her slender frame would be marred by this small decision, so opted for a plain pineapple ring soaking in its own juice.

Then he asked me a question I couldn't answer. 'Why would the woman order two desserts, one way superior to the other in pleasure? Why did she tantalise herself with the two things before her?'

'Dunno, Dad. Maybe she's just a thick cow.'

Talking of which, on the way to Kully's new house Kiz

made Pardeep do five pit stops at well-known shops and shout, 'Oy, hurry up, love. Got the Jag waiting.' At the last stop – Pete's Asian Video and Music Centre – Mum cursed Kiz, my sister with the killer smile, when she got out to buy a pirate video release of *Bhangra Kings, Gidha Queens*.

'I'm in that,' said Kiz, cooing at the thought of seeing herself on screen.

Telling her to put a sock in it or she'd have had a fist in it if Mum heard, we all waited silently for Mum to return.

Mum was caught unawares by a Mrs Purewal, who swore blind she knew Mum, but Mum swore blind back, saying she'd never seen the woman in her life before. Still, we ended up giving Mrs Purewal a lift to the Gurudwara, making us twenty-seven minutes late at the Rais'. Never mind, I thought. That's twenty-seven minutes less we have to stay there.

When Pardeep pulled up at his house, Mum was so astonished that she had to hold her knees to stop them banging together. Their garage looked bigger than the plot of land our house and garden stood on.

'Must be the size of Himley Hall,' guessed Kiz.

Before I could start taking measurements a girl in a bright turquoise sari stepped out and showered the car with rice. She was followed by an alarming number of people who supposedly had come to meet us but I sussed were actually there to judge and rate us.

'Here we are,' announced Pardeep as if the name plaque – '*The Rai Residence*' – hadn't given the game away. 'Our humble abode.'

'Very humble,' I said innocently, attracting a glare from Mum as she marvelled at the gravelled path, oohed at the double-glazed doors with their stained-glass flowers, and aahed at the huge patio with two wrought-iron benches. This impressed behaviour continued as we entered the hall with a staircase in the middle. The veins in Mum's hands were popping out with her being so close to real velvet curtains and a 100 per cent wool Wilton carpet. I don't know why she was so excited, 'cos she wasn't getting any of it, but I suppose she must have been pleased that her daughter had landed in the lap of luxury, even though most of it was insipid-looking.

Tea and spring rolls were distributed round a grand oak table. Kiz and me were told off by Kully and Rai for sitting on the floor to eat.

'All Indian people have a dining-table and chairs,' I said. 'Nobody ever actually *eats* at them, though – that would be mad.'

'We're not like them,' said Pardeep, quickly changing the subject by asking whether we'd like a tour of upstairs.

'No,' I said firmly. 'Your bedroom is your business.'

Upstairs, he flung open a door to reveal a huge bedroom with the sort of dark-red velvet carpeting only ever seen in the Savoy (not that I'd seen it), and walls covered in a two-tone classic wallpaper priced at more per roll than it cost to paper our whole front room. Pardeep went straight to a small walnut-wood drinks cabinet in the far corner of the room – impressive enough to house the world's best liquor, given to him on his travels around the world.

Then he started – and went on and on – telling me and

Kiz about how he went on business trips to search for what he called 'new ideas'. Most of his journeys were impulsive, like the time he flew to San Francisco just because an air hostess he fancied was on duty on that plane. On the day-long flight he observed the way she walked up and down the aisles in her stiff navy-blue British Airways uniform. She in turn hovered about him so that she could smell his aftershave, which he reckoned she couldn't put a name to but could tell must burn a hole in the pocket of any man.

In their new bedroom the couple stood as far apart as the room allowed, probably scared that I'd creep to Dad. Damn right I would. Kiz stared out of the window, watching more guests congregate underneath the security lights mounted on grand pillars, while Pardeep poured himself a shot of Indian Bacardi, which he'd become accustomed to drinking whenever he was down there, supposedly to visit relatives. He then poured Kully a G & T. God, you get a girl married and she starts acting real sophisticated.

'I want this honeymoon never to end,' said Pardeep, glugging down the last of his drink and heading for the drinks cabinet.

Kully looked adoringly at him. 'So what you saying? You want a never-ending honeymoon?'

The conversation was killing me, so I escaped out into the corridor, where some children were playing Scrabble. It made a pleasant change to be met by an imperfect smile, its bottom teeth crooked and a side tooth missing with the stub of the new one showing through. A small girl like a rag doll with pigtails held out a box of chocolates with one hand, the other being crammed full of her favourite truffle and coconut sweets. Smiling at her, I dipped into the box and took out a montelimar and orange. I'd no intention of eating it, but the kid had offered so it would have been rude not to accept.

'You can have the whole box if you want. I've got mine,' she said handing over the gold-foil carton. She waved her other fist in my face, showing me her selection, then stuffed a caramel in her mouth.

'What's your name?' she asked.

'What's yours?'

'I asked you first.'

'I asked you second.'

'Dippy.'

'Sushminder something.'

'What type of name is that?'

'Oy, you cheeky little nit, it's better than Dippy.'

'Isn't.'

'Is.'

'Isn't.'

'Is. My name Dippy's on my passport but it's not my real name. My Nana named me something else but it's got too many letters and it's too long to say so they made me into a Dippy.'

'You know what? I have the same problem. I'm a Sushminder, Susham or Sushi, depending on who you are'

'That's not good' remarked the girl, sitting down on the top step of the broad staircase and swinging her feet like twin pendulums. 'Your sister's the new one around here, ain't she? Now they can stop picking on me. They sent me to some special school. I'm not ill or anything.'

She spoke very quickly as if there was a time restriction placed on her. 'This new school I'm at, it's a long way from my house so I have to catch a bus. We haven't got a car and Mum won't let me take a taxi like the other children in my class. I get angry sometimes 'cos they ask me questions when I don't know the answers but they don't ask me questions when I do.

'It's my birthday tomorrow. I'm gonna be nine. Don't time fly? I'll get to hand out sweets to the rest of the class and to people I don't like. The teacher locks away the sweets in a drawer and says I can only share them at playtime, but I say I want to share them now. It's my birthday now. Mrs Foggarty isn't nice. She never listens and she's an ugly person. Her hands are always talking, pointing to me if I spill anything or swear. She wears big thick skirts that end at her knees and it looks like dog-hair. They swear all the time, but if I do it isn't right. Nothing's right. I'm going to save up my money and buy fireworks for Diwali. Lots of them from the corner shop.

'Nana trusts me and lets me serve behind the counter sometimes, shutting and opening the till. Sometimes he even lets me stack the shelves. I put the rice in a neat line, with all the veg stuff on the left side and the non-veg on the right. Yes, that's the way Uncle Rai likes it. He says it's customer service doing it like that. He gave me five pounds last time and said I'd done a good day's work. I swept that floor – mopped it, even – but I couldn't get some of the dirt off so I used a knife to get the black bits off. They stick there because people chew the stuff and then spit it out for me to clean. Lots of people come in

Nana's shops and some I don't know hang around the potato box outside. They pick up the potatoes like they're going to get in the box and touch them all. They prod and make faces at the rotten *galiya* ones and then when they've filled the brown paper bags until they rip they come in and pay for them. I'm gonna be an astronaut. That way I get to fly five miles every second. How do you piss in space?'

'Huh?'

'Piss in space. How do you do it?'

'Oh, there's a Hoover for that.'

'Yeah? That's good. I'll definitely go to space, then. Sometimes I'll think I'll meet the aliens.'

'If they wanted you to visit them, they'd have asked you round for a cup of tea by now don't you think – that's if they drink tea, of course.'

'I don't like it when the meat van comes on Tuesday at ten o'clock. It smells because the meat-man hasn't washed it for years. That's what he says, but I don't know if he's lying. Why would he lie? Uncle Rai says it won't harm me if I help him a little but I say I won't touch the blood on the animals, 'cos I might get mad cow disease or salmonella poisoning. The van really really stinks, and the old women cover their noses and mouths with their *chunniya* when they walk past. Then some of them spit in the drainpipe, like this. I feel like that sometimes when I see the pigs hanging on the hooks. They just hang there, except sometimes they swivel, like this. When I go home and Mum's made me sausages, I say no, 'cos they make me see the pigs' faces. I have toast and beans instead, but she still complains and says the sausages aren't made from

211

meat or anything. My brother's clever 'cos he can do sums without a calculator.'

Dippy got to her feet, shook my hand and wandered off, muttering, 'Well, I hope I get to be an astronaut but I don't think an ethnic minority has been in space yet.'

'Ethnic majority,' I cried, looking down at the Scrabble word she had made with the small cream tiles – 'vociferous'. I do meet some strange people. Think they're trying to tell me something.

When His Majesty Pardeep and Her Royal Highness Kully had stopped complimenting each other on how daintily she breathed and on how he folded his arms when he was interested in a conversation, and we'd seen the art-deco-cum-Indian-classical-inspired en-suite bathroom for the second time, Pardeep began to give Mum tips on the stock market. This was quite difficult, since Mum wouldn't know what shares were even if Pardeep had given her a thousand of them. After an hour she was able to say that the subject had something to do with owning a company. It wasn't really her fault she couldn't understand, because Pardeep's Punjabi was enough to send me and Kiz into fits of laughter.

Afterwards Kully's mother-in-law began to interrogate Kiz and me about our futures and how well we had planned for them. Not so well, she found out. Although she didn't say much to our faces, I sensed that Mum would hear about the career advice. Then, as if to distract me from the interrogation, Mother-in-Law began to introduce the family to me because Mum had said I needed to be told just one more time because amnesia can set in quickly with some girls. She really wanted me to become acquainted with Birmingham's high society.

'This is Pardeep's younger brother, Jagdev, this is his elder brother, Sanjeev, and this is our eldest daughter-in-law, Pretty.'

They were all pleasant and polite, nodding and smiling where appropriate, and when even their mother turned on the charm I began to think the 'nice' gene must run in their family. She suggested that we take a day trip to Blackpool. After all, if the couple had got to go to Bermuda, it was only right that we poor folk should go to Blackpool.

'Na,' I screamed with a sudden flashback to the day when Mum and Dad dragged us to Skeggy. Mum began by saying, 'Now, don't say we never take you anywhere,' which in my experience isn't the best way to start a visit.

We kids had never seen the sea before, and it made me tingle with excitement just looking at it. Like a person just let out on bail, I headed towards the Skeggy sea with my eyes glazed and the thought of swimming in the strong tides drowning me.

'Susham, you are not here to go in the sea, you see?'

I looked at her, wondering what on earth she was going on about. For pity's sake, there was the sea, and here was me and my lot – children competent at swimming and with proficiency certificates to prove it.

Mum's melodramatic performance of 'What if you get eaten by sharks? Don't think I'll be coming to save you – I can't swim hahaha' persuaded me not to break Rule No 41: When by a considerable amount of water of the natural kind, don't swim. It doesn't matter if you try with your clothes on, it still isn't appropriate.

Dad tried to mollify me by helping me build a sand-castle Indian-style. Now, don't think this means it looked like the Taj Mahal or something, it just means that we used more advanced equipment, that's all. Empty Vitalite and yoghurt tubs and big ladles worked well as improvised bucket and spades, but they did tend to draw attention from passers-by.

Having deprived of us of the fun of going in the sea, Mum then made another impossible demand: she told us not to get dirty in the sand. Fun really was not on the agenda, so after only an hour and a bit we headed home to good old Dudley from whence we came.

Now I think about it, I'm sure Mum and Dad used to have competitions in who could have less fun, in which case Dad would have been the champion. His winning entry was when he said the local community centre would be going to Alton Towers and if we children wanted to we could go with him. We all said yes without hesitation.

The trip started off fine, 'cos Dad let me eat five doughnuts. Then he near enough copped Budgie one, who was doing Chinese burns on my wrist for the heck of it. I don't think Dad did it on purpose, though, when I got left behind at the castle and had to spend much of the day being led around by an oversized dog in a costume 'cos I'd been abandoned by the adults. Tannoy messages went out for Dad to come and collect me and eventually, after the longest time, he did. I was grateful that he was pleased to see me, but was very sour at having been dragged about by a supervisor dog to help welcome all the other younger children by handing out helium-filled balloons.

So mother-in-law's suggestion fell like lead: I was not about to sign up for yet another fun-free day. Unfortunately, everyone else seemed keen.

'We're going to Blackpool, all right?' said Mum in her gritted-teeth voice, thinking she wasn't losing her temper when in fact she already had.

'No,' I screamed, stamping so hard on the Wilton carpet that my footprint could be seen. 'I've got to work.'

'Where?' they all shouted one after the other.

'At Tamber's Cash and Carry, that's where.' I'd got the job because Kully's marriage had strained us financially. Mum hadn't let on throughout the whole wedding ordeal, and this made me worry for her.

The massed ranks of Dillons and Rais gasped in unison, as if they'd rehearsed.

Then, after a long pause, Pardeep stood up in front of me. 'They're our competitors.'

'Yes they are.'

Suddenly that Rai barged in. 'Did I hear Tamber's name in my house?'

They all pointed at me. I swear they'd been taking point-the-blame-together lessons.

'Yeah, I'm working there,' I told him calmly, shaking my head in that really loose way when you feel quite like you know it all. 'What of it?'

Rai circled round me with his hands behind his back and his head nodding away in anger. 'I'll give you double what he's giving.'

'No can do, Rai. Me and my dad can't be bought like that. You'll never have us.'

Smiling smugly, Rai sat down in the big leather chair reserved exclusively for him. Nobody spoke, for I'd said my bit simply and without emotion getting in the way.

When the silence became oppressive, Mrs Rai leapt into the breech and tried to make something resembling normal conversation. 'Susham, would you like some *roti-shoti* or *chai-vai*?'

'Er, can I have some *shoti* and *vai*?' I asked.

At once they all shrieked with laughter, scaring the pants off me. 'Oh, that's too funny,' they cried. '*Shoti* and *vai*! What a funny girl she is.'

Then without fuss, without fury, I walked out of the house, turning back only to wave to Dippy, who called goodbye to me from the first-floor bay window.

Later that week, when Kully turned up crying on the doorstep with her belongings in a Sainsbury's carrier bag, I got into trouble for not letting her into the house. It wasn't that I didn't like her, it was just that I objected to Mum and Dad wasting their money on her wedding if she wasn't going to go away for good, because like it or not if she ever separated she'd get not a penny from Pardeep, even though the geezer was loaded. Rule No 42: Never, ever divorce. That option is taken away once you get married.

Mum threatened me with a rolling-pin when I wouldn't unlock the door, but I didn't relent until I'd made Kully say, 'I love Tony Benn. He's the best.'

Mum spent much of the day trying unsuccessfully to find out why Kully was back in our house when she had a mansion of her own only nine miles away. Kiz and I didn't have the will or the energy to care. We were too shattered from the toing and froing from the kitchen, cursing our married sister on our travels.

'Get me some sugar. Get me some *pakore*. I'd like a chocolate biccy to dunk in my tea.'

'Would you now?' shrieked Kiz, ready to take Kully to the top of the stairs and throw her down.

I realised the truth while I was stirring our Kully's third cup of tea with ground cardamom and a tinge of *jeera*: the in-laws had kicked her out 'cos she was a bossy cow. So what if that graduation picture in the living-room showed her holding a scroll? Didn't mean to say she was any cleverer than me.

Then Kiz, tired of the slave treatment, could resist the urge no longer. Up she got, grabbed Mum's *chunni*, waved it about and sang, 'I have a sister who has a degree but she's as thick as a brick. She has letters after her name but can't tell a pig from a chick. Even then she walks around, all mighty, all hoity and toity. Sometimes she pats me on the back and offers some of her sympathy. She says, "We can't all be clever, my dear. We can't all be as clever as me. You see, my sad, jealous sister, I have been to university. My university is the best, it's the most renowned in Midland. People come from ever so far just to shake my professor's hand. So don't you worry your cogs, my dear. Don't you worry one little bit. I am clever by far, my dear. Says so in this here certificate." And I turned round to that girl who thought herself so great.

217

I know inside, so I shared it aloud: "You, dear, are a reprobate!" '

I clapped heartily. 'Va, va,' I cheered. 'You, Kiz, speak the truth in the most fashionable way.' She and I shook hands because we were fighting against a common enemy, the perfect elder sibling.

Rule No 43: Never curse your sister after she's married. Just because you feel like a punchbag doesn't mean you should give her reason to treat you like one.

Mum didn't say anything when Kully jabbed me and Kiz in the arm with her lethal nails. She was too occupied with scrutinising the wedding film for the second time, to encourage Kully to think about her marital obligations. Just when Dad was on screen tap-dancing gracefully, the doorbell rang.

'Going,' I said loudly to the rest of the household, who pretended they hadn't heard it.

'Coming,' I shouted as the knocker began to bang and slam the letterbox. Whoever it was didn't realise that there was only one slave in this house.

I should have guessed. On the doorstep stood Pardeep wearing a sharp suit but looking not so sharp. Why didn't he and all his family just move in?

Once he'd got through the turquoise front door, painted by Dad some years ago, Pardeep said he wanted to talk in private with Kully. I said there was no such thing as privacy in our house so they'd best come out with it, but Mum undermined me by telling him we'd be willing to give them some space.

She pushed Budgie off to the Pind Pub, and told me and Kiz we'd have to go with her to pay the final bill at the *mithai* shop. So off we toddled, me in my brown duffel coat, Kiz in her jacket with the fake fur collar, and Mum in her patchwork cardigan over a thick, shiny *salwar kameez*.

As we reached the shopping arena of Dudley's downtown, Kiz suddenly thought that a calamity had occurred and so did I because it looked as if she was having a heart attack. A minute later, after all Mum's '*Hi meri mari kismet*', we found that Kiz had left the shop money in Mum's purse at home.

'I'm not going back,' she said.

'Well, that complicates the situation,' I said, 'because I'm not going to be your retriever dog.'

'I've got a bad leg,' said Kiz, pretending that it was suddenly giving way.

'I've just had two broken arms. Beat that.'

Mum agreed that my near collision with the Escort might have had some lingering effects on my mental powers in the pursuit of physical exertion, but she argued that I would be the better sprinting candidate since Kiz couldn't run with the sharp type of heeled shoes she wore. Anyway, she went on, Kiz was near enough a dunce when it came to finding things. I reminded Mum of the asthma I'd suffered from since early childhood, but she played it down, saying it was only a bit of a breathing problem and a fit young girl like me shouldn't be so preoccupied with minor ailments. That'll be the last time I put up with one of her 'I've got a killer headache, I think I've got a brain haemorrhage' routines.

When I got home, I barged into the living-room to find Pardeep and Kully arguing loudly. I told them not to worry about me and continue hurling obscenities at one another as I was only looking for Mum's purse. Pardeep asked how much she'd lost. 'A round a hundred and fifty quid,' I said not really knowing. Then, just like that, he pulled out a wad of notes and peeled off three crisp fifty-pound notes.

Kully at once started ranting on about how he should stop giving money to people he didn't owe it to. That got me mad enough to tell her that she was a leech and a money-grabber and our parents had spent all they could on her just to give her a high-class wedding, so she'd better watch her mouth 'cos she owed them a lot. Before long, Pardeep began to defend her and sure enough, after a little bit of verbal abuse directed at me, the two started hugging each other as if they'd been parted for years.

Pardeep sat down on our rarely used front-room sofa, but shot up again as if sitting down was offensive. I spied Mum's pursed squashed down the side of the settee, grabbed it, threw the three fifties at Kully, and accused Pardeep of being a thief just for good measure. Then I legged it out of the house.

'Did you hop there or summat?' asked Kiz when I got back to them, purse in hand.

'Ten minutes there and ten minutes back usually, and I've made it back here in fifteen minutes flat.' That shut her up.

Once Mum had checked that all her money was there, we carried on walking downtown, eventually arriving at Worzel's fabric boutique or, as Mum called it, the suit shop. The door was jammed so Mum and I gave it a good punch to loosen the rust that fixed it, but as soon as we trotted inside I wanted to trot right out again, because there in the middle of the shiny velvet-leaf-patterned material section stood Arjun with Mrs Kaur.

I tried hard to remain true to Rule No 44: Never, ever acknowledge your friends in front of your mum. The last time I'd done it was when Mum saw me chatting to our local elopee, Tejinder. That was bad news for me 'cos now Mum assumes it was Tejinder who'd put ideas in my head of running away to the allotment. I told Mum she'd best apologise for embarrassing me and Tejinder like that and that one should always be polite in front of one's children's friends and not accuse them of becoming the community's local slapper. Rule No 45: Get used to your parents never apologising. It's impossible for them to be wrong.

I knew Arjun had seen me as soon as the fabric rolls fell on me, but still I pretended he wasn't there and I hid behind some green polyester hanging from the ceiling by way of merchandising.

'What are you doing there?' asked Kiz in a clear and penetrating voice.

'Nothing,' I muttered, hoping she'd pay no attention to me, but before I could say 'Look there's So-and-So outside' to send her away, Mum called out, 'Oy, *kuriye*, come and look at this. It will be nice for your *massi*, no?' Somebody shoot me.

'Er, yes,' I whispered, standing behind the drape of fabric with only my trainers peeking out from underneath.

'Come here,' said Mum loudly.

I should have realised she'd be unhappy with my answer, and would want me to take into consideration the weave and heaviness of the fabric she was looking at. I budged not an inch.

'Come here now,' yelled Mum, edging closer, ready to yank me by my hood.

'Why?' I moaned. 'My God. Can't you people make a decision without my help?'

They always want my informed judgement when they deal with small matters such as what colour to paint their fingernails, or whether the *rotiya* should be buttered or not, but when it comes to real decisions, like whether or not to get Indy married to Pinky because he's up-and-coming, nobody ever asks me. They just go right ahead and make life-changing decisions without my invaluable input.

Mum tutted at me and gave me three rolls of five-yard fabric to hold while she weighed up the pros and cons of each fabric. She made it an art form accessible to no one else, so I peered through one of the rolls like it was a telescope, trying to do so as inconspicuously as possible.

What I was peering at was Arjun, who was having an even lousier time than I was. Great. He was laden with six rolls of fabric, a bag of sequins and a pot of hooks and eyes from Mrs Kaur. His hair was dishevelled and had fallen down over his face, but it couldn't hide the frown staining it, which I carried on admiring until – *Wham!*

'Ow! Watch it,' I yelped, covering my right eye, which he'd walloped with a roll of blue cotton.

He apologised hastily. 'Didn't see you camouflaged there.'

'You see me now?' I groaned, my eye throbbing with pain.

'It's gonna go black, that is,' said Mum, fingering a roll of *devoree*.

Serves me right for ogling him like that. I was ashamed of myself. Ogling was something I did not do, for a girl like me had better things to do of an intellectually challenging nature.

Arjun smiled shyly, as if it was the first time he'd laid eyes on me. I don't know why I frowned so fiercely in return, but it may have had something to do with the temperature rising and my family being there in front of him. With Arjun being the perceptive lad he is, an immediate look of concern took over his face. It was good to see him looking like that, 'cos a girl can stand only a certain amount of that cool, aloof type of look without getting agitated.

Mum at last decided that *devoree* was in fact her thing, based on the consideration that Kully's mother-in-law had a *salwar kameez* made of material exactly like it. I followed her to the counter, carrying the rolls horizontally – carrying them vertically looked silly, she said.

We were harassed by Kiz who had dropped some silver beads on the floor and was manically searching for all of them, crawling around on hands and knees. That girl wreaks havoc wherever she goes.

Then Mum called out, 'Oh, Painji, *sat sri akal*' – that's Mrs Kaur to you and me. 'How are you? Very lovely choice in fabric you got there. Good old Arjun *beta* out shopping with you, then?' She said, tugging his chin as if he was a toddler.

'What you been up to?' asked Arjun trying but failing to go down the casual-conversation route.

'Oh, leave me be will you?' I muttered.

Arjun looked his version of hurt, rolling his eyes in frustration and folding his arms all defensive like. Well, it was his turn for a change.

He waited until Mum and Mrs Kaur were absorbed in discussion of the *devoree*, then drifted closer to me and said quietly, 'Look, give us a chance, will you?'

'What for?'

'The same thing I'm giving you a chance for.'

'You what?' I said. 'A chance? You aren't any such thing. A hindrance, that's what you are.'

'There you go again.'

I said nothing and waited for him to elaborate but he just stared at me over a roll of that blue cotton, probably hoping our mums would think we were talking about whether it was the right shade.

'Look,' I said, 'you asked how I am, all right, so I'll tell you. I've been fine ever since I adopted an elephant in Sri Lanka. My three pounds a months buys him enough food to survive and let generations of elephants trample the plains, so any donations you care to give me will be appreciatively passed on to Divvy – that's his name. He's a short, stumpy-looking thing, abandoned by his parents. So there.'

Arjun looked quite taken aback. 'How's your dad, anyway?' he asked.

'Fine,' I said, and for the first time in my life I meant it. Then I could control myself no longer. 'You're glib,' I said angrily.

'And you're a no-map girl.'

'Sorry.'

'Sorry.'

'You and me mates, then?'

'More than,' he whispered.

This was how IT was meant to be. I smiled.

Arjun went on to tell me things had been difficult for his mum ever since she'd come here to repay the debt his dad owed to their uncle.'

'One thing I forgot to ask you,' I said. 'How come your mum's a Mrs Kaur and you're a Dhaliwal?'

After another dramatic pause, he said 'She wanted me to keep Dad's name alive.' Arjun grinned a little, then turned away to pay for his mum's suit.

My mum, Worzel and Mrs Kaur were busy looking through the wedding photos Mum carried in her carrier bag of the week – this week it was Asda's.

'Who's this uncle of yours?' I asked, though I could already predict the answer.

'Uncle Rai.'

'No.'

'Yes.'

'Pukka?'

'Pukka. That's what I've been trying to tell you all along – I'm expected to lick their boots just as much as you are. That's why I couldn't say anything at your uncle's about the clubbing. Mum would have had a nervous breakdown.'

'So it's got nothing to do with me being unladylike?'

'No way. That's the best bit about you.'

225

'Right,' I muttered, unsure whether that was a compliment or a put-down.

'Sammy isn't anything—'

'Compared to me?' I interrupted, all agog.

'I wouldn't compare you with anyone.'

Haiyo Rabba. I wish I had a remote control to replay the moment all over again.

He looked as though he was going to give me some more verbal admiration, but Worzel came in and switched on the telly that sat high in a corner of the shop.

'Aaah,' sighed Mum.

Seeing Alpha Punjabi obviously reminded her that she lacked something. We couldn't afford it any more, so Budgie's Music Channel and Mum's Alpha Punjabi subscriptions were the first things that had to go. I think it was then that she began giving her own dramatic performances. Now she was glued to the screen with her jaw drooping and her eyes scanning each minute detail, each pixel, and revelling in every second of Alpha. She hummed every piece of background music as if she herself had composed it, and she beamed with a joy I hadn't seen for some time.

Kiz went over to Mum and held her hand while they jiggled a little to the Punjabi folk. Mum giggled like she was back at her village school. She seemed so at ease with herself, but when I walked over the smile vanished and she stood still, staring through me. Did I smell or something? Kiz's eyes were fixed, too, not on me but on the television behind me. They all stood like soldiers at attention, Mrs Kaur, Worzel, Kiz and Arjun, all of them with the same gormless expression and none of them saying anything.

'What is it?' I asked.

Kiz didn't answer; she didn't have to. I followed her long index finger with my eyes as she pointed to the telly, but soon I wished I hadn't. You know when something you accidentally did in the past comes back like a hurricane, nearly taking you up in its ferocious vortex, but unlike Dorothy you still end up on Earth? Well, that's how I felt. There on Alpha Punjabi, was that thin-gummybob dancing in the foreground and I in my peacock head-dress was doing star jumps near some sheep. Gulp.

'That isn't me, just a girl who looks like me,' I said, trembling at the sight of Mum's expression, which was of utter disgust. Her ears twitched in spasms for she was finding it difficult to remain standing and was already faking a heart attack.

'It's only a promo,' said Kiz like that would assuage Mum's growing despair. 'It ain't coming out for another two months.'

'Here, have a chair, Mum.' I only just managed to get the chair under her bottom in time – I knew that if she'd fallen, so would have I.

Mum put her hands in the air when Worzel came to hug her, offering solace, I think. 'Why does my own daughter carry on like this, behaving like some *lafangi* without moral upbringing? Look at her! A bloody uneducated, cartoon-drawing peacock. Will she always bring shame on us?'

'No, I bleedin' won't,' I said defensively. 'Only some of

the time.' That last comment of mine can't have helped, but to Mum's credit she ignored me.

'I can buy the ticket now if you want,' whispered Worzel in Mum's ear.

I scowled. 'Heard that Worzel.' What she had to do with anything, I don't know.

Mum looked surprised at Worzel's offer but nodded all the same

'Can I go?' asked Kiz eagerly, completely misreading the tense, suffocating atmosphere.

Mum got up very quickly and looked at me eyeball to eyeball with tears streaming down her cheeks. She cupped my face in her hands and tidied a flick of my hair behind my ear. 'You, my dear, have lost it. You must go to India to find it.'

'What?' I cried, for never in a million years would I have foreseen that Bohemian line of thought coming at me.

'Mr Dindsa and his family in Delhi are waiting for you.'

'Well, they can wait all they bleedin' want. I ain't going. I don't know 'em. I only know India through you, Dad and Sholay.'

'What are you going to do here, then? You're not even studying.'

'So, studying isn't just about a textbook,' I howled. 'Remember when we were stripping the wallpaper in ninety-six and I was chalking the bare walls with *my* cartoon characters? Well, that was studying for me. You just never wanted to know. You said it was thick people's work but I'm *not* thick.'

'Taking M&Ms, was that studying, too?' said Mrs Kaur with her hands on her hips.

Sneering at her cheap shot, I shook my head. 'No, that was just me stealing.'

Mum stroked my face. Her hands were rough but warm. 'I do love you,' said Mum. 'You know?' Well that well and truly did it. She'd said that to Dad before he was taken, and now she'd said it to me. 'You, my girl, don't know who you are. You're like your father.'

'I know more about who I am than you ever will. *Haiyo Rabba*, what am I saying? I know more about *you* than you ever will.'

'Tell me, then,' ordered Mum, tapping her foot on the floor. So that was her game: catch me out in the detail.

'Well,' I started, 'what was Rai doing in our kitchen, flipping eggs like that?'

'He was hungry.'

'Yeah – for you,' I blurted out. 'Nobody makes omelettes like Dad, and you let him use Dad's best frying-pan like it meant nothing.'

'It's a cooking-utensil,' squawked Kiz, undermining the tension.

'But it belongs to Dad, just like he did to Mum and Mum to—'

There I stopped. Didn't want to go on any more. For the first time ever, I realised that what I wanted to be wasn't the same as what I was. Diving deep into the miscellaneous barrel of fabric remnants I wallowed in the silk, the viscose, the canvas, the polyester, all of it suffocating me. 'Just leave me alone. I've had enough. You lot are never gonna give me a satisfying ending.'

Bedlam in the bazaar

I've heard that the sun in India feels as if it's only a few metres away from one's very being, which I'm sure is true. I'd find out soon enough but it did pain me to think that I'd miss all those things here I'd grown to love and detest. Above all I'd miss the grey places; they're so underrated. I'd probably get withdrawal symptoms from the colour that has shrouded me so much. I only hoped to Dearest God that Mark Tully had told the truth – I'd never been to India, you see.

Indy went to Punjab last year and he reckons that the inferiority complex in India is bubbling up and will explode some day, and when it does all us lot won't go over there so high and mighty, like we should be walking on red carpet all the time. I told him it wasn't us lot who told them to roll it out in the first place. I mean, I'm as inconspicuous as they come but they can sniff you out before the first beggar does.

I tried to get my jabs at Dr Sharma's but they were having none of it. The receptionist said I had to be going on holiday to get holiday jabs, cheeky tart. I said I was, and that Scotland still counts as a holiday destination. I couldn't tell her about India or she'd have not only phoned Mum and the police but given Dad's shrink a buzz as well – the NHS have connections. Anyway, she said Scotland wasn't overseas, so I said, well, that depends on what you class as overseas 'cos there are a few rivers on the way, and if I went from the Shetland Isles then I certainly would be going overseas, so there. But she was having a bad day and wasn't up for my so-called time-wasting. I'd have to go to India unprotected against the harmful elements, but what can a bit of malaria do to a person like me?

I'd been packing furiously anything that looked handy, because I found it difficult to imagine India as a place that would acknowledge, never mind accommodate, my needs. So far, Customs willing, I've bought enough pasta to make the Italians give it up, ten hand-held fans – two of which have already broken by getting tangled in my hair – three bottles of Head and Shoulders, one emergency can of baked beans, a watch which cost me a fiver in the market, some Murray Mints, which haven't hit my tastebuds since my fourteenth birthday, and three bottles of the highest-factor sun-block lotion because coming back a different shade just makes life more difficult. Oh, and toilet rolls. That's all we really needed, said Dad. Toilet rolls.

'Where do you want to go?'

'India, sir.'

'How many going?'

'Two.'

'Where to exactly, miss?'

'Delhi, sir.'

'Are you sure?'

'Yes, sir. Why? What's the problem, sir?'

'No problem,' said Balu Lalu Travel Agent's Mr

Customer Service of the Year with a grin wide enough to make me wonder whether my skirt was tucked up round my knickers even though I was wearing trousers, so I looked over my shoulder and checked. I realised I'd noticed a lot of surreptitious smirking going on lately, and I knew it was them holding back everything they know about India in case it affected the perception of us young 'uns. They've failed to realise that Indian cinema has well and truly won the award for that one. Courtesy of the Indian film industry, I saw India through a lens coated with *filmi masala* and expected either very rich or very sullen beggars who'd harass you because their life depends on it, and the police to arrive at every crime scene late or during song sequence, at least. Oh, I couldn't wait.

I couldn't believe I was going. Whatever made me book those return tickets to India on the trustworthy Turkmenistan airline had better be the same thing that would get me through this trip. Already I had visions of my thirst for adventure drying up as soon as I toddled into Birmingham airport. It was almost a shock to realise that this time I'd be the traveller myself, and not coming to drop off yet another relation with the house in their suitcase to show off in Punjab. It was me this time, and I found myself eager to go and get slapped in the face by resident Indians who'd know me only as yet another NRI, and not as the more complicated multifaceted personality I had carved for myself.

I'd miss Dudley, though. Already I was remembering loads of stuff like how the only thing that brought our family together, made us one, was the Channel Four

Indian Film Matinée. Suddenly I remembered everything about our semi. The way it looked like a derelict building from the outside, with only clean curtains to tell you that anybody had ever showed it the slightest bit of love. The way it had paper-thin walls which meant you could hear even whispered conversations in the next room. The way people used to cherry-knock and I'd go out and swear at them and threaten to put Fairy Liquid in their eyes if they came back. The way I used to go out into the road and prune the weeds at the front of the house so that the dandelions would grow in more abundance. The way I used to sit and stare out of the window made for a shop-front as the rain flooded the gutters and drains, carrying with it the waste and litter of people passing by. The way I'd do roly-polys on the discarded old double mattress in the garden, which on sunnier days dried up and gave me a bumpy castle of my very own. The way I collected ladybirds from the allotment and trapped frogs under a holey bucket. The way . . . Oh, I seem to have gone on. Forgive me, but that's what the suppression of memories does to your thoughts. I was a broken dam.

I didn't have many answers but I wasn't going to India to seek them out. For one thing, Rodney and Del Boy had already given me most of them. For another, when I go looking for answers all I get are more questions. Having already made my list of things to do, I read them out to myself as I sat by my bedroom window They included riding on the top of a train, pretending to be a maharani touring on an elephant, sitting in a cinema watching any old blockbuster, and haggling for an ornament I didn't really want but insisted on having because I got it cheaper than dirt.

Bimla, Worzel and some other relations in the Midland vacuum had been coming by the house to give me tips on travel, all of which strangely ended with them giving me a parcel to take out to their relations. Oh, it's all right, Worzel, I really don't need to take my stash of Salbutamol inhalers with me, just as long as there's enough room for your Debenhams carrier bag full of children's vests and knickers. I'll die for your cause, just so long as your nephews and nieces have their underwear. Rule No 46: Always take people's gifts to India without question. It doesn't matter if they've given you illegal drugs: your duty is to your community.

When I at last strolled into the airport and across the marbled floor, with a glee that marked me out as a first-time-abroad traveller, I wondered whether I should go back to Dudley and say goodbye to everybody properly. Naaa. It would have taken too much explaining. 'Why are you going? Who with? What for?' I couldn't exactly say, 'Oh, I'm kidnapping Dad because him and me, well, we're giving ourselves a good old brush-down so we can come back different people.'

The only person who knew was Indy, 'cos I'd borrowed Dad's air fare from him. He's real decent like that. I mean, I didn't even have to ask him for the money: he offered it. He knows I'll pay him back from my cash-and-carry earnings.

I steered my brand new black suitcase into the main entrance, with Mum, Budgie, Kiz, Kully and Pardeep trailing after me, trying to keep up. I was worried Dad would show earlier than he needed to, so checked to make sure he was sticking to his side of the plan. He was. There pinned to the front of the Turkmenistan check-in desk was a Post-it with the secret code name 'Rafi' scribbled on it. Now I was content, and that airy-fairy feeling airports give me took hold.

The glossy interior always makes me wonder whether airports are actually more exciting than your destination. I mean, they're big enough to be mini-cities and they welcome you and your cash – especially your cash – like a relative returning from exile. So I tripped along on my merry way, searching for the disorderly queue that would be lining up at the Turkmenistan check-in, only somehow I ended up at the pick 'n' mix section. What? It was on the way and Indy'd told me that India isn't hot on hard boiled sweets. Mum made a dash to claim the peanut cracknell, while I shoved a hazelnut caramel in my gob.

'You don't eat wine gums,' said Mum, doing a detective's inventory of my sweets.

'Er, I do sometimes,' I said, not very convincingly.

'Wine gums are your father's favourites.'

'Yeah, I know. Just taking them with me to remind me of him.'

I don't know if Mum believed me, but she seemed OK with that reply. At any rate, she said no more, just led me firmly back to the check-in. Phew.

'Now, make sure you stick with that woman there. I know her – she's a friend of a friend of a friend, and very nice, too. She knows where she's going. You, Susham, *beti*, do not.' And with that she pushed me into the depths of the queue – or at least the ruins of one. An Indian queue? No such thing, mate.

After waiting what I thought was half an hour but turned out to be double that, I was further agitated by a middle-aged woman (therefore my anti) who was trying to persuade the frosty pink-lipsticked check-in woman that thirty-seven kilos was nearly the same as twenty-five. Usually I see no cause for concern or embarrassment when a member of the public harasses a customer services person, but when it means I have to stand next to a stripy man who communicates only through belches, piety soon disperses.

After another five minutes of wrangling, the anti gave up, lunged her suitcase on to the floor and began looking through a bunch of keys tied to her handbag to unlock it. Her two sons, helpful as they were, blushed with sheer embarrassment; know how you feel, guys. It happens all the time. Anti packs into her suitcase the whole of what she'll be leaving in her last will and testament, hoping to spread her affluence among her brethren. Alas, she finds that the only place it'll be spread out is at the feet of other passengers. Ten *salwar kameezes*, three bags of almonds and a package of cardamoms later, the OK signal was given for Mrs Carry My Whole House on my Back to board the plane: make way for the Champion. I then watched in dismay as yet another anti paid obeisance to God, hoping that she'd get the blonde, permed woman who looked like a bit of a soft touch. Get on with it. By now the circulation in my left leg had lost its way completely.

When I at last reached the head of the queue, 'Did you

pack your luggage yourself?' inquired the tough-looking redhead confronting me; her name badge said she was Mrs Walters.

'Is that a trick question?' I asked uncomfortably.

Mrs Walters was nasty. Her eyes pierced through me as though she were an X-ray machine herself. 'No. Did you pack your luggage yourself?'

Woah, the comedy gene was missing in her family. She never heard of Julie Walters?

I nodded furiously, with a quick, loud 'Yes.' If only the twits knew the truth.

When Mrs Walters told me to put my baggage on the scale, I nearly burst a blood vessel heaving my suitcase off the ground and staggering up to the desk. I used my full strength because I didn't want to look like a weakling, but the case felt at least four kilos heavier than it should have been. God, I thought, those bloody pistachios will be the death of me. I smiled innocently as the digital scale clocked up twenty-nine kilos. I wanted to shout that if I'd had my way I'd only be taking a briefcase with me like those businessmen flying business class do, but seeing as I hadn't had my way airport luggage rules should be relaxed for girls like me.

Mrs Walters totted up the calculations on paper, because mental arithmetic was far too much of a strain. I had to put right Mum's overloading mistake by handing Mum my huge compendium of things to do and see in India, a radio and some sketchbooks. Upon this sacrifice I was cleared. Realising that I was gonna die without that compendium, I ran into WH Smith, frantically looking, searching, for written advice on India. I was dismayed to find only a crappy *Wish You Were Here* book on South Asia. I didn't need anybody to tell me what to do off the beaten track, or that I had to cover my head when visiting places of religious or cultural importance. I needed information about how to stay alive on GT Road. But apart from that dismal holiday book everything failed me, so in the end I opted for a bag of Maltesers – gone off M&Ms, you see.

Before going through to the departure lounge, I turned to Mum and the others. Tears scurried down Mum's cheeks, as if I was going abroad in order to have a life-saving operation, this embarrassed both of us. Then she took my hand and placed a Snickers bar in it. 'Here, you'll need this,' she said, trying to offer me some comfort.

I squeezed out a thank you and hugged her.

'You'll need this, too. It's got Uncle Dindsa's telephone number and address. He's picking you up from the airport.'

'Thank you, Mum.'

'Oh, and the cash and carry phoned me. You're sacked.'

'Why would they phone you?'

'That's what those Tambers are like,' said Pardeep innocently. 'Should have worked for us.'

'You still here?' I asked.

'I'll still be here when you get back.'

'Oh. I'll look forward to it,' I said sarcastically. There went my resolution.

Budgie smiled, shook my hand and informed me that the car park would wait for no man. After that he headed off, shouting over his shoulder that alcohol miniatures would be much appreciated. So there I was, Snickers bar in hand and Mum sobbing over her once-repressed profound love for me. In all the years I'd known her, she'd never once let on about how much she approved of me.

Heart-wrenching though this was, it was only a momentary lapse and soon she was giving me spurious advice, which only a girl who'd been in a coma for the past twenty years would have required. Rule No 47: Remember to be polite. Rule No 48: Always comb your hair. Rule No 49: Do as the Indians do when in Rome. Rule No 50: Beware of the lizards. Rule No 51: Don't talk to palm-readers about science. She gave me one last bear hug, informed three stranger passengers that I was her daughter and needed taking care of because flying wasn't my thing, then bade me farewell.

'Bye, Mum,' I whispered giving her a kiss on the cheek. 'And, Mum, thank you.'

She walked away. Her cotton *salwaar kameez* was shrouded by yet another patchwork cardigan. Still, she looked a charming sight as she turned round, probably to remind herself what I looked like. I'd certainly be able to remember her face as she looked at me then.

Mum had left the departures entrance with another woman who only moments before had said goodbye to her mid-twenties son. He was allegedly going to find his roots. Mum was always comforting someone else.

That left only Kully, Pardeep and Kiz for me to say goodbye to. 'See ya,' I said cheerfully.

'Hold up,' squeaked Kully. 'You going just like that?'

'Well, you did.' She looked hurt, so I apologised

quickly, not meaning a single word of it, so that she and Pardeep could walk off hand in hand.

Kiz then gave me a light hug so her foundation wouldn't smudge.

'Bye,' I said.

'See ya, you lucky cow. Hey, if you see any film producers or actors tell 'em about your talented sister, will you?'

'No problem.'

'Aah, ain't you kind?'

'Yeah, I'm a real diamond,' I said.

'And don't worry about Dad. I'll rota everyone to see to his needs. He'll be just fine.'

'Thanks, Kiz.'

'You silly cow, you're taking him with you, ain't ya?'

I nearly fell over.

'How do you know?' I asked.

'Bumped into him, that's all.'

'You won't tell, will you?'

'What do you think?' I didn't know. 'Of course I won't.'

'Thanks.'

'Don't be stupid. You're taking him to India for his sake. Just bring back my normal Dad with you, that's all I ask.'

Before I could reassure her that Dad certainly would be better when he returned than when he left, Kiz was heading for the British Airways desk.

'Must find out what the height requirements are for being an air hostess,' she said over her shoulder.

It was strange standing there on the marbled floor with

nobody to bark at or bite me, so I was glad when Dad emerged from the gents' toilet, looking a little like Michael Palin in his brown blazer.

'Come on, then,' I said. 'Where is it?'

'*Ki?*'

'Your *tetchi*, that's what.'

'I haven't got one. Didn't have much to pack, so just put some of what I needed in this.' He held up a Somer-field's carrier bag so crammed with socks that they were overflowing at the sides.

'Here, put it in my backpack,' I urged.

'I can look after my own things, thank you very much.'

'I don't mind, really I don't. Come on, let's have you looking like a real refined first-class passenger – like you've got nothing to carry, nothing to worry about.'

'OK, then.'

We crammed his stuff into my small but capacious backpack till it was nearly bursting. A little while later we had to take the whole lot out again when I realised that the passports were right at the bottom, underneath his medicine. The medicine that I hoarded. Dad was all composed getting through check-in. That unsure smile of his seemed to make people feel that they'd intruded on him. Still, I was doing enough fretting for the both of us. Surely the authorities would be looking for him by now? After all, he'd hadn't turned up for his appointment with Dr Sharma, and she was keeping a close eye on him. 'Wouldn't want a relapse, would we?' she said.

'Aye-up.'

'OhmyGod!' And then, with vast relief, 'Oh, Arjun, it's you.'

241

'Hello, *beta*,' said Dad.

'*Sat sri akal*, Uncleji. You all right?'

'I'm *teek-taak*. Do you know, Sushminder, that this boy helped me down when I was hanging from that shop window?'

'No I didn't, Dad. No one ever said.'

'You never asked,' Arjun pointed out.

I stood there a little sullen, a little baffled, because some things go past you as if you weren't meant to catch them in the first place. Other things go past, then come back like a boomerang and smack you on the head.

'You weren't going to say goodbye?' asked Arjun.

'Er, me and Dad, we're taking a trip, that's all.'

'Oh, Sush, quit playing the pretender all the time. I know.'

'So why ask?'

'Just wanted to know if you trust me enough to tell me yourself.'

'It ain't nothing to be ashamed about.'

'Didn't say it was.'

'I'm not very good with words. With words I'm not very good. I know how I could, how I would, and when I should, but still don't get my message across, get all muddled, and holler, when I'm in distress, and then sometimes I whisper, like that makes a difference, and sometimes I stutter. Communicating, isn't so great, when that's not what I can do. It's all a hullabaloo of a mess when I dribble and drabble in talkless babble.'

'So what *are* you saying?'

'Dad's gonna exorcise his demons.'

'What about yours?'

'I haven't got any.'

Arjun smiled. 'You sure?'

I didn't answer straight away – I was too freaked out by his mind-reading.

'I'll ease things out for you here.'

'Thank you.'

Arjun smiled again, then strolled away. When he'd gone a few yards, he turned and gave me a slow-motion wink. *Hai.*

Dad and I eventually found seats 26 and 27A. After cramming my backpack into the overhead cubby-hole I sat down. Damn, I'd wanted a window seat. Moments later I got up to tackle my backpack again and got out the Murray Mints. There was only twenty-five minutes left before take-off many of the seats were still empty.

I knew I'd get some sado-masochist sitting next to me, so wandered through the types of scenario that might occur. Fingers in the eye should work, but if it didn't, Dad said, the thing to do was to act crazier than the other crazy person and then they'd surely be scared of you. I asked if that's why he'd started acting crazy, but he replied, 'No. I was the genuine article then.' With only two inches of leg-room my left leg had lost feeling. I ordered a cup of water because the air-conditioning had dried me up.

All of a sudden passengers flooded into the cabin, elbowing each other as they struggled along an aisle just wide enough for one chubby man. A liberated toddler climbed over the seats in front of me, screeching,

'There it is, there it is. Twenty-one. Look, Mummy, look.'

'Ooh, you little runt.'

After gulping down the water in one go, I sank deep down in our battered seats. In front of me was a television screen displaying the map of our journey. It told me I was beginning my journey in Kazakhstan.

'Hope the pilot's geography is slightly better,' said Dad.

I began fidgeting with my five-quid watch. Annoyed that the second hand was stuck, I tapped it three times to bring it to life. Just the trick. Now, I wondered, is India five and a half hours ahead or five and a half behind? As I twiddled the hands back and forth, trying to make up my mind, two men grunted and started speaking over me as if I didn't exist. Welcome to the Punjabi plane. They moaned about how little time they'd had to say goodbye to their loved ones, which got me thinking about how I hadn't said goodbye to Indy or Saira. I don't like goodbyes.

Investigating the elastic-topped pouch on the back of the seat in front of me, I found the in-flight magazine on Turkmenistan: 101 things to know about it, and all that. As I turned to page five – and it was a wonder I'd got that far without keeling over – a man's hand tapped me on the shoulder. Oh God, the plane hadn't even taken off and oh God, oh God. I was in big trouble. Should I plead insanity or should I pretend to be Jackie Chan and kick them till they were down?

When I finally came to, with a slap on the head from Dad, the man said he'd mistaken me for somebody he'd seen in a *Bhangra Kings, and Gidha Queens*, promo, and apologised.

'So you should,' I said, taking a swig from my second glass of cold water.

All around us women put their hands over the mouths of toddlers, to shut them up. The air hostesses must have wished they could shut our mouths, too, as they tried their best to tell us how to fasten our seatbelts and how to use our oxygen masks and life jackets. They were on a loser there. I mean, how did they expect us to listen when they weren't doing a song-and-dance number? Some people.

Dad stared out of the porthole in that reserved excitement of his. He hadn't been back to India since he was nine. Something had always stopped him. That something was usually him. When the plane roared down the runway, Dad looked at ease – whereas I was busy having a heart attack for the both of us while the plane shook from side to side.

When at last we were airborne, our ears popped away happily. This was the right time to ask Dad those questions he used to answer without me making an appointment to see him.

'You know if you're not happy. Are you sad?'

Dad nodded, but then shook his head, then nodded and then shook his head again.

OK, that question was a write-off, so I tried another one. 'Dad, why do people in the army polish their shoes in wartime? It's not like the enemy's going to spare you if you've got shiny shoes.'

'It's all got to do with the state of mind, see?

'Dad . . .'

'*Hai*, Sushminder, *beta*, do be quiet. You never ask simple questions about things like times tables.'

'I haven't got a simple mind.'

At that point I was interrupted by the air hostesses, who brought along a trolley loaded with plastic dinners. Everything I'd read about the food on planes turned out to be true.

When Dad and I snapped out of our three airline-food-induced coma, half a day had passed – even our ears popping hadn't been able to keep us awake – and we were coming in to land at Delhi. As we said farewell to the rickety plane, the first thing that greeted us was our nosebleeds. It must have had something to do with the atmospheric pressure in the scalding heat.

Holding tissues to our noses we found our way along plant-lined corridors to the airport proper. Despite the plants, it looked curiously sterile, like we were the first human beings ever to pass through it.

Every airport security man in his khaki uniform sported a moustache and an 'I'm off duty' look. 'This way, madam,' one of them ordered as I was about to infringe their precious security by going into the ladies' toilets.

Dad and I finally reached Customs after having got stuck for ages behind a mooing cow which had escaped from God knows where.

Our Mr Customs had orange lips and was backed up by a soldier with a rifle, but he didn't seem hostile. Rubber stamp poised, he asked, 'Can you teach me how to British? I'm hoping to get my visa.'

'Yeah,' I said, praying they'd heard the right thing and he'd let us through, 'I'll teach you how to British.'

Thump, thump, *thump*! he went. We were legit!

Passports in hand, Dad and I toddled off to look for the nearest relative or rickshaw, whichever came first. At the exit, despite the humidity (when we were expecting some fog) we hugged each other: we'd made it, and without a word from the loony brigade.

Mum had said Mr Dindsa would be meeting me, but we waited fifty minutes and not one Fair Isle sweater was there to be seen.

'Damn the sun,' said Dad.

To cheer him up, I went to go get him a *panir tikka* from the cleanest-looking vendor.

As I was walking back, Mr Dindsa jogged in, shouting, '*Sat sri akal.*' He always loves to make a grand entrance.

A thin, frail-looking young man behind him with jangling puppets stopped chasing him and began to harass a woman who looked less penny-pinching.

Mr Dindsa had been expecting to meet just one delinquent girl at the airport, so he just couldn't believe his sunshades when Dad appeared. After hugging Dad to make sure it really was him, he shook my hand – the one that wasn't holding the *panir tikka*. Mr Dindsa was dead chuffed to see us. Even his comb-over was waving hello.

'My hotel is only a twenty-minute drive away,' he told us, taking charge of the luggage.

After getting hold of a coolie, who heaved our stuff on to his head, Mr Dindsa set off briskly to his Ambassador, which came complete with the grumpiest chauffeur this side of Snow White's house. When Mr Dindsa swore at the coolie, we were off. Being unable to untie the curtains of the inside, I saw very little of Delhi except for the back of a turban and a sweaty head belonging to Mr Dindsa.

All too soon we ground to a halt. There'd been an accident, and bales of hay piled higher than any tower on the back of a truck were strewn across the road and the pavement. There seemed to be not one inch of space to spare anywhere. People trundled along between the bales like they'd seen this sort of thing many times before, but the stationary cars, rickshaws, tempoos, motorbikes and bicycles all honked furiously, each expecting someone else's to be the Chitty Chitty Bang Bang that would fly away over it all.

'We'll have to walk,' moaned Mr Dindsa, who looked ready to sack his chauffeur, as if he had caused the accident.

As we dodged through the Delhi public, I saw men loitering everywhere, moving in no particular hurry or direction. This got me wondering what had happened to all the women.

'Still alive,' said Mr Dindsa, laughing so loudly that a young beggar-boy stopped and gaped at him.

Dad and I trailed after Mr Dindsa, clambering over people's feet while Mr Dindsa showed us up by moving in and out of the crowds with the ease of long practice. Canvas bags bulging with veg and dhal obstructed the dusty pavements, making me feel as though I was strolling through an oil painting. Trying my best to breathe through the dusty heat, I knew that if an asthma attack came on here I was sure to die. The ambulance men round here aren't the quickest. It's got nothing to do with the potholed roads, the mood swings of the traffic controllers or the ambulance sirens not working. The crew just want to sip more *cha* that's all.

We arrived at Hotel Quality hoping it would be. On entering the lobby we scanned the mirrored ceiling and sleek marbled floor. Both reflected our souls, making us feel larger than we were. I had a sudden urge to skid across the lobby in my boots, but was unnerved by the sight of a bunch of guests who looked like they'd just come from a funeral. In front of us a concierge flitted around with his clipboard of duties. His long, coiled moustache like a snail's shell had a fleck of pastry still in it. The viscous sheen on his black suit reflected all India's heat energy, making me and Dad want to move into the shade of a potted palm.

'Vow!' I gushed in my most convincing Indian accent.

Budgie had told me that if we pretended to be more Indian we'd get better service, but I don't think the Quality's maroon-clad employees fell for it. Their eyes, already suspicious, wandered over us with a look of contempt. Another moustached man winked like it was an affliction, so I pushed Dad quickly towards Reception.

At the desk was a conscientious-looking woman with her *chunni* hanging at exactly the right angle to give her an air of respectability. 'Welcome to Hotel Quality. What can we do to service you?'

'I *beg* your pardon?' I asked. Dad elbowed me in the ribs.

'We're with Mr Dindsa,' I said, as I looked around for him so he could confirm. Mr Dindsa was, however, deeply involved in settling a row between a eunuch and his or her friend.

'Okey-dokey,' said the receptionist in the most cheerful way.

While we waited in the guest lounge Dad swallowed some of his pills. 'Phone your mother. Tell her we arrived safely.'

So off I went back to Reception to use the international line. After three attempts, the phone finally rang in Dudley and Budgie answered.

'Who's that?' He has such a charming telephone manner.

'It's me, Sushminder.'

'Oh, hi, Sush. You and Dad got there all right, then?'

'Yeah.' I answered, surprised worried that he wasn't shouting obscenities at me. 'Is Mum OK?'

'She's at the factory. Early shift.'

'She doesn't know *yet*?'

''Course she knows. The whole of Dudley knows.'

'Tell her I miss her already.'

'Will do. You just look after Dad.'

'Will do.'

'Can I go back to sleep now?'

'Sure . . . See ya, Budgie.'

'Take care.'

I put the handset down quickly. What did he mean, 'Take care'? I don't ever remember him saying that to me before. If he meant 'Keep looking over your shoulder',

250

why didn't he just come out with it? What's with the euphemism?

'That will be ninety-seven rupees.'

'No it won't,' said Mr Dindsa, appearing like a squirrel for its nut. 'She is with me.'

Looking annoyed, the receptionist began typing away.

'You two look tired,' said Mr Dindsa. 'Shall I show you to your suite?'

'Only if it's the ambassador one.'

He patted me on the head and pushed me and Dad towards the lifts. 'I have a surprise for you.'

'I'm not very fond of surprises, Uncle Dindsa. Can we not have one?'

Scowling at me, he shoved us into a very large lift. 'You'll like it here. Taken me a long, long time but I have made this hotel work. When I came it was but a pile of crap. Now it's—'

'—A bigger pile of crap?' I laughed nervously, but stopped when I realised that Mr Dindsa wasn't amused. In Dudley he even used to laugh at my knock-knock jokes. What had happened to him?

'I'm afraid the rules here are different. Your sense of humour won't wash in Delhi,' he informed me.

Mr Dindsa dished out luggage-carrying orders to a beleaguered-looking bellboy and snapped at him, 'Press the button then.' Why press the button yourself when you can get a bellboy to do it for you! Straightening his double-breasted blazer, Mr Dindsa mopped his shining forehead. He looked very uncomfortable.

'Where are your Fair Isle sweaters, Uncle Dindsa?'

The answer to this question was clearly painful, and,

upset that I'd had the insensitivity to ask, he wrinkled his nose. 'You won't believe it, but they've been stolen, the lot of them.'

'No!'

'I wouldn't lie. It happened on the second night I took over this hotel, at around twelve or one p.m., would you believe. A launch party downstairs in the lobby was being held in my honour. All of Delhi's elite was there but none of them could sympathise with me. We never did catch the thief.' Mr Dindsa looked quite overcome with emotion, as if he might start sobbing and go on till tomorrow. 'I know who it was, though. I know, I know. You won't believe it, but I think when Rishi Kapoor came to stay here he took them.'

'No!'

'Yes. He's the only man in India who's as proud of his knitwear collection. Too much of a coincidence, wouldn't you say, Amarjit Paji?'

Dad nodded to show he'd been listening. He hadn't.

At that point we arrived on the third floor. I thought it would have been quicker if we'd taken the stairs, but Mr Dindsa said I should stop being so funny. He hurried us along the corridor, waddling almost like a penguin in his excitement, while Dad and I duly played his follow-the-leader-game. Dad walked along calmly and I kept anxiously close to him – thoughts of the Delhi police nabbing us and taking Dad away were swarming in my head.

Mr Dindsa diverted my thoughts by flinging open the door of Room 99 and pushing me and the luggage-laden bellboy inside. Dad and he strolled in after us.

The room was both spacious and comfortable, and its decor was simple enough to let you think. I was impressed. But the heat soon deadened my excitement, because it made it difficult for me to move. My white muslin shirt was sticking to me so tightly that it had become a second skin, so I sat underneath the ceiling fan to try to cool off a little. Dad went and washed and changed into a plain navy *kurta*. He looked brand-new again.

'Thanks for the surprise, Mr Dindsa,' I said. 'It's really lovely.'

'Surprise? This isn't it my dear. You and Amarjit Paji are in for a real treat.' Mr Dindsa rubbed his hands.

'Don't tell me it's the Palace on Wheels?' I hoped.

'No, it's something much better.'

The moment Dad and I sat down on the hardest leather seat in the world, Mr Dindsa clapped his hands, jumping on the spot. 'Our Mr Tempoo will give you an unforgettable tour of Delhi.' Without asking us whether we wanted to go, he shouted, 'Take them away.'

After bunging a cassette into the player to blast his latest Indian flick number like it was urgent, Mr Tempoo obeyed with alacrity. The auto-rickshaw's G force clamped me back against a metal bar behind my head. No need for seatbelts, then. I wondered how the vehicle had survived his driving for so long and why there were no doors. You couldn't go at nearly forty miles an hour without a door, could you? All three tyres squeaked as the rough roads battered their already bald treads, but the noise was nearly drowned by the jingle-jangle of Mr

Tempoo's hanging ornaments and his loud-as-humanly-possible singing to an Asha Bonsle track.

Dad looked comfortable in his seat, like he was remembering the feeling all over again. His grey hair waved in the breeze as we swerved in and out of traffic. The frenzied beeping, unlike anything I'd heard before, made me tense. Sometimes Mr Tempoo beeped to tell a bigger truck to get out of the way, but most of the time it was just because he had spasms in his hand when moving to the music.

'No, stop! You're gonna kill her!' I screamed as Mr Tempoo shaved past a poor old woman carrying a basket of roasted peanuts on her head.

I realised then that India needed only one thing to keep itself safe. It wasn't a big United Nations peace treaty. It wasn't even a hold-hands-all-round-the-world record-breaker. It was the bleedin' Green Cross Code. God bless the bright spark who came up with that idea.

'Please, Mr Tempoo, go a bit slower.'

'Any slower and we'll be in a stopped mode.' Mr Tempoo spat out some deep-brown saliva, which landed on a disgruntled cow that had made its bed in the middle of Delhi's M1.

But he did oblige – for all of two seconds before muttering, '*Besti!* What becomes of a car-driving man when he is overtaken by a scooter-riding girl?' he clamped his foot to the accelerator again.

'Oh, be quiet. Keep your eyes on the potholes.'

'Don't you worry, madam. I know these Delhi roads like the back of my hand.'

'That's what I'm worried about. No one knows the

back of their hand. Not me, anyway,' I said, examining the back of my hand.

As we zipped past one smell after another, I felt as though I was being possessed. My mind hovered in some computer motor-racing game: memories of Budgie and me going to the chippy on Friday nights to play on the arcade machine came pouring back.

'You got a tempoo where you come from?'

I looked at him, stumped. No, Dudley didn't have auto-rickshaws but one of my Folk Friday uncles had a Reliant Robin, I said proudly. Mr Tempoo wasn't too impressed as he drove into the thick of Delhi.

When he came back from finding the picnic hamper that had fallen off the front passenger seat some yards back, he assured us that tying it on with a *nala* from his jogging bottoms would stop this caboodle happening again – 'caboodle' was his word, not mine. Then he sped off through the densest part of Delhi, half the time driving partly on the pavement – never mind the pedestrians.

Eventually, he decided to stop at a red traffic light, but this was only so he could forage for another cassette in his specially commissioned cassette carrier.

'You like Gurdas Mann?' he asked.

'God bless you!' cried Dad, perking up.

As soon as Mr Tempoo cranked up the volume, Mann's voice echoed all around us. The odd Delhi driver smiled, accepting that their shoddy selection of Indi-pop music was taking a plummet for the greater good.

'Nai reesa desh Punjab diya'.

'Aaaah,' sighed Dad, humming and tapping his feet.

Mr Tempoo swooped through the traffic, keeping time

255

with the beat. The dust smeared our cheeks and covered our lips. Delhi was having a spell of early sun, said Mr Tempoo, so we outsiders shouldn't worry too much if we'd overloaded our suitcases with bulky winter clothes, he'd buy them for a good price.

Before Dad could tell him to stop talking *buk-buk*, a beggar-girl stuck her pigtailed head through the window. Although quite young she was already adept at batting her eyelashes and smiling in such a way as to have the most pity bestowed upon her.

'Please help me,' she asked in a painful voice.

'Why don't you help me?' I asked.

'You have money.'

'Who says?'

'Your linen shirt does.'

'Look, all I can offer you is advice.'

'Don't want it.'

'Well, bog off, then,' I snarled. 'Charming. Dad, you try and make the world a better place and all you get is aggro.'

'Welcome to the land of your ancestors.'

Undeterred, Pigtail Girl began dancing up and down by the tempoo, screeching her head off.

'You won't get a rupee out of us,' I told her, sitting very straight and shaking my head to convince her. 'Not one single rupee.'

Before I'd finished speaking, Dad had lobbed ten rupees her way.

'May you live a thousand years,' she yelled, all delighted, as she headed smartly to a white Maruti not far behind us.

'That's impossible, Pigtail Girl. Come back and give my dad a realistic piece of blessing,' but before she could ask what 'realistic' meant, Mr Tempoo was again pretending he was in the Monte Carlo grand prix.

'Please let us see Delhi in one piece,' I implored him. 'I don't want to say farewell to the world on a Delhi Road.'

'Don't you worry, madam. Not one teeny-weeny bit. I know Delhi road's like the back of my . . .'

I glared at him in the rear-view mirror, which he apparently used only to re-grease his hair.

'. . . like the back of my wife.' Mr Tempoo laughed a lot, honked a lot and swore a lot before shutting up.

From what I could see, which wasn't a lot, what with the dust in my eyes, Delhi was too much. The intensity and brilliance of its flickering colours, its smells ranging from a reeking stench to fragrant musk, its noises like a fanfare, smacked my senses. Humans who were both strange and familiar looked at me like I was lost, but there was no way any of them could give me directions because they seemed just as lost. Delhi made no sense at all.

Mr Tempoo skidded round a stubborn Maruti (there were thousands of them) and honked, enraged by the other driver's playing *ghazals*. 'No wonder he's driving too slow – slow music.'

'*Bach ke!*' shouted Dad all of a sudden. The next thing I knew I'd been flung out on to the roadside. Rule No 1 in India: Don't stick your head out when sightseeing in a tempoo.

While cursing Mr Tempoo with my eyes, I watched in

amazement as the trucks, buses, cars, bicycles – anything with wheels – skimmed past me like I wasn't there.

'People would pay good money to see this sort of thing in a circus,' said Dad, who'd got out of the tempoo to check if I was alive.

In the middle of a Delhi flyover, it dawned on me that here among the lunatics, among the cows, among the honking, among the stench, Dad and me would prosper. The sparkle in his eyes, missing for so very long, had returned. Even the dimples in his sallow cheeks seemed to have plumped up.

When Mr Tempoo realised that flinging an NRI out of his tempoo was a heinous offence and would merit severe punishment, he legged it.

Dad wandered out into the middle of the traffic, towards a concrete bollard which I assume he took to be a podium. The sun beating down on our already tanned skins was glowing all around him. Raising his right fist slowly in the air, he shouted something that should have been shouted a long time ago.

'Think what a shame for this day gone. Don't tally them off one by one. For livers of life, take destiny's hand. Shake her and break her, then make your demand. You may love her but do not revere. Life's driven at your speed, in whichever gear. Plan not the day nor map the route. So what if you're lost? Your judgement's astute. Think what a shame for this day gone. Don't tally them off one by one.'

'Welcome back, Dad,' I whispered to myself.

Then, well, you know how long-lost parents and their children run into each other's arms in Indian flicks? Dad and I didn't do that. Instead we skipped to the Bedlam in the Bazaar *dhaba*.

There was only one thing Dad wanted to eat.

'An omelette, please. The best you've got.'

All BlackAmber Books are available from your local bookshop.

For a regular update on BlackAmber's latest release, with extracts, reviews and events, visit:

www.blackamber.com

one straight away. If there's one thing I hate, it's eating cold food which should be piping. Dad refused again, shaking his head. He shouldn't have, because he looked frail and grey, so I shoved one into his hand anyway, and without argument he took a bite of it. Afterwards me and Dad played count the woodlice; six altogether. Although we didn't talk much I was glad he was nearby.

We must have been there forty-something minutes before we realised it would be at least another six hours before the clan dispersed to their various parts of the world. 'Stop the wedding,' mumbled Dad over and over again. One way or another I knew he'd try.

Dad isn't like either of his brothers – he's by far the noblest of the lot. If he says something you take notice. Even his face is straight to the point. His long, defined nose, jaw and forehead have aged well. His poised stature gives him an air of gracefulness; not at all like me, all gangly and cumbersome like, banging into things I can clearly see. Like I say, of the three brothers Dad is the most noble. Dudley Chacha's all right. His name isn't really Dudley, that's just where he lives – come to think of it, he actually lives in Croydon. Come to think of it, I don't know what his real name is. Anyways, there's also Wally Uncle from Wolverhampton who's divorced now with two children. I'm quite fond of his youngest daughter, Guppy.

On Mum's side of the family there's Brummie Uncle, who's married to Mum's youngest sister, Worzel (aka Gurmej), and Greavsie from Gravesend is married to Bimla, Mum's other annoying sister. We don't often see much of Greavsie on account of him thinking that he's all

and Budgie's best mate. Dad's never banned anyone from our house except him. I think it was that day he rapped me on the knuckles with a pack of cards because I'd lost a game, the rules to which I still do not know. It could also have something to do with the day that Dadoo decided to take up rapping as his future career.

Apparently he's MC Didoo Dadoo or something like that. Now he talks like he's a rapper, walks like he's a rapper and, worst of all, dresses like he's a rapper. The funny thing is – wait for it – he can't rap. Hah! So really he isn't a rapper at all. He's just a baseball cap, Caterpillar boots, signet ring, designer jersey and bomber jacket. Dadoo's like that in summer, too.

The thing I don't understand is how Dadoo can have such a genial giant as a father – I mean his dad can do all sorts of things with his arms and legs in a real nimble way and can levitate you on just one hand. Not only that, but he can put his arms right the way round his back and twist his legs to look like flumpalump marshmallows. Dadoo's elder sister, Jagdev, is pretty decent, too, and I can talk to her for ages and a lifetime and not know it. She knows loads of stuff but doesn't ever brag about it. She's away at university doing Economics, probably just to get away from that rapping.

I once told Dadoo he wasn't his parent's real son 'cos he'd been left on his mum and dad's doorstep by some girl who'd got herself impregnated with alien bits and bobs. Naturally, he thought I was using warped psychology and he started telling the whole of Dudley I was a big softy. So now when he winks at me I dimiss his sign of flirtation and take it as an insult 'cos I really mean this when I say it: Dadoo is one thick breed.

Exchanging my polystyrene plate for a china one, I began piling on the second helping of food until the mango chutney threatened to spill over the edges on to the maroon deep-pile carpet. Dadoo stood there staring like it was his hobby and was joined by a few uncles, who must've thought me greedy for not offering them more food like a dutiful buffoon, but what was there to ask? They already had their hands full with the shot glasses of Bell's from Blackpool. Some people! 'Main jat yamlaa pagla dewaana . . . oh ho ho.' Then they all started singing like drunken Punjabis with only one mission: to get bladdered on their sorrows. The Folk Friday uncles kicked up their feet and frog-leapt into our furniture, all twelve of them doing the Cossack dance Punjabi-stylee. When Wally Uncle nearly kicked the shins of a beleaguered toddler gone astray, I saved myself from being crushed by darting straight to the cupboard under the stairs. The dancing was getting far too dangerous for me. The stairs would have to be my sanctuary – well, it was either that or go to the girls' room and listen to them talk about their fates.

Inside the cupboard, 'Dad!' I screamed, hurling myself into his arms for a bear hug.

How he'd got past the three witches in our house with their body-heat-sensing eyes amazed me. Crammed into the cupboard, Dad's five-and-a-half-foot frame reminded me of Dadoo's dad, the contortionist. I wedged myself between him and the door, and he giggled while making a shadow picture with his hands – I think it was a dog. In the faint light that forced its way through the cracks of the MDF doors, I saw his bleak smile. His beautiful wispy grey hair hadn't been combed in days, and his normally large black eyes were only half their former size from lack of rest. His hands were cold, too, so I rubbed them in mine to force the blood to circulate, but try as I might his fingertips would not thaw.

Tucked into a pocket of Dad's blue parka, I could see a small Nivea container. In it were assorted smarties to control aberrant thoughts – funny that: coloured pills to dampen coloured thoughts. With only a few of the pills remaining, I added the ones that had been saved in my duffel coat to his collection.

The noise outside of chatter, crockery and bhangra was strange as it filled the silence under the stairs. The two of us, hiding in our own home.

Dad found a loose screw on the floor and, with shaky hands, used it to etch his name on the sloping ceiling: 'Amarjit Singh Dillon wasn't here.' When he'd finished, he chortled again and whispered, 'There. I'm permanent now.'

The cupboard was a snug fit and we had to crouch in tight so that our knees touched our chins. Them lot outside couldn't get at us, making it all the more cosier. Near my feet was a small bottle of Bell's, which had probably been hoarded by Brummie Uncle or Budgie. Pouring a little into the cap of a Mr Sheen can, I offered it to Dad. He refused it, but a convenient ledge just above my head allowed me to rest the shot (talking like a real pro there) and on my lap was the feasty plate ready for me to devour. The samose were still warm, so I offered Dad middle-class just 'cos he uses words like 'Sunny Jim'. Yes, I'm still confused, too.

Outside I could hear Dudley Chacha chatting to someone up near the stairs. Knowing all too well that Dudley Chacha doesn't do discreet, I began humming. He helped us out when Dad wouldn't get off the number 32 because it hadn't arrived at the Pind Pub. The bus driver nearly called the police when Dad offered to take over the wheel and make the bus float in the Dudley canals.

That was last summer and I hadn't seen Dudley Chacha since he got himself a job down South which he won't tell us the title of but pays well. 'Business,' he says, 'that's what I'm doing.' He's probably been too busy looking at some more girls for himself, at the same time pretending it's all such a chore by embracing the speck of doubt telling him she's not the one. He's seen them all: tubby, lardy, skinny, in-between, high-pitched, perfect, flawed, domesticated, clubby, well-off, poor, all sorts of jelly babies and he gets to choose; yet he hasn't submitted himself to a single one of the sixteen Miss Worlds.

Antis are therefore allowed to kiss their teeth at another perfectly matched proposal wasting away. 'Who does he think he is? The Maharaja of Punjab, I s'pose.' Well, if he isn't that, I must admit he could definitely be the Maharaja of Dudley. He's the bee's knees and elbows and he knows it.

If everyone isn't getting married around here, they're looking for someone suitable for someone else. It's a bit disheartening, really, thinking that's the only aim in life. There I go again, talking like a careers adviser: aims,

aims, aims. I got quite sad in the cupboard under the stairs, thinking about all the people I'd once known who'd vanished into the abyss of marriage. Hope they're all still alive.

'Oy, get out. It's photo time,' shouted Dadoo.

'*Pare mar*,' I shouted back.

'You've got to be in the video,' he insisted, trying to yank the door off its hinges and managing to open it a crack.

'Noooo. Get stuffed. Leave me alone.'

Fighting to keep the door shut so he couldn't see Dad, I sizzled, trying to threaten him and make him back off. But his long, skinny arms were surprisingly strong and I had to use all my might to stop him.

There was no way I was smiling for no camera, only to get the mickey taken out me of for the rest of that video-tape's living days. No, Dad and I were going to sit there and conspire and let the sound of Rafi's singing waft through the house the way it had always done in the days before Budgie drowned it with his garage-cum-*ghazal* mishmash. Rafi's voice I adore; it's my uncles' voices that scare the human out of me. When they're drunk they lose the power of speech, and on top of that they try to sing, hitting notes that haven't even been heard by a dog yet. They make me want to roast myself in the oven. I could, if I'd really wanted to, have gone out, turned up the volume and drowned sweetly in Rafi's soothing voice, but they'd have spoilt that. Nope. Dad and I stayed put in that dingy cobweb- and woodlouse-ridden place, staring at the shot of whisky near the air brick.

Nina, my eldest cousin, once told me that whisky was an acquired taste, and she'd know because she lived at Brummie Uncle's house when she was studying at Aston. I said, if it burns your oesophagus and tastes worse than vinegar, why acquire it? Adults will do anything for acceptance – except my dad, that is. Here he was, one of life's ninety-nine per-centers. While watching him munch the last bit of pakora, a sudden urge to hug him tight came over me.

'Everything's gonna work out fine, Dad,' I told him. It had to.

Then Dad said something I'll never, ever forget: 'I believe in you.'

Nobody had ever said that to me before. Liar, sure, failure, certainly, but believe in me? Never, ever.

'Come out, come out, wherever you are. I am near, you are far,' crooned Dadoo, banging on the door again, If he hadn't stopped when he did, I'd have gone out and bopped him one. You see, that Dadoo sits at a synthesiser all day so just assumes us humans are like the flicks and switches on which he can play any beat he wants. There's no way I'd ever listen to anything he has to say, even if it was for my own good. 'I'm not a rapping nerd,' said Dadoo when I called him one. He's nothing but, I tell you. When his sister fell off the roof of their garden shed and broke several bones, Dadoo wouldn't let their mum ring for the ambulance because he was using the phone line to download samples off the net.

Suddenly the cupboard door swung wide open, almost off its hinges. It was inevitable, I suppose, because nobody ever leaves anybody in peace round here. The unwritten but constitutional law is that if you're not being harassed you're not being caressed. Rule No 9: Privacy is something you aren't entitled to.

'*Arre, arre, arre*, look at her Painji, come look. Your daughter is an alcoholic. Come, come quickly,' whined Bimla, exaggerating like her knickers were on fire.

'Paji is also looking rather wayward, wouldn't you say?' said Worzel, trying to look serious.

'No! I've not even touched the bloody stuff, and my dad's no more wayward than me, you fat cow,' I shouted, immediately revving my defensive engine. 'Here, smell my breath.' Opening my mouth wide I exhaled into Mum's face to convince her somehow that although there was whisky on the ledge I had no intention of drinking it.

By now the whole clan had formed a semicircle round the cupboard door, blocking all the exit routes. To them I was nothing but guilty. The more benevolently curvaceous gifted antis and pot-bellied uncles, who'd have had difficulty fitting into the cramped hovel of a stateroom on a cruise ship, had to resort to standing one behind the other, waiting in turn to take a peek at the culprits.

Then I was nearly blinded by a flashbulb and a camera came rolling in with its zoom lens fixed on my half-empty shot glass. I lashed out but missed, so had to resort to covering my face with the empty plate. This failed to deter either Nina, who went on shoving the camera in my face, or Bimla, who went on pushing her daughter forward to get the best angle. Disentangling my legs I stood up, ready to whimper at eyes unforgiving in their pleasure at my misery. Glaring at me and Dad, they were. Yeah, that's what they were doing, glaring.

Of all the glares, Sammy's shone the brightest. 'Ha,' she sneered, 'you always get caught, Sushi.'

'Look, try it,' I said, shoving the shot glass in Mum's face. 'A person must be smashed out of their brain in the first place if they want to drink that stuff.'

'Aah, Painji,' sighed Bimla, 'Sushi – your own daughter – calling you a drunk.'

'Shut up, Bimla. My name is Sushminder or Susham.' I waited a moment for a response but none came – that's if you don't count the smug faces looking at me. I don't know why I open my trap sometimes; it must be because I have an obligation to my 'put your foot in it' history. This time I couldn't help myself and my mouth ran away with me.

'You're all so, so, so tabloid. All you ever do is freak out at other people, pretending they're the weirdos and then give them advice so you come out looking like Rab has only given you the gift of wisdom.'

'That's it, you join in and stir the cauldron, you goblin,' said Mum through gritted teeth. 'Why must you bring us all down to your level?' Before I could answer, she said, 'I'll bloody well see to you later.'

Snatching the empty plate out of my hand, Mum apologised to Brummie Uncle for the chilli chutney that splattered his surfing shirt, and dragged me out of the cupboard.

'It's not goblins who stir cauldrons, Mum, it's witches, OK? At least get your derogatory terms right.'

While Mum towed me along our carpet towards the front room, I pointed at Worzel and Bimla and told them to leave my dad be. But they ignored me, helped him out

45

of the cupboard and, dazed though he was, led him towards the living-room. The guests running behind him told him they missed him and asked, 'Where have you been? You all right?' Dad didn't answer. I had just enough time to warn Worzel and Bimla that if they got my dad taken back I'd see to it that their darlings Sammy, Pinky and Nina would end up in the *Des Pardes* matrimonials. That would kill them for sure.

In the front room, the kids had rebelled and put on *bhangra* mixed with Asian under-overground.

'Shut up, now. Dance. Have some fun.' Mum gave me one of those looks that mean 'It ain't over yet.'

'Yeah, Ma, I'll do exactly what you say.' But I said it in my head, 'cos there was no need to go right out and ask for a slap.

This is perfect timing for Rule No 10: Don't walk around or hide under the stairs with shots of alcohol. If getting drunk is a necessity, get well and truly bladdered, then you won't feel the slap.

Mum swept out, slamming the door behind her, leaving me to sulk and split the split ends in my hair.

My twelve-year-old cousin Guppy dug me in the ribs. 'Look, Susham, your dad's going ape.'

Angrily, I barged her aside with my hip so I could investigate. She was right.

Through the keyhole I could just glimpse Dad being made to sit on a pine stool so high that his feet dangled. He was mumbling to himself again because everybody else lacked the patience to listen. Like a toddler he smiled courteously at the very relatives whom years ago he'd rightly labelled '*haramde*' – that's a naughty word to you and me. That wasn't my dad there, the unhappy bloke wearing his flat tweed cap indoors and with a hole in his navy wool sock in the sharp October wind-chill, was it?

'Coom an' join in,' said six-year-old Preetam, whom I'd last seen when she was four.

'Do that Dixit move again,' demanded Guppy, trying to aim popcorn in big-mouth Baldev's gob while the mob cheered for Jyoti. She was a fourteen-year-old child prodigy who'd be entering some high-fly uni next year and had begun to shake her body like a banshee. While she was in the middle of a routine which put Morris dancers to shame, in came her dearest mother to calm the tempo down with a handy slap on the backside for thrusting one's pelvis towards onlookers in a loose-woman way. Oh, and it was just getting to be such fun.

That Poor Child Prodigy had developed a liking for bopping her bust up and down, thanks to the influence of Kiz, who pretends she's the young headmistress of a big drama school. The thing is, her students are never gonna end up on stage – shame, that. When Poor Child Prodigy sat down to join my 'not having a good a time club', the opportunity to play paper, stones and scissors was seized. The best out of two hundred and one. I won. Afterwards we gazed out of the window at the cars going by. My colour was blue and Poor Child Prodigy's red, and because I'd won, on account of more blue ones went by, she had to go get us some more roasted peanuts. Life doesn't get more dull than that.

I must have fallen asleep on the sofa for ages, 'cos when I surfaced my back ached like somebody had stomped on it the night before. These household parties, exciting as they were, had that droning hypnotic effect, so to pass yet more time I counted the red berries on the middle border of the blue-patterned wallpaper. No doubt Mum would redecorate that as well, seeing as she was doing up anything that looked slightly worn.

Even she'd have to go in for her MOT sooner or later. It's not that she's not pleasant to the eye; it's not even that she doesn't work hard; but she's got sagging eyelids and drooping cheeks, the kind of stuff that would be instantly put right by Worzel. All those crinkles that deepen with more frowning and even more worrying. One thing Mum hasn't got is laughter lines, 'cos her skin's wrinkle-free there. Maybe she hasn't laughed much in her life.

It was way after twelve when Dadoo, completely smashed, left. The last of the big benders, he is. Always announces he's leaving an hour or three before he actually does, so that when he slams the front door behind him I think he's still lurking somewhere around the house. This time, though, he really had gone, leaving me to wait impatiently for Mum's sisters to barrage her with advice on how to keep a well-ordered family without an ISA to their name.

Dad was still dangling his feet from that high seat and mumbling what seemed like bitter nothings to himself. He spoke beautiful Punjabi. His voice was soft but strong, taking all the coarse edges off even the harshest sounds. Creeping up behind him to listen, I could just make out those same old words: 'Stop the wedding.'

When I took his hands, which were still shaking, Dad

48

stopped talking to himself. We headed towards the kitchen, only to be stopped by Kiz who was searching for the paracetomols.

'What you doing?' she asked, kissing Dad on the cheek.

'Nothing,' I answered.

'Is he all right?'

It didn't take much to pacify Kiz, 'cos no sooner had I said, 'Dad's perfectly fine, don't fret,' than she found the paracetomols and said, 'Goodnight.'

I wasn't sure where I was going to take Dad, but it had to be somewhere out of harm's way. He couldn't stay in his own home.

'Where ya going?' asked Budgie, as he tried to cram the seventh bag of rubbish into the wheelie bin outside our kitchen door

'Er, nowhere. Fresh air,' I said, pointing out of the window as an added visual clue. Dad inhaled and exhaled, to elaborate the point, but that *bandar* Budgie didn't shift in the slightest. Enjoying the way we squirmed under his gaze, he straightened his smart grey shirt like it made him a better person. I smiled back and looked the other way. It wasn't that I was scared of him but Budgie's the biggest dobber ever. If I'd walked out with Dad then he'd instantly have tannoyed to the rest of the household what we were doing and before I could come up with a taunt cheeky enough for a slap those lot would have taken Dad.

Trying to outstare Budgie across the kitchen lino was hard. His steely eyes were fixed on me like I was his target. Do I move or not? I wondered. When his mobile rang in the nick of time, I nearly jumped with glee. It was Dadoo. Even though he only lived ten metres away, he found the need to phone. Budgie soon immersed himself in talk of the latest gig in Birmingham, so Dad and I took our chance and legged it through the front door, only to be met by Mum, Worzel, Bimla and two policemen.

Nearly smacking myself in the face with panic, I pushed Dad hard. '*Daur*, that way. Run, run!' I screamed, but when my words fell to the ground so did Dad.

From his knees, Dad looked up at Mum with eyes full of despair. She, biting the side of her sequinned *chunni*, gaped around to see how many people were staring, but the dark that had fallen on our semi-detached road was drowning everyone. I'd never known the road so quiet.

It wasn't quite the white-coats who carted Dad away. It was those Russian dolls in their *salwar kameezes*, their *chunniyan* drifting in the wind like their loyalty.

Hide away

The whiff of vomit welcomed me through the door that led into Dad's ward. The waiting-room was no better: the smell of filthy detergent clung to the inside of my lungs. And they wanted Dad to stay in this!

As I sat waiting for Dad to come out, I noticed a manila folder which had slipped down between my chair and the wall. There was no one else in the room, so I fished it out and flicked through the official-looking papers inside. To my astonishment, among the many patients' names was Dad's. I read on.

I knew things which those idiots in their guise of the sane did not, and my heart felt good. My legs swayed as I sat on the sill dangling them out of the second-floor window above our corner shop. Listening to the wind creak through the damp-rotten holes, I was slowly being eaten away. I was glad of it.

Down there on the road they listened, their necks cranked up, straining to watch me and revelling in the drama that had interrupted their dull daily schedules; the halal meat man, the video-rental woman, Mrs Kaur, the *mithai* man, the material woman and the lollipop lady. I remember it now as I saw it then. They and caught-up pedestrians stared at me, the man who had been sitting in the window for the past forty minutes, not threatening to jump but not ruling it out, either.

'Get down. Get down you mental spastic,' wailed Mrs Kaur, above all the babbling talk. 'I'm losing trade.'

I'd lied to her. I told her I needed the toilet or there would be an accident. She obliged, but began cursing me when I locked the door to her flat above the shop.

I heard the crowd's whiny voices, but chose not to listen. 'If I die, *budiya* going to jail. *Chaki* peesing and peesing and peesing' – my body whirled in a vortex as I imitated the actions of grinding a wheat stone – 'and peesing and peesing and . . .' I threw down four knives and six forks.

Everyone speedily stepped back, and Mrs Kaur tripped over her own feet. She warned the crowd to get back for their own safety before the madman they were all so intrigued by killed them. 'He'll get out a gun, you know. Then will you stop looking, when your brains have been blown out?'

'Ah, shut up,' said the material woman. 'He's not crazy. That could be any one of us.'

'Not crazy?' said the halal meat man. 'I know crazy when I see it, and he gets a certificate of authentic-iteee.' His butcher's knife pointed upwards to indicate that if danger struck them they couldn't say they hadn't been warned.

Every time I threw down some more cutlery, the crowd veered back into the street, pretending to be scared. Those who were stubbornly engrossed and